The Unlikely Angel
of
Casco Bay

A Novel

Keith Christian Milne

Published by Keith Christian Milne.
Hardcover: ISBN: 979-8-99267-59-17
Paperbacks: ISBN 979-8-99267-59-24
ISBN 979-8-99267-59-00

About the Book

In the quiet coastal town of Casco Bay, Maine, widowed lobsterman Benjamin Morse Scot struggles to rebuild his life after the death of his wife and a battle with alcoholism. Just as he finds new hope and love with Janine, a compassionate counselor, Ben's dark past comes crashing back when a ruthless cartel demands his skills for a deadly smuggling operation. Forced into an impossible choice after Janine is kidnapped, Ben embarks on a high-stakes mission to outwit his former partners, survive a daring escape, and protect the woman he loves. But when a shocking betrayal shatters his world, Ben must face a final showdown with enemies both seen and unseen.

THE UNLIKELY ANGEL OF CASCO BAY is a gripping tale of love, redemption, and survival that will keep readers on the edge of their seats until the very last page."

Dedications

Many thanks to my wife, Connie Milne, for her constant support, encouragement, and editorial eyes.

Thank you, Ingrid Russell, for your support, for encouraging me to write, and for your editorial feedback.

Thank you, Helen Wise, for your editorial eyes, your thoughtful feedback, and for your encouragement.

Thank you, Gayle Salter, for encouraging me to stop thinking about writing fiction, and to finally get started actually writing it, beginning with finishing this original short story by the same name, at keithmilne.com. Your need to know what happened next with Ben, resulted in me writing this novel.

The original short story was adapted to become chapters one and two of this novel.

https://keithmilne.com/2023/12/21/the-unlikely-angel-of-casco-bay/

"The scariest moment is just before you start. After that, things can only get better."

—Stephen King, *On Writing*

TABLE OF CONTENTS

1

HAVING ANOTHER ROUGH ONE

Louis, the mail delivery person, could tell something wasn't right with Ben. He could see him slouched over in a chair next to his boat. He half ran, half waddled down the dock towards him. Ben wasn't moving, and Louis couldn't tell if he was breathing or not, so he decided to give him a little shake, "What the? Ben. Hey . . . Ben!"

Ben suddenly came to life like someone had flicked on his power button. "Hey, leave me be . . . who are you?" He stood up fast, then realized who he was looking at. "Geez Louis, you had me thinking I was about to be robbed, thunked on the head, and thrown in the marina." His gravel voice always sounded so indignant and commanding.

Louis looked annoyed and a little angry too, but lightened up a little as he explained, "I was coming down the dock and saw you slouched over and not moving. I called your name, and you didn't move or answer or do anything, so I ran to see if you needed any help or resuscitating or something. Sorry. I didn't mean to startle you, Ben."

"We're fine, Louis, and I appreciate your concern. I really do. Thank you for coming to my rescue, but I'm fine. Really. I went out early this morning and didn't have any coffee. When I got back, I ate a huge meal over at McGiddy's tavern, and washed it all down with a nice, big, dark pint. I came over here and decided to have a seat in the nice sunshine before going back aboard *Bessie*. Well, between me being old and not getting enough sleep, combined with having no caffeine and eating a big meal, that alone would normally be enough to put me to sleep. Add drinking a little alcohol and sitting in the nice warm sunlight, well, who am I to say no to the wave of fatigue that suddenly swept over me as I sat here. How about we start over now that we're face to face and still alive?" Ben smiled tightly, then cracked up laughing for a few seconds.

Louis smiled, "Sure thing, Ben. I'm just glad that you're okay. Phew, that was a close one though! It got my blood pressure sky high. For a moment there, I felt like I was having an out of body experience, then it settled down. Anyway, here's your package."

Louis handed Ben a small box wrapped in brown paper addressed to his son Andrew Scot with % Benjamin Scot on the second line. Across the bottom of the package it said, *For Andrew Scot Only* on both the front and the back. That was strange.

"Thank you, again, Louis. You have yourself a great rest of your day. I'll see you soon."

"Glad you're well, Ben, and glad to have been of service to you. I know you'd do the same for me. Can't have a great community to live in without everyone helping their friends and neighbors."

Ben smiled, "I couldn't agree more! My wife used to say something similar. She often said we have to be good friends and *better* neighbors."

"Oh, I like that one." Louis said with a wide smile before turning to leave.

Feeling a little off center now, Ben held tightly onto the rail of the walkway leading down to *Bessie*, his 40 foot fishing vessel. He turned and waved again, and watched Louis finish waddling his way down the long floating dock towards his mail truck like a fast-walking emperor penguin.

Ben and Bessie were married for thirty eight fast, wonderful years. Bessie passed away four years ago, and Ben missed her terribly. Everything reminded him of her, or of both of them together, or of their family time together while raising their two kids, Andrew and Celia.

Not quite ready to go into the cabin, he started thinking back to when he was young and in crazy love with his then wife to be. "Ben and Bessie. That has a bit of a ring to it. Hmm . . .," he flashed back, picturing himself at their formal wedding. He saw himself standing at the altar, exchanging vows with Bessie. Afterwards, his best man promptly announced their marriage to everyone who had gathered for their ceremony, *Ladies and Gentlemen, I am happy to present Mr. Benjamin Morse Scot and Mrs. Bessie Grace Scot, Mr. and Mrs. Benjamin Scott.* Everyone stood and began clapping. They kept clapping and turned towards Ben and Bessie as they walked down the aisle together towards the front of the church after exchanging their vows. It was fun for both of them. They were radiant together. Happy, and, at least for now, on top of the world. The people all around them were celebrating the two newlyweds, while they walked the aisle together, smiling and nodding back with gratitude and love in their hearts.

Reliving this again, Ben started crying and laughing at the same time from a mixture of the joy of the memory, the pain of Bessie's loss, and his steadily deepening loneliness, all coupled with anxious feelings about his own aging and pending demise.

Now, the more he laughed, the more the laughter seemed to want to keep coming out. He laughed so hard his eyes grew hazy with tears. He had a hard time seeing, and began to stumble around on the deck, laughing so hard that he got to the end of his breath, and had trouble inhaling again. He started coughing like crazy afterwards. He kept replaying that announcement in his head, and each time he did, it made him start laughing all over again.

Ben was laughing and stumbling along at a good rate of speed, his eyes full of happy tears, when he misjudged his distance to the cabinet at the aft end of the deck. His left foot ended up hitting the cabinet hard, ejecting him straight forward at an odd angle, and he landed over the aft end of the boat. Luckily, at the last second, he'd managed to grab one of the deck cleats to stop himself from going completely overboard.

Now, he was left lying on the edge of the boat face down over the bone-chilling, 51 degree water, with only the thin top rail under his waistline. His left hand holding onto one of the deck cleats with all the strength he had. He took a deep breath, then pulled hard with his left arm, while at the same time swinging his left leg over the rail. Luckily, it gave him the momentum he needed to roll back into the boat. He stayed sitting on the deck, trying to calm down and still processing what had just happened.

Once he managed to calm down, he started chuckling while replaying what had just happened in his mind, while also being careful not to let himself get caught in another blinding laughter loop again. He really liked the feeling of a belly laugh, and who doesn't? It was the first one he'd had in years. *Laughing hard is amazing, even if it did almost cost me serious injury or death*, he thought.

Ben stood on *Bessie's* deck, taking in Casco Bay, and the oncoming evening. He was born not too far from here, grew up here, married someone from here, worked on the water here his entire life, and had seen what seemed like a million beautiful, colorful endings to other days.

Over time, from fishing and lobstering, he'd made enough money to buy the land and the house his grandfather had built. Shortly after that, he and Bessie had moved in and improved the place to the point where the original was unrecognizable; if someone had left when it was still the original house, they would now think that someone had torn down the original house and built a new one.

Over the years, Ben had kept adding on to the original house. Now, they had 5,600 square feet of living space. There is a huge new entry, a dining room big enough for fifty guests, nine bedrooms, twelve bathrooms, and a parlor that doubles as a dance floor. A barn, a four-bay garage, and lots of elaborately landscaped gardens in various places over the remaining twenty acres between their nearest neighbors and where the house sits near the water's edge. He remembered all the blisters and calluses, the two broken toes, and the one broken finger, all happening during the first big expansion. He had no idea, then, that there would be four more expansions over the next twenty years.

Ben was proud of his family, and he was proud of his success as a lobsterman and fisherman. But the cherry on top of it all was what he managed to do with that house. He sometimes still can't believe it when he sees it in total. Remembering all the phases is simple, but taking in the final result takes adjustment of one's ideas about what is possible in creative building.

The last few groups of seagulls were flying off into the rapidly setting sun. The sandpipers were sticking around for a while to see what might pop up for dinner. They cruised the coastline in large groups, like a squadron of stealth planes. They flew low and quiet, scanning the shoreline below for anything edible, finally landing en masse, then rapidly walking in all directions while poking the wet sand with their long, stick-like beaks.

Ben watched them fly, admiring their precision, noticing and observing with reverence their flawless execution of their survival instinct. The onshore winds were beginning to pick up and the sun was getting low in the western sky. A swirled collage of pink, orange, purple, blue, and gray clouds painted the sky in a three dimensional pattern reflecting their different altitudes.

Ben couldn't believe he was already sixty-eight; nevertheless, he had no current thoughts of retiring. He still loved being out on the water, it was his passion in life. Ben was sometimes called an *old salt*. He is unassuming at just under six feet tall, with blue-gray eyes that seem to mirror the color of the water when out at sea. His full beard and still thick head of hair have become mostly white now, but are still tinged with red, and his face and neck look equally leathered by decades of hard work, sun, and salt air.

Being a lobsterman, Ben always dresses the same from day to day. He wears a black knit watch cap, a long sleeved, cotton t-shirt with a flannel shirt over it. He wears rugged jeans, a little worn out at the knees, and keeps them up with a thick black leather belt. He covers his feet with either lined steel toed work boots or tall rain boots.

Ben is stocky, and still stronger than many half his age. When he's pulling traps up, he wears a rain suit as needed, and heavy, wool-lined, suede gloves. He keeps half a dozen pairs handy at all times. He is kind, but stern, and doesn't have too much to say most of the time. When he does speak, he doesn't mince words, but gets right to the point.

Going through life as a lobsterman, he had sometimes fantasized about doing something less physically challenging, but he hated sitting at his own desk, even on a stormy day with nothing else to do. He certainly couldn't imagine having to dress up, drive somewhere, sit at a desk all day shuffling papers and attending meetings. Pure torture for Ben.

Here, on Casco Bay, off the coast of Maine, Ben has seen whale pods, Japanese poachers, pirates, treasure hunters, refugees, survivors of shipwrecks, scuba divers, chartered fishing boats, and more tourists than the stars that shine at night. Everyday is a new adventure out on the water. Ben enjoys having the solitude and time alone, something most people never know.

Even when Ben isn't working, quite often, he'll launch *Bessie* back out into Casco Bay. Leaving the man-made world behind, and cruising out across the vast liquid tundra of water that is always teeming with marine life, is the best drug Ben has ever been exposed to. Every single time, the calming effects on both his mind and body, from being out on the water, take effect very quickly. The profound solitude is never lonely, but often feels like a pair of warm hands gently embracing him.

Once or twice over the years, Ben rolled up his sleeves on unusually hot days, letting anyone nearby who wanted to, get a glimpse of his one and only tattoo. He got it three weeks after getting married. Right in the middle of his right forearm in a big, beautiful, cursive font,

BESSIE.

So far today, Ben estimated that he had already pulled up nearly one hundred pots, and he guesstimated that he had about fifty more to go. Right now, he's super tired, not only from all the hard work, but also from not getting enough sleep, not having adequate caffeine, and from drinking that pint at lunch instead of eating real food. He was starting to get a headache, and felt achy and sore. "Ah, heck with it! Where's the whiskey?" he asked no one in particular. Looking forward to his drink, Ben picked up his pace a little walking down the ladder to the galley thinking, *I'll get the rest of those pots tomorrow. I'm not going back out today!*

Ben found his way down to the galley and opened the cabinet where he always kept the Irish whiskey. He grabbed a drink glass, sat down, poured himself a double, and downed it all at once. He quickly poured another, and downed it just as fast. Finally, he poured one more double and, this time, seemed content to sit tight while letting the other four shots settle in.

The whiskey started hitting his brain quickly on an empty stomach, and that always put a smile on his face. He loved that first rush from alcohol. He took another good sip, and let his mind wander back to his early days with his wife, Bessie.

He saw her dancing provocatively, coming towards him with only a minimal, see- -through, silky, night gown covering her gorgeous naked body. She loved doing that for him. He loved watching her and seeing the obvious joy she derived from dancing for him. It was the way they'd always been. Pure love and understanding, conveyed by simple eye contact, or a knowing glance. They simply got each other.

He imagined Bessie baking in the kitchen with both Andrew and Celia next to her, watching her make bread dough. Both children helped knead it. The smiles. The warmth. The smell of yeast and flour. The feeling of warm, sticky dough. The sharing of knowledge and of love. The making of warm memories for all. So beautiful.

Ben felt the pain of Bessie's loss stab his heart all over again. He wondered if it would ever stop and leave him alone to live in peace, and he wondered if he would ever know that depth of love again. She had died years ago, and all the distractions, work, and booze, have not worked in making his pain about losing her stop, or get any better. He wakes up every morning thinking about her and their time together, and, since her death, she is always the last thing he thinks of before falling asleep at night.

He poured himself another drink, this time a triple. He half downed it wanting it to hurt, or at the least burn like hell. Ben could feel so much emotion overwhelming him: Anger, rage, emotional pain, loneliness, helplessness. He finished the last of his drink in one big slug, then slammed his glass down on the table.

"I know how to make you stop. You will stop now!" Ben shouted, stumbling towards the berthing area. He rummaged around under his rack for a minute then stood tall, shouting "YA." There you are, you son of a bitch."

The reflection of the berthing light slowly traveled down the barrel of the loaded .357 Magnum as Ben, holding the gun with both hands while in a crouched stance, slowly turned back towards the door. "That's right, you'd better back the fuck away . . ." Ben slowly walked still in a crouched position, holding the gun out in front of him, as if he could see an invisible intruder that no one else could.

Now, back out in the galley, he sat down, putting the gun down in the middle of the table, and poured himself another stiff drink. He was already drunk, but, as always, he never seemed to know where the line was and stop short of it. Now, even though someone might be able to hear him, they certainly wouldn't be able to understand him. His speech was slurring to the point of incoherence. He was just about ready to pass out when his phone started ringing. He fumbled for a moment, then managed to get it out of his back pocket and saw that Andrew was calling. He let it go to voicemail. Somehow, in the back of his mind, Ben knew that he was missing something or that he was forgetting something important, but couldn't think of it. He was feeling woozy and very tired, but he was still angry, and still haunted by fond memories and visions of his life with Bessie. He didn't want to talk to anyone right now. He just wanted to be left alone. Ben's loss sometimes felt like a black hole trying to suck him in—heart first. He looked at the gun. He realized that it would be so easy now. He was drunk and alone. He had the weapon. He had the nerve. He had pain. He picked the gun up with his right hand and turned it towards himself, slowly moving it towards his right temple until he felt the cold steel touch it. He held the gun there for a long time. He could feel the weight of his loss, the weight of his loneliness, and the weight of the steel against his head. He moved his forefinger a little, feeling it pull the trigger a tiny fraction more, right to it's maximum tension point—and then his phone rang again.

The sound snapped him out of his trance and, at least temporarily, stopped his crazy, drunken, highly dangerous, behavior. He retracted the trigger mechanism and put the gun back down on the table. His hands were trembling so hard he could barely coordinate his movements. He reached for his phone laying face up to the right of the gun. A full screen picture of Andrew smiling while holding a big sea perch he'd caught while helping Ben out on the boat a few years ago. Ben barely managed to tap the button to answer the call, before falling face first onto the table with quite a thump, followed by the whiskey bottle tipping over, emptying itself first all over the tabletop, and then onto the floor.

"Dad? Dad." Andrew half shouted, sounding perplexed and worried.

Ben tried to answer him, but all that came out was a bunch of slurred gibberish.

"Dad, what's going on? Are you okay? Talk to me." There was no answer, only silence.

"I'm on my way, Dad. I see on my GPS you haven't left your dock yet. I should get there in about an hour. Don't leave, please. Just stay put." Ben was still passed out on the table and hadn't heard a word of what Andrew had just said but, for the time being, he was at peace.

2

THE SURPRISE PARTY

When Andrew arrived at the dock, he quickly parked, then ran down to where Ben's trawler was docked, and rushed inside. Following the strong scent of whiskey, he completed the handful of steps to the galley, and then he saw his father, sitting in his chair, with most of his upper body lying face down on the table. A gun was being held loosely in his hand, and the source of the odor, an overturned whiskey bottle, was lying next to him on it's side. He rushed over scanning the area for any signs of blood, but didn't see any. He saw that his father was breathing and appeared to be sleeping, and just fine. After a big sigh of relief, he managed to get Ben back into a fully sitting up position.

Once Ben was safely propped up against the back wall behind the table, Andrew prepared a pot of super strong coffee. While the coffee was brewing, he rummaged around under the sink and found an empty spray bottle and filled it with ice cold water. He turned and quickly walked up to his dad and sprayed him right in the face with it at point bland range. A couple of seconds later Ben woke up with a start.

"What the hell . . . Andrew, stop."

"Dad. Thank goodness you're okay. It was getting late back in Portland. I wasn't sure if you were lobstering off of Cape Elizabeth or Small Point today, so I checked your whereabouts on my phone."

"Your phone? What the heck are you talking about now? I can't remember where the hell I am other than on my boat! Where am I docked?" Ben asked with a slur.

"Dad, you're docked in Elizabeth City."

"How the hell did you know where I was anyway?"

Andrew poured Ben a big mug of his special brew. "Don't you remember, when you got your new phone, I showed you how I set it up so that I could always see where you are as a safety precaution?"

"Yeah, . . . no, . . . I don't know." Ben took a sip of the coffee Andrew had just set in front of him, and almost dropped it trying to get it back to the table as fast as possible. "Shit! What did you do, make this pot with an entire bag of coffee? It tastes like mud!"

"Sorry, I just wanted to make sure you would be able to really wake up. We have places to go, and people to see tonight. Don't even tell me that you forgot that tonight is that surprise that I was telling you about a couple of weeks ago?"

Ben looked confused for a minute, "Ah, Christ, I'm sorry, Andrew. I *had* forgotten. I wanted a drink, but I wasn't even sure that I had a bottle on board. When I found one, I started drinking. Then I started feeling sorry for myself again thinking about your mom, you know, back in the day. Then I started getting really drunk, and I got really mad, and super sad, and I thought I'd just better stay the night with my ass docked right here, safe and sound. You know?"

Andrew gave his dad a reassuring smile. "Yeah, Dad, I know. I get it. I'm glad you chose to stay put here on account of how drunk you are. What's up with the gun?"

Andrew gave Ben a deadly serious look that commanded a straight answer.

"I thought I heard something outside and fetched it out of my hiding spot in my berth. That's all." Ben said, while looking down at the tabletop instead of his son.

"Did you ever see who, or what made the noise you heard?"

"No, there wasn't anything there, so I came back inside and sat down and had another drink, and that's the last thing I remember before you woke me up."

Andrew noticed the way his dad stared at the gun on the table while he explained how it got there, but never once looked up and into Andrew's eyes with sincerity to reassure and reinforce to him that he was really telling the truth. That did not go unnoticed, and really concerned him.

"Have you ever had issues here with people trying to rob you, or hurt you, or do anything bad to you Dad?"

Ben was trying not to hang his head. He took another sip of the muddy coffee, then set the mug down and looked at Andrew's eyes with a penetrating look, "No, I haven't, but today I did, so I fetched my pistol just in case, okay?" He paused for a moment, then shouted, "Case closed for crying out loud!"

"Okay, Dad. I believe you. Sorry if it seemed like I was doubting you, it's just that when I find you drunker than a skunk on whiskey, and there's a gun on the same table as the bottle, and you're lying face down when I walk in, well, I thought the worst, I did, I'll admit it, and it scared the hell out of me."

"Oh, I'm so sorry, my sweet boy, come here." Ben slowly stood and turned towards Andrew who moved in fast for the hug. They hugged tightly, smacking each other's backs, then pulled away laughing and smiling.

Andrew helped his father find something decent to change into, and promised to drive him back in the morning so he could finish collecting the rest of his lobster pots. He helped his dad into the passenger side of his car, getting a scornful look from Ben for treating him like a frail old woman. Then they headed over to Ben's house for the surprise that Andrew mentioned a week or so ago.

The big house that Ben and Bessie built together thirty years ago, stood on a foundation of granite on the northern coast of Portland, Maine, in a place called Falmouth. The house used to be the only one on Kelley Road, all the way down near the end, near the water's edge facing the Presumpscot River where it exits into Casco Bay.

Despite the grandness of the house, there was a time when they were both worried that they may lose it to the bank after a couple of bad lobstering years. They'd decided to subdivide some of their land, and then sell building lots to raise additional cash to live on. Those who bought the lots and built houses are all nice, decent people, who have been perfect neighbors over the years. Ben had never regretted that decision.

Ben's house offers a stunning approach, with a big turn-around driveway, a big covered porch outfitted with plenty of rattan furniture, and at least a half dozen rocking chairs, all painted different colors. The entire house has large, open rooms, and the walls, ceilings, and floors are all covered either in hardwood or stone, or a blend of both.

As they pulled into the long driveway, they both commented on the curb appeal of the house, how grand it appeared, and how the look of it had a way of instantly making someone feel welcome. Pulling up in front, somehow visitors knew they were going to be enjoying themselves, and would finally be able to really relax. Years ago, when the house was only half its current size, the rumors around town abounded about how a simple lobsterman could afford to be doing so much to his house and property. The last rumor Ben heard was that he had a wealthy, estranged from the family, grandfather, who'd left him all of his vast wealth upon his death. Whenever Ben had heard this in passing, or if someone had asked him directly if it was all true, Ben would just stay quiet and give them a Mona Lisa smile until they excused themselves and walked away.

Andrew parked in front, got out, and came around to the passenger side to help his dad, but Ben had already exited. Before going in, Andrew asked if they could just stand there for a moment taking it in. He hadn't been to the main house in quite a while due to business travel.

As they stood there together, Ben watched his son. He was proud of Andrew for a multitude of reasons, but he also simply enjoyed seeing how much his son looked like he did when he was younger. Shocking red hair, a full, well-trimmed beard, the same blue-gray eyes, and the same firm, formidable jaw line, like Kirk Douglas, but without the dent in the chin. The biggest difference besides their age, was their dress. Unlike the commercial fisherman look, Andrew preferred business attire and suits most often. Casual for him was a golf shirt and slacks with casual dress shoes. He looked like someone who lived in the Hamptons in New York.

As they walked up the long walkway to the porch, Ben felt a mix of emotions. He was starting to realize that, if he was ever going to know true peace and, perhaps, be able to live life without having almost constant painful thoughts about his dear, departed Bessie, that he may very well have to sell their home. Since he'd worked so hard to make it what it is today, it was more than painful imagining not owning this grand house anymore.

One thing he knew for certain, but hated to admit to himself, was that Bessie would never want him to be suffering like this, especially about her. No. She would've wanted Ben to be happy, and even have another woman in his life to come home to every day. No doubt.

Ben paused after climbing the stairs to the main porch to catch his breath. It had been a really long day. He looked at Andrew, "Let's get us something to eat, son, what do you say?"

"Sounds perfect, dad."

As soon as they were inside, Ben flipped on the lights and almost fell down from the percussion of fifty or so people all screaming *SURPRISE!* all at the same time.

Ben caught Andrew beaming from ear to ear, "You knew about this, didn't you?"

Still beaming, Andrew said, "Yep. I set the whole thing up starting eight months ago. It's not easy getting all these people here at the same time you know." He finished with a laugh and the rest of the room followed suit.

In small groups, his daughter, Celia, and her husband, Jake, and others moved in to say hello, as did Ben's younger brother and sister and their families, and some of Ben's old fishing mates that had worked alongside him, off and on over the years, usually during peak season.

Once everyone had extended their greetings to Ben, had some food and drink, and had spent some time talking and swapping stories, Ben suddenly interrupted the peaceful gathering by loudly clinking the side of his glass with a spoon, "Can I have everyone's attention, please? Just for a minute? Thank you. Thanks. I love that you're all gathered here today, but I'm wondering why you have all come up to greet me as if I'm the Pope or someone important? Can someone please tell me what the occasion is? It's not my birthday. There was no funeral, and it's not a holiday. As far as I can tell, no one is getting married here today either, so what gives?"

The only noise that could be heard were people's breathing. Andrew looked around, "Would someone like to answer him?"

The room stayed silent, then Celia said, "I'll tell him. I'm so excited! I've been keeping this a secret for so long it will be a relief to finally be able to get it off of my chest." She looked at her father and said, "we are all gathered here to celebrate you. Yes, you!"

Ben looked extremely perplexed, "I don't understand, why celebrate me? For what? Why? What did I do?" Ben looked around the room, and was genuinely confused. *I am just Ben. No big deal. What, is this some kind of weird intervention?* he thought.

Celia looked around the room, "I'll start, then let's all share what we know and what we've seen from him all these years." Without waiting for anyone to answer or agree, she continued, "Dad, we want to celebrate you because you have led a life of quiet solitude with your nose to the grindstone. Whenever someone looks at you, you smile at them. When someone asks you for help, you always give it. You never complain. You'd get up everyday, and do your thing by going out on the water, even when it was really dangerous, to ensure that we always had what we needed. Me, Andrew, Mom, we never did without anything in life that really matters, and it was all because of you." Tears were now streaming down her face as she recounted all the things about her dad that she was grateful for, and she was struggling hard to keep her voice from wavering.

Andrew, choking his tears back, added, "Yeah, Dad, she's right. You always taught us good from bad, right from wrong, and you managed to do it without hurting us. You taught us by your own example. You went out, worked hard, brought home the bacon, and never complained. You always made time for us: me, Celia and Mom. You came home every night for dinner, and I knew and felt that you truly cared about us. You always asked how our day was, and really listened to the answers. You built this amazing house for us to live in, and made sure we had what we needed. I can never thank you enough for all that you've done for me, our family, and our community over the years."

With little pause after that, Tom, one of Ben's oldest buddies, and a former employee, told everyone about the day his truck broke down and wouldn't start.

"Shoot, I couldn't believe it, I didn't know what to do. Damn truck had always started just fine, but not this particular morning. So, I left the kids at home with their mom, forcing them to miss school that day, and me to walk four miles to work and show up late."

Everyone in the room got quiet, as they tuned in to Tom's story, "So, tired as hell when I got there, Ben could tell something was wrong and that I was upset, and he asked me what was going on. When he heard what happened, he put off launching the trawler, giving the other fishermen going out that day a big head start on the day's catch.

He told me to get in his truck and he drove me home. We picked up my two kids and took them to school. After that, he drove back to my house and called a tow truck. He told the man on the phone to tow my truck to Gill's garage over off of I-295 and have the truck fixed, and to put the whole thing on his credit card. On the way back to the dock, he told me I could pay him back over time, and it would be for me to decide how much and how often, and whatever amount I came up with would be fine, and not to worry. Who does that?"

The room remained quiet and people were mesmerized by Tom's tale, but they were also looking at Ben, who oscillated between looking down while he listened, and humbly looking around the room, never letting his eyes stay locked on any one person for too long.

Tom continued, "Ben didn't want to hear any of my objections or anything. He kept saying that he was just happy to be able to be of service to me and my family. Can you believe that? I have never had something like that happen to me before, and I've never met anyone like you before. Ben, you are the best man I've ever known. I'm not a church-going man, and I'm not even sure if I believe in any kind of traditional God, but man, you really saved me back then, and I know I'm not the only one—look at all these folks. From the top, and the bottom of my heart, Thank you." Tom raised his glass, "Let's hear it for Ben! The unlikely angel of Casco Bay. Oh, and folks, before I forget, I tried to pay him back, and he took my monthly payments, but then gave them all back to me at the end of the year as a Christmas bonus."

Everyone raised their glasses when he shouted, "Here's to Benjamin Morse Scot, the best friend anyone could possibly have!"

Ben was flabbergasted and felt himself blushing. He was completely speechless for a while. He fought hard to keep the tears from streaming down his cheeks, eventually succumbing and letting them flow while he listened to the deep expressions of gratitude and felt everyone's love, and kindness, and caring in his heart.

The speeches continued flowing and, one by one, each person told a meaningful story about Ben. The rides he gave, the money he 'lent,' the free repairs he gave, the gardening advice, and his wise financial insights about how to handle money as a fisherman. As a person, people expressed their gratitude for Ben's patience, his kindness, his obvious love for his fellow man. Many of the things or incidents that he was responsible for, those he had helped, were brought up for everyone to know about so that the true scope of his goodness would finally become visible and made public for all to see, know about, and share with one another.

Everyone felt it was imperative that Ben know just how much of a positive impact he had made on their lives. They wanted to share the countless ways over the decades he had done so much good. They wanted it known that in good times and bad, Ben never complained, never asked anyone for anything, was always ready and willing to help his fellow brother, sister, or neighbor in any way that he could, and always with a smile on his face. Everyone told him that night what a great, valuable, respected, and beloved individual he was. The evening was utterly serendipitous.

After the evening's activities ended. Ben took a long shower and, in his mind, replayed the speeches he'd heard that night. His heart had soared hearing all the kind things that people said about him and about how he had impacted their lives positively, and how much they cared about him. He had no idea that so many people saw him in the ways they described. He had been blind about his sense of value with the community, or even within his own family.

Lately, he had been feeling pretty darned worthless, and his feelings were somewhat validated by the complete lack of any visitors, phone calls, or people needing or wanting his help too much anymore. For a second, he flashed back on the gun, and his flirtatious dance with death only hours before, and felt a jolt of guilt pass through him. He forced himself to try and continue replaying the good memories while embracing his good feelings.

The next day, when Andrew dropped Ben off at the marina in Elizabeth City, Ben remembered the package Louis had brought him the day before. He asked, "Hey, what about that package you sent? I got it yesterday, and it says, Andrew is the only one who can open it. I meant to give it to you last night. Let me go and get it, I'll be right back."

"Ah, actually, that box was for you, Dad. I just wanted to make sure you didn't open it before the party. Open it at your leisure. I'll call you later. I can come by later at eight?"

"See you then, Andrew. And, hey, I can't thank you enough, but let me say it again—thank you."

You're welcome, Dad. See you later."

"See you."

The first thing Ben did after getting back onboard *Bessie* was to put a pot of coffee on in the galley. Afterwards, very curious, he sat down and opened the box. Inside was a slightly smaller cardboard box with a lid. Ben pulled the lid off. Inside the smaller box were letters attached to gift cards or letters of credit!

Fred McGillicutty, whom everyone called *Cutty,* owner of the general store, wrote about how he'd lost track of all the delinquent bills from friends, family, and former workers of Ben's that Ben had paid off, always in private, always instructing Fred to keep him anonymous. Fred had enclosed a gift card for $2,500.00.

Clair, over at the fish market, wrote about how she'll never forget how many times Ben came over and mowed her grass, and then played ball with her son, David, whose dad had been killed in Iraq.

Christian, at the garage, wrote about how he had developed deep respect for Ben over the decades, watching him give rides and money to his friends, relatives, employees, and strangers when their broken down vehicles needed expensive repairs that they couldn't afford to have fixed. Ben stepped in, and stepped up, and made the difference for others consistently. He enclosed a card that would allow Ben to get gas for his personal vehicle *free for the rest of his life.*

Phyllis, of *Phyllis's Style Salon and Barber Shop*, Ben's barber, wrote that she has listened to others tell her stories about Ben's philanthropy for almost twenty years now, and has come to learn what a fantastic human being he is. She included a homemade coupon that reads,

This coupon is good for a haircut and/or shave for Benjamin Morse Scot for the greater of the duration of his natural life, or mine, whichever comes first!

At the bottom, was a small picture of smiling Phyllis. Ben couldn't believe all of this praise for him. It was more in one day than he'd received in his entire life combined. He loved how it made him feel inside, though. He thought, *this must be what it feels like to win a million bucks in the lottery or an Oscar for best actor.*

When he finished, it seemed as though he might never have to buy food or gas or clothes or pay for a haircut, beer, or shot of whiskey ever again.

Ben got up and found the gun he'd almost used to end his life the day before. He emptied the chamber onto the table. He scooped up the bullets and hustled up to the top deck. Once he was topside, he walked over to the aft end and threw the bullets and the gun as far as he could. He watched the bullets spread out like a fan before disappearing, and saw the gun spinning end over end until hitting the water, instantly disappearing beneath the cold water. Ben smiled. He finally felt liberated and happy inside for the first time in four years. Afterwards, he sat at the helm for a couple of hours thinking about his life, his age, and his secrets, then went down below to face the truth.

3

JUST ME AND MY MONSTER

Once down below, Ben took stock of all the liquor he had on board. He had more than he could believe, and he knew that unless he got straight with himself now, he would likely keep drinking heavily, and eventually drink himself to death.

Ben gathered up everything except one unopened bottle of Irish whiskey. He went back topside and, one-by-one, opened and emptied all the bottles into the ocean. As he poured out each bottle, he could hear the ocean hissing in satisfaction, pleased with each offering. He threw the bottles into the recycling bin and headed back in for the day.

Once home, he wrote a letter to both Andrew and Celia letting them know that he would be out to sea for a week or two and to please not bother him, barring a serious emergency. He told them he was going out much farther on this trip, looking for the prize lobster that would pay him well for bringing in that kind of size and weight.

He finished the letter and left it on the kitchen table, then gathered up some food, water, personal items, and toiletries, and headed back to the marina. Ben had paid Daniel, one of the marina's helpers to fuel Bessie up so she'd be ready to go when he got back. He had plenty of supplies for at least two weeks, and had prepared well for the trip.

Ben fired up the twin engines and headed out for the second time that day. This time, he was heading far out into the Gulf of Maine, and planned to stay there until he was dry. If he succeeded, he would be living his life without drinking for the first time in nearly thirty years.

This was one of the single biggest, most important tasks he was going to face in his life, other than choosing the correct woman to marry. He knew it in his bones that he had to choose. Either it was him and good health, or the booze, and a premature death. He also knew that he'd been living on borrowed time with this little secret habit of his. Last year during his wellness check, Doc Fitzgerald told him that he would be dead in five years or less if he didn't immediately change his ways.

Ben didn't bullshit himself about quitting drinking. He knew it would be the hardest thing he'd ever do. Hell, if he didn't have a little whiskey in his coffee in the morning, he'd have a mini-case of the DT's by eleven a.m. Besides, he'd really grown to like that drink. The strong, muddy coffee would wake him up, and the whiskey would keep his nerves calm and take the edge off of the coffee buzz. It was a match made in heaven, and a perfect way for Ben to hide that he was drinking. If anyone came around, there he was, usually working on something, a coffee mug right next to him, and an ironclad reputation as being someone who really loves his coffee.

Once under way, Ben put the helm in auto pilot with proximity alarms enabled, and headed down below to make himself something to eat, and then open the last bottle of Irish whiskey he would ever let touch his lips. Ben was going to slowly drink the entire fifth of whiskey, and then live up to his new vow to never drink another alcoholic beverage again, for the rest of his life. It was non-negotiable.

After a quick dinner of a lobster omelette with bacon and toast, Ben was full and felt strong. He also felt more determined than ever to stop drinking once and for all. It was a life lesson that he needed to learn, and a life issue that he needed to be able to overcome. He had to prove to himself that he was the good man everyone else thought he was. Guilt shot through him while he looked over some of the cards he'd received at the party, and in the mail, thanking him for being such a good man, and praising him for his angelic ways. If they only knew, Ben thought.

Ben cracked open the bottle of whiskey and took a big drink directly out of it, like a homeless boozer in a dark alley behind the garbage bins, who'd just received an entire bottle for Christmas all for himself. He felt the familiar warmth and mild burn as gravity pulled it down into his stomach. Once in his stomach, it felt like a warmth bomb exploding in all directions as the whiskey coated the omelette and toast, settling in his stomach with a slight weight.

A short while later, he felt a very mild but distinct buzz hitting his brain, as the warmth from his stomach continued spreading outward in all directions throughout his entire body, warming every single cell simultaneously. Ben loved the feeling that alcohol gave him when it first hit his brain. The mental topsy-turvy and the dizziness, followed by some giggling and the need to want to converse more, but usually with a sharper tongue.

Ben knew in his own heart and mind that he, in many ways, was a good person, and every bit as good a man as many made him out to be, but it was what they didn't know that made him feel the most guilt. He knew that many who honored him wouldn't have if they'd known the whole truth about him. He wanted to be the man they thought he really was, and the man he knew he really was, or had been, and now would become again.

Yes, he had done a lot of favors for a lot of people around town, but so what. He knew that most of them would've done anything to help him if he'd ever needed their help. Somehow, in the past, when presented with the ugly truth about how bad someone else's situation was, he always felt compelled to do what he could to make things better for that person.

Ben had a great track record over the decades of hiring men and helping people down on their luck, and could usually tell a good person from a truly bad one. The bad ones seem to exude an energy that is unmistakable evil. The folks he had helped over the years never asked for anything, and were just experiencing some hard times for various reasons. He'd known most of them. The people that he'd just met, and that he ended up helping anyway, were also good people. There was no doubt in Ben's mind or heart.

Ben kept looking at the cards, and the pictures that people had sent to him, many with their smiling, grateful faces, and letters promising him a lifetime of gas, or food, or supplies, and he felt like a total fraud. He took another huge drink from the bottle and swallowed hard. Yep, this is it, the last of it. Forever. This is one secret that they'll never have to know about, he thought.

Ben took his bottle topside. It was already dark. He looked over the gauges at the helm. He was already twenty miles off the coast and, now that fall was coming fast, traffic on the water had diminished over the last several weeks, just as it always does this time of year, so there was nothing on the radar for at least ten miles or more in any direction. He slowed down and then let the engine return to idle as he came to a stop and dropped anchor.

The night sky looked like it went out to infinity with a trillion stars twinkling. Some of them seemed almost woven together, loosely connected by the hazy band of the Milky Way. The gentle sound of water lapping at the side of Bessie, and his own heart beat were the only sounds he could hear. Ben sat at the helm and took several more swigs of whiskey. His thoughts kept bouncing back and forth between the past and the future, with a brief slice of time dedicated to the present. He felt scared all over again, remembering the day Hernandez appeared on the dock asking for a few minutes of Ben's time.

He finished the bottle in record time, and promptly stood up, firmly gripping the wheel at the helm to keep from falling. Once stabilized, he found his way back out onto the deck. He slowly walked over to the bow and, just as he had done with the pistol a short while ago, he threw the whiskey bottle, and his drinking habit, into the ocean with all his might. He watched it become a temporary beacon, reflecting the moonlight with each revolution, spinning like a precision top to its final, and ironic, liquid destination for all eternity.

Ben stood at the bow, looking out across the black ocean towards the knife-edge line delineating the point where the dark horizon meets the star-filled sky. He felt deeply relieved. Now, there wasn't any more liquor on board. He had food supplies for two weeks and, despite thinking it was going to be pretty rough, he felt up to it.

Thinking ahead, he began looking forward to no longer having to feel like he needed alcohol to smooth out, take the edge off, or just recreate with. Now, he knew he couldn't control himself around liquor, and that was the truth. That night, he slept better than he'd had in a long time, in part from feeling so good about his new resolve to live sober.

The next morning, the sun came up casting white hot light in all directions, simultaneously turning the ocean's surface into a field of sparkling diamonds. It was going to be a beautiful day, and the only thing besides eating and reading, was going to be a little fishing. So far, Ben felt good. He'd slept like a rock. Indeed, things were now looking up. He really was truly all alone, out here twenty miles off of the coast of Maine with only his own thoughts, and his own capabilities to survive on. No booze. No distractions. Only rest and relaxation.

By two in the afternoon, he was bored as hell, and he missed the buzz of relaxation he usually felt by now. He missed feeling like he wanted to laugh more than anything. The only thing he really felt now was pain, and fear. All the nerve endings in his body were beginning to feel raw, and on edge, and it worried him.

Great Scot, it's only been six hours and I already feel super edgy, uptight, and snippy. All of my nerves are buzzing, and my whole body feels like it's aching from the nerves not getting what they need. No what they're used to getting.

Ben took a Naproxen and a time released, extra-strength acetaminophen and grabbed his fishing pole. He laid it down on the deck and fetched the jar of pre-shucked mussels that he'd brought to use for bait, opened it up and pulled out a nice fat one. It looked like it needed a little trimming. He pulled his knife out of the sheath on his hip and reached down to trim the mussel and missed, slicing deeply into his left forefinger. Blood began running everywhere. Ben dropped the knife and grabbed the topside first aid kit near the helm. He tended to his finger as best he could, then finally got his line into the water.

He sat back, finally feeling somewhat relieved, but he had to constantly fight the urge to think about booze and drinking. The thoughts kept coming around, he kept visualizing a bottle of his favorite whiskey sitting on the table waiting for him, or a freshly poured one sitting in front of him on the bar.

The sun was very warm, and Ben began to feel sleepy and before too long, he nodded off. After an hour or so, he woke up with a start, wondering where he was before quickly remembering that he was onboard Bessie, and the sound he was hearing was the whine of the reel on the fishing rod turning at high speed. A fish had taken the hook, and ran the opposite way with it.

Ben's mind was still in a dense, alcohol-withdrawal fog. It took him a few seconds to realize what was going on. When he did, he didn't think, he just reacted by reaching out and grabbing the line instead of tightening the drag on the reel or trying to reel the fish in.

As soon as Ben grabbed the thirty-pound test line, the strong nylon instantly found its way to the spot where the bandaid covered his injured finger. Like watching a high-speed movie, Ben watched the nylon fishing line rip right through the bandaid, dive directly into the previous cut and, just like a band saw, cut the tip of his left forefinger right off, and with enough velocity that it flew overboard along with some fresh blood—all before he could blink twice.

Now, blood was literally pouring out of the end of Ben's forefinger. He grabbed a rag and wrapped it around his finger, squeezing hard. He stumbled a little trying to stand up, still unsure of what he had just witnessed, which was absurd, considering that he was now staring at a profusely bleeding forefinger stub. Luckily, the first aid kit was still sitting close by from the earlier incident. Ben used an entire roll of gauze to try to stop the bleeding, but he could still see the blood already starting to soak through the multiple layers he had just put around it.

Ben outwardly remained calm, but was smoldering with anger and fear inside. Goddamn it. Of all the times for this to happen. Well, Benny boy, how are you doing now? You know this is what you're going to have to get used to. When stress like this happens, guess what, Benny boy? No booze to help you deal with it. Hahaha. What? Did you really think I was going to let you off that easily? Guess again, Benny boy. Guess again! Hahahahaha.

Ben could feel his heartbeat pounding inside his finger as hard as a bass drummer in a marching band. The huge, white gauze wrap was rapidly becoming the huge red gauze wrap. Ben knew now that his plan to stay out to sea and away from others while he withdrew from alcohol wasn't going to happen the way he intended. He started the engines and headed back to shore for medical help before another problem, like an infection, happened.

When Ben finally docked Bessie in the marina, he was in so much pain he could barely think. Every time he tried to use his hand, which he needed to often, a jolt of fresh, high-voltage pain would shoot up his arm, which was aching from his shoulder all the way down to his fingertips. He managed a minimal lockup, and found his truck in the lot.

Driving the old truck was more difficult than anticipated. The large steering wheel required two hands doing the hand-over-hand steering maneuver when making turns.

Somehow, Ben managed to get to Maine Medical Center's emergency room, but not without hearing a few honking horns and angry drivers shouting obscenities at him. By then he was sweating and trembling, mostly from the emergence of the first wave of alcohol withdrawal, but also from the pain and the intense stress from getting back to shore from so far out at sea, and then driving.

The intake nurse took one look at him and called for someone to take him in immediately. After that, Ben passed out. A short while later, while they were moving him on a gurney, he became semi-lucid. He watched the images of various parts of the hospital from a supine position passing before him like a strange movie. Only the upper part of the walls, the ceiling, and the face of the person pushing him, beginning with his chin, were visible from his vantage point. The inside of the ER had chrome plated stainless steel everywhere, gleaming and reflecting the bright overhead fluorescent lights. He heard what sounded like an almost constant murmuring and mumbling, and the sound of an intercom voice off in the distance. The smell of alcohol, disinfectant, and floor polish were, at times, a bit overwhelming, even causing him to wake up from sleeping.

A skeletal male doctor with thick red hair and equally thick glasses, appeared and began talking to him, but Ben couldn't hear him. He watched the doctor's mouth moving while he unwrapped Ben's finger, but didn't hear a word that he said.

Ben looked down just in time to see the tip of the bone of his forefinger looking back at him. The entire finger had turned several different shades of purple, red, and black. Ben passed out.

4

TWO ANGELS MEET AT A REHAB CENTER

A few hours later when he woke up, there was a nurse loading sheets and extra supplies into one of the closets in his room. He watched her for a moment. When she finished, she turned and started to leave. She glanced in his direction and noticed he was awake.

"There you are, Mr. Scot. Good to see you! Did you have a good nap? Are you feeling better?" Ben didn't feel as though he was able to answer, and he had a lot of questions himself.

"I'm going to let Dr. Munson know that you're awake now," she said starting to leave again. Ben struggled to get any kind of an answer out, and was getting angrier by the second that the nurse couldn't slow down and notice him struggling.

When she got about halfway to the door, Ben finally managed to blurt out, "Wait!"

The nurse came back and stood next to his bed smiling. "Yes?"

"What's your name?"

"Oh, gosh, I'm so sorry, my name, of course, My name is Janine, Janine Thompson. I'm going to be your nurse during your stay. Is there anything else I can get for you right now?"

"Hi, Janine. Yes, some cold water, preferably with some ice would be really good. How long have I been here? And, where have I ended up anyway?"

Janine looked at Ben like she wondered if his mental state had somehow become impacted from infection from his wound. "Why, you're at Maine Medical Center, silly. You brought yourself here."

"I barely remember the trip back. I was out on the water. Twenty miles out when I cut off my finger fishing. I could tell I needed professional medical treatment, so I managed to get myself to shore and get here." Ben paused, then his tone grew stern, "The thing I'm struggling with is why I was checked in and housed in a room when I have an outpatient injury?"

Ben's headache kept pounding inside his skull like a blacksmith hammering steel on an anvil. He was confused and just wanted to get stitched up, get some pain meds, and be on his way. He started trembling and sweating again, and he also had the strangest feeling that Janine was some sort of alien spy who was disguised as a nurse the way she kept sliding suspicious looks in his direction.

He was convinced that her true job was to make sure that he was kept alive so they could use him later for a secret project. He wasn't sure when it was going to happen, yet, but he knew it would be soon. He saw everything as sinister rather than kind. He knew one thing for certain: he didn't trust her because she made him feel things, and that meant she was powerful and dangerous.

"Take it easy. You're being kept overnight for observation, that's why we checked you in. You seemed pretty delirious when you came in. It's just a precaution to ensure that you're okay before we discharge you. If you need anything else, please don't hesitate to ask, but don't get snippy with me or I might just 'forget' to come by with your pain meds for a few hours past time for you to take them, if you get my drift," Janine said. Her tone was daunting and she maintained tight eye contact with him. He knew he'd better do what she said.

Ben was shocked. Apparently, this attractive, petite woman wasn't going to put up with his crap or anyone else's.

"I'm sorry. I apologize. It's just that . . . that . . ."

Janine came closer and put her hand over Ben's injured hand resting on its own pillow, and looked into his eyes with so much caring, love, and understanding that Ben was taken aback.

He paused for a moment, then looked right into her eyes, "I'm going through alcohol withdrawal and now that I've injured myself, I'm not certain how I can deal with everything all alone. I wasn't counting on being injured. I thought I was going to be spending the next two weeks on the water, alone, to deal with what's coming from withdrawal without having to burden others, or put up with anything from them either."

Janine didn't flinch. "What was your plan?"

"I was out on the water with enough supplies for two weeks plus, and I just wanted to do this alone. I got myself into this mess, so I wanted to get myself out. That's how I've always done things."

"Well, I'll give you credit for not wanting to be a burden, and for taking responsibility for your own fate but Ben, what you were actually doing, whether you realize it or not, was taking your life into your own hands. Without medical supervision, alcohol withdrawal can cause things to happen physiologically that can make your heart stop. In some instances, without a doctor and paddles close by to zap your heart, you're a goner. It's that simple. Losing the tip of your finger was actually a blessing in disguise. It may very well have saved your life."

Ben was speechless. Now that she laid it all out like that, he knew she was right. He had been foolish to think he could do this all alone, especially while out at sea. What if a big storm had come along? What if he had gotten so hot and delirious that he had jumped into the water and been badly clipped by a shark? What if, while in the water, he swallowed some salt water and drowned while trying to cough it out?

"Now that I know your real issue, I can tell you that, with your insurance and Medicare, you're all set for becoming an alcohol recovery patient, if you'd like me to change your status."

Ben hadn't thought about that. "Really?"

"Really. In fact, I can have you moved to the wing that I work in, and that way I'll be able to stay with you, follow you, and make sure you have good care, if you'd like." Janine gave him a big smile after finishing. She could tell that Ben liked her.

Without any hesitation Ben answered as enthusiastically as he could muster, "Yes, please," adding, "Can you please get me another blanket? I'm so cold and I just can't seem to get warm. What's the temperature anyway?"

"The temperature in the hospital is kept at a constant 72 degrees at all times. If you're feeling cold it's from lack of activity, your healing, and your withdrawal. I have to go and check on other patients now. I'll check with you later in your new room. Someone will come for you in a little while and get you moved."

Ben felt like shit, but he was so grateful for Janine. He felt so much better for telling her the truth, and now his plan could proceed, but this time with professional supervision. Being instantly rewarded with immediate professional assistance right after confessing, was like getting an extra cherry on top of a sundae.

Nurse Janine was the first woman that Ben had felt caring from since Bessie passed. It felt amazing. It made him realize how many feelings he had suppressed, and now he knew just how much he really missed being with an amazing woman.

An hour or so after Janine left, a tall orderly with long braids named Jeffrey came and gathered Ben's things. He took careful inventory, announcing each item that he placed inside a big bag that had a label with Ben's name on it, then he put the bag under Ben's hospital bed.

Ben watched him taking inventory and said, "I could just get dressed."

The orderly looked at Ben, his braids swinging around, "I was told to move you to the rehab ward, section C, as is, that's all I know. If you want to get dressed, I'm not going to stop you, but if you're planning to stay and get well, you might as well just stay as you are, cause you are just getting started." Ben didn't need to ask Jeffrey what he really meant, he already knew, and he was absolutely right.

Ben wanted to just get up and get dressed, then drive home and pour himself a nice big glass of whiskey. After that, he'd flip on the tube, and maybe take in a taped NFL game and just zone out for a while pretending that this whole incident was either a figment of his imagination, or a weird, somewhat bad dream. Thinking like that is how you got here in the first place. Look at you. You can't stop drinking without help now. If you don't do this, you may never have another chance. Maybe it's all downhill from here with my health if I don't do this. I'll stay drinking and get worse, he thought.

Over the next three days Ben felt like he'd gone to hell, visited the devil himself, made a horrible deal with him, and now owed his soul to him for all eternity. Then he realized he was safe because by going to rehab, he had made a pact with an angel first.

The shaking grew worse and he developed a nasty fever. Before it got too bad, the shift nurse hooked him up to an intravenous drip to stabilize his electrolytes and then, per doctor's orders, sedated him, sparing him the worst effects of alcohol withdrawal. He never noticed or woke up when the nurses changed his gown, sponge bathed him, or tucked him back in again.

After four days of withdrawal, Ben was over the worst of it and didn't even notice it too much. He had slept almost the entire time he went through it, and was grateful for the relief he was beginning to feel. On the fourth day, the doctor reduced his sedation by half, and by day 10 Ben felt physically whole again, so they discontinued it altogether. He was surprised to learn that he had been unconscious for the last ten days, remembering only a handful of frightening dream fragments while out.

Ben felt starved and asked for a double portion of everything, which they brought to him with a smile. He quickly ate all the food, and sat up in bed so he could better look outside at the bright sun filtering through the tree in front of his window. The tree housed a large wren population that had turned the tree into their personal condominium complex. Ben could hear the little wrens chattering away, communicating with one another, while a full one quarter of them were continuously coming and going, flying into, and back out of the dense branches.

Janine came in quietly. She stood inside the door for a few seconds, and saw that Ben seemed to be in a trance watching the wren's activity. She quietly tip-toed over to his bed. Ben noticed a movement in the corner of his eye and turned in time to see Janine finish her Ninja slide to the side of his bed. "Hey. Hi. Jeez, you startled me a little. Janine, right?"

"Right. Hi." Janine just stood there looking at Ben with an ear-to-ear smile. Ben stared back with equal enthusiasm.

With the curtains open, and the daylight streaming in through the big picture window, Ben could see her better than he had earlier while in the midst of the thick onset of alcohol withdrawal. But even then, he hadn't been mistaken at all. She was extremely attractive, and he could see that she was closer to him in age than he had previously thought. Ben felt excited by her presence. He felt his heart rate increase. He hadn't experienced feelings like this in years. He didn't want to take his eyes off of her. The bright illumination in the room seemed to backlight her, surrounding her like an aura, magnifying her beauty. Right now, to him, she looked to be a vibrant, healthy, well-proportioned, sixty-something Angel.

They both started to speak again at the exact same time, twice, and then gave up, but kept laughing. Finally, while still giggling a bit, Janine asked "So, are you settled in? After the first two weeks you will be allowed limited visitations from friends and family, but not until then."

Ben's eyes grew wider when she said the next two weeks, so she quickly followed with, "That is, if you want to be a part of the hospital's recovery program for alcohol dependence."

Ben felt alarmed, but played it cool. "Well, I think I do now that I'm here. But, what exactly is left for me to do, other than continue healing and recovering?"

"Well, you're probably not going to like this part, but the remainder of the time you spend here is in post withdrawal support. Group therapy, private therapy as needed, and just time away from all that may have contributed to you becoming dependent on alcohol and staying that way. A break from life for a while with no worries or temptations to drink."

"Why did you think that I wouldn't like it?" Ben asked, his voice rising a little.

Janine answered him very matter-of-factly, "Experience with men in your age group. The therapy part is, as I've heard it put before, too touchy feely for many older men. They opt out of that part, and go home. Most of them go right back to drinking again, usually in a very short time frame. They didn't learn the strategies for fighting cravings. They didn't get to know the other members, who help support one another, and they left without a sponsor, which is probably the single biggest piece of assistive care there is. They come from the generation that believes that they should always take care of their own business privately, like you were attempting to do."

Ben looked back out at the beautiful sunlit day with a million things racing through his mind. Janine stood by anticipating his answer. Finally, Ben turned and looked straight into her eyes, and said, "Sign me up. I'm in," then smiled from ear to ear while still looking at her.

Hearing him say this, Janine let out a little squeal of approving delight, and briefly clapped her hands while smiling at him.

"I'm so happy to hear you say that. You have made a really great choice for yourself. We will be able to help you if you let all of us inside your thoughts and feelings. If we are able to learn what precipitated your addiction and help you to reframe the trauma, you will finally be in charge, and your addiction will no longer control your subconscious urges to continue to want to drown the pain. Get used to me checking in with you, because you're going to see my smiling face, like it or not, at least two or three times per day for the next month. This is it for me today. I'll see you tomorrow. Again, congratulations on your decision!"

She leaned over and gave Ben a quick kiss on his left cheek afterwards, whispering, "Have a great night, Ben." Afterwards, she stood up and gave him one more quick inspection with a very pleased look on her face.

Ben looked back at her with warmth in his heart. He noticed her joy, her warmth, the life force in her chestnut eyes—flickering, teasing, flirting with him—whether she knew it or not. One thing was certain, Ben already felt a strong magnetic connection between them.

Somehow, she gave him confidence, and made him feel good about making a great decision for himself today. He felt settled and resolved to go through the entire program doing what the doctors and staff wanted him to do. He was sick and tired of feeling chained to booze.

Ben still couldn't believe that he had let himself ever get so addicted. He denied it for a long time, but in the back of his head and in his heart, he knew the truth. It all seemed so manageable for quite a while, and he always assumed it would stay that way until about a year ago.

The first sign of alcohol dependency arose when he went out lobstering one day, and he went down to the galley for his late morning break. He always had coffee on his morning breaks, and had started making Irish coffees a few months before, and really liked his coffee fixed that way now. This particular morning he went in, poured the coffee and left a little head room for the whiskey. Then he opened the cabinet and discovered that there wasn't any.

Normally, this would not have been a big deal, but for some reason, this morning it was. Where the hell did I put that bottle, Ben thought. I know I didn't finish it. Damn it! His search became more frantic. He could already feel a knot of dread rapidly forming in his stomach, and his heart rate picked up a few notches. As the minutes passed, while Ben frantically opened cabinet after cabinet, he felt his panic rise, and he grew increasingly angry that he couldn't find what he knew was there . . . somewhere.

Finally, in exasperation, he sat down hard at the galley table, tired, angry, and exhausted. He took a deep breath and let it out. Some of his anger hitched a ride on the exhale. He took another huge inhale, and could feel the tingle of excess oxygen beginning to hit his brain. This time, he let his breath out very slowly with his eyes closed. *Why the hell am I so angry about not being able to find something*, he thought. After sitting at the table for quite a while it hit him. *It's the booze. I'm not angry about not being able to find something, I'm angry about not being able to find the booze.*

Ben went back up to the topside deck and began tossing traps again. He was frazzled by what had just happened, and he couldn't stop thinking about it. Two hours later, his hands were trembling, and it wasn't from tossing traps for too long. Once he noticed his hands trembling, he took stock of himself. He felt his insides trembling too, like being cold and shivering. He felt mentally foggy, and nothing seemed to work right any longer. He headed in early, denying the lack of whiskey had anything at all to do with his decision. As he neared the main dock in Portland, he felt irritated to no end, and impatient. Come on, come on, come on, he thought, watching a smaller vessel pass in front of him at the last second just as he was almost there. He pulled into the dock, killed the engine, grabbed his coat and lunch pail, locked the door and ran to his truck.

He drove straight over to Maude's Dockside Spirits a couple of blocks from his docking berth as if he were in a Formula One race. He made his purchase quickly, then drove his truck directly behind the store and immediately opened the bottle of whiskey, drinking directly from it. He was so desperate, he actually managed to take a couple of gulps without stopping, then put the bottle between his legs and just sat back, letting the feeling of the whiskey spread through his veins, soothing his ragged nerves, and relaxing every part of his body. Just like a heroin addict Ben thought, before closing his eyes. He let the whiskey seep into his system. Within minutes, he received the relief he had sought so desperately to get, as he felt the whiskey begin to take away all the stress, pain, discomfort, anger, and frustration he felt.

5

PURGING THE PAINFUL PAST

The rehab center had strict rules around mobile phone use, but before being formally admitted to the program, Ben was allowed to use his phone briefly. He thought about his situation, and decided to go ahead and let both of his children know he was changing his plans by group texting both of them at the same time,

Hi, I wrote that I went fishing, and I did. However, I was also going out on an extended trip to be alone and give up drinking. I've developed a serious dependency, and I've kept it hidden from both of you. I'm sorry for doing that, but I felt ashamed and, of course, was living in denial for a long time about my dependency. I had an accident at sea, got back in safely, went to the hospital, and I'm now safe and getting well here at the rehab center. See you around the tenth of next month. P.S. Andrew, please water my plants for me in the main parlor and my den. My bills are on autopilot, so no worries about losing power from non-payment. :-) Thanks! Love, Dad. P.S. I'm fine, no worries.

Over the next several weeks, Ben struggled with getting in touch with his real feelings. Gradually, he came to know more about himself, and he was better able to see himself more clearly, through participating in group therapy and hearing other people's struggles with alcohol. He learned some strategies for staying sober once back on his own, in order to minimize the chances of relapsing.

Ben was impressed with the staff and the alcohol recovery program at Maine Medical. Janine came regularly to check up on him, and it was absolutely the highlight of each day for him. They began having lunch together, and chatted about everything: life in Maine, their past, their former spouses, their likes and dislikes. At the end of his first week on the ward, Janine let him know that she had asked to be transferred to the rehab clinic full time, and that her request had been granted.

The following Monday, Janine shared some of her past with Ben. She was formerly married for 23 years to her one and only husband, Bill, before he died at work of a cardiac arrest. That was twelve years ago. As Janine put it, "Bill worked for Merrill Lynch, and hated it, especially after they merged with Bank of America. He stayed frustrated, ate too much, didn't exercise enough, and was far too angry most of the time. One day it all just came together like a perfect storm of death leaving him hunched over, dead, lying on top of his tuna fish sandwich. His secretary found him that way after returning from her own lunch break. She called 911, but it was too late. He was already long gone."

"How horrible. That must've been hard for you to learn about when it happened," Ben said, in his best, neutral tone.

Janine smiled, "I could think of many other ways of dying that are far worse, but thank you."

"I know first hand the horrors of losing a spouse and how it feels." Ben added matter of factly.

After Ben said that, Janine insisted that he tell her at least the short version of his experience of losing his wife, just as she had about Bill.

Ben shared his story about Bessie going through cancer, and how hard it was to be a witness to her demise, watching her wither away into nothing, then dying in a drug induced haze. "Christ, in the end, poor Bessie didn't even know who was in her room. She was barely able to stay awake for more than a minute or two." Ben looked at Janine with tears in his eyes and his voice trembling as he fought his emotions, which were now bubbling up like lava from a fresh volcanic fissure, "Watching her slowly shrink down to little more than a skeleton, and knowing that when I said goodbye to her for the last time, that she really didn't hear me, or know that I told her I loved her that one last time, well . . . that was one of the most painful things I've ever experienced."

No longer able to control his emotions, Ben looked down at the table and silently sobbed, tears pelleting the food on his plate, his whole body moving with each sob.

Janine came around from the other side of the table and sat close to him. She turned towards him, wrapped her arms around him, and pulled him in so she could hold him closer. Ben cried for nearly five minutes straight, staring down at the table the whole time.

"Let it out, Ben. Let it all out. It's going to be okay, I promise. Play the tape as much as you need to. Mourn her loss, Ben. I know how much you loved her, and I know she loved you equally. I know she is watching over you too, Ben. It's no accident that you hurt yourself.

That's what saved you and brought you here. Bessie knows about your pain, Ben. She does. She doesn't like it at all, and very much wants you to be happy. I know she does, and you know it in your heart, too. The pain is hard, I know. It gets easier, but it never goes away completely. There, there, my friend. I'm here. I'll stay here as long as you need me or want me to. I'm not going anywhere, Ben."

Ben finally managed to compose himself enough to look up at her again. "Thank you, Janine. Thank you so much." He gave her another hug, then excused himself, promising to return shortly. When he returned as promised a few minutes later and sat down, he sat across from her again, instead of resuming his seat next to her.

Janine protested a little, "Ahhh, you're not going to sit next to me anymore?"

"Sorry," Ben retorted, "I want to maximize how much time I have to look into those gorgeous chestnut eyes."

"In that case, let me get us some more coffee then. Back in a second."

Ben watched her go across the room to where the coffee dispensers were lined up. She seemed to half glide when she walked, and she looked fairly athletic. He could tell that she kept herself in good shape.

Later, she shared that Bill and she were never able to have children. "After giving it almost ten straight years with nothing to show for it, I just grew tired of trying. I told Bill he'd better find himself another wife if he wanted kids. He told me he was fine without having kids, but I could tell he was super disappointed. A year later, I was cleaning out a drawer in the den and I came across a lab test result that was stapled to a letter from Dr. Peterson, Bill's former doctor. The lab result showed that Bill's sperm count was really low. So low, that the odds of me being able to conceive a child were worse than the odds of winning the lottery. I was livid. The letter was dated almost six months prior to me telling him I was giving up."

"What did you do? Anything?"

"Yes, I confronted Bill about it, and I also saw Dr. Peterson and gave him a piece of my mind about it. The doctor cited federal privacy regulations, but I told him I didn't care. How dare they keep that information from me when they knew how much we both wanted a child. Well, I thought we both did. I couldn't believe it. I felt so deceived."

"That is very disappointing for sure. After ten straight years of having your hopes up. Did he tell you he was going to have the test done to see if the reason for you not being able to conceive was his fault?"

"Nope, not at all. He just went on his own. Maybe he suspected it, I don't know. But here's the real kicker, Ben, when I saw Dr. Peterson, who assumed that Bill and I shared everything with each other and, after citing HIPAA regulations, he just happened to say, Well, Ms. Johnson, I'm not certain why you're upset with the results considering your husband's masturbation addiction. Janine looked disbelievingly at Ben, like she had just learned this for the first time herself all over again, "Can you believe that?"

Ben half shouted, "Hell no. That's highly unprofessional."

"So, I told him that, first of all, I wasn't upset with the results, per se, but more upset that this vital information wasn't shared with me. Then I thanked him for telling me about my husband's issue, and drove home to confront Bill about it. When I did, Bill sheepishly made excuses, and said he just wanted to check his count for himself to make sure it was good, but when the low result came back, he felt like he wasn't a real man anymore and had begun to question his masculinity. I asked him why he didn't seek help if he had an issue with self-stimulation, and he immediately snapped that he didn't have an issue. I didn't want to press it. Apparently, he was masturbating two, three, sometimes even four times per day. No wonder his sperm count was low. No wonder why I couldn't get pregnant. I'm sorry, I know this is way too much personal stuff."

Ben quickly answered, "No, it isn't. Please continue. I'm listening." He was fascinated that someone he met just a short time ago could be this intimate with him already, but he felt warm inside from the candid, intimate discussions, and shared stories.

Janine continued, "After that confrontation, he looked away from me a lot, and hardly spoke to me anymore. I could tell that he was depressed all the time and asked him to please get some help, but he would either stay silent and move away, or just walk past me giving me a grunt instead of a real answer. Two weeks later, he had the fatal heart attack while sitting at his desk. I became speechless for a while after that. I felt guilty that I had been seriously thinking of divorcing him for the first time in our marriage, and that I let myself become so alienated from him."

Janine's tears welled up in her eyes as she stared off into the distance. Finally, she shook her head and took a deep breath, then looked at Ben. Their eyes met and they held their gaze for a few seconds. She smiled and, without any warning, leaned over and kissed his cheek slowly, but firmly whispering, "That was then, and this is now," as she slowly pulled away.

Ben fell into a trance listening to the sad ending to Janine's marriage, but he snapped to attention when she moved in for a kiss. Feeling her warm breath, and the tenderness of her lips on his cheek, sent tingly, electrical sensations radiating throughout his entire body, giving him the first reactive and spontaneous stirrings he'd had in years, and it felt delightful. He laughed nervously for a second, and felt his face grow hot from blushing.

After Janine left for the day, Ben headed back to his room to rest before dinner. Only two more days to go and he would be graduating from the alcohol rehabilitation program. He was looking forward to getting home, seeing Andrew and Celia, and he was also looking forward to getting back out on the water for at least a few hours a day.

He checked his email. Andrew wanted to know if he needed a ride and, if so, what time to come on Friday. Ben let him know that he had his truck out in the parking lot, and the graduates were all getting released right after lunch, so he'd be home by 2 p.m. at the latest, and thanked him for checking about the ride.

Ben appreciated Andrew always being there, just checking in, making sure that everything was okay, and asking if he needed anything. Ben was getting older, so it was a good thing, and it didn't go unnoticed.

Every so often, Ben and Andrew would go out on the water together, just like they did when Andrew was back in college, helping Ben out with lobstering to earn money for tuition and fees.

Oddly, even though Ben and Bessie had saved adequately for his education, when it was offered to him, Andrew had said, "Oh, thank you very much, but I've made my own arrangements and wish to pay for my own advanced education. You guys use it to take a big trip, or two big trips, or something!" He wouldn't take the money no matter how much Ben and Bessie offered.

As it turned out, Andrew did so well his first two years, that he applied, and received a scholarship that paid for most of his latter two years, plus he graduated with honors, a 3.97 GPA from University of Maine at Augusta, with a BS in Psychology. He then went on to Yale Law, graduating again with honors, Summa Cum Laude (4.0 GPA). Ben and Bessie could not have been more proud of him. Even Celia had said, "We're not worthy, we're not worthy," bowing to him repeatedly as he walked to see them after receiving his diploma. Later, Ben was even prouder of him when Andrew became partner at Smith, Kline, and Scot, Attorneys at Law.

Celia is so much like her mother was, certainly with her looks, but also, just like Bessie, Celia is soft spoken, pleasant, even tempered, and fair. Always a word of encouragement and something positive from her. Ben always thought Celia did God's work as an elementary school teacher. He remembered how she used to play teacher all the time as a little girl. Knowing her then, it would have been easy to guess what she would end up choosing to do with her life as a grownup.

The next day at the rehab center seemed to fly by. Ben got up a little early to write in his journal. He started keeping one since entering the center on Janine's advice. She said it could help reveal useful elements, patterns, or experiences of Ben's early life that may have contributed to him becoming alcohol-dependent. She said that by identifying these elements, Ben could learn to remember his trauma, feel it again, and then learn to reframe many of the experiences with fresh, more forgiving eyes. Doing so, would help him develop a deeper understanding of his own history, and himself, and help him adopt a new, healthier attitude towards living over time.

Ben fought the idea at first, but after doing it for a couple of weeks he began to enjoy it, and found himself looking forward to making time to write entries of his thoughts and feelings. He found that it helped him clarify his thoughts, and put things in a more realistic perspective. Today, he decided that he was going to continue writing even after leaving the center.

Friday finally came. Ben woke up with a smile on his face. He had been successful! He had worked the program and was feeling better than ever. He felt strong, even about his prospects for being able to stay away from alcohol on his own. He had hardly thought about alcohol the entire prior week. When he had, it had been during group therapy when he was required to discuss his former habit. With her permission, Ben chose Janine to be his sponsor. What a godsend he thought. His entire group attended the lunch graduation ceremony.

It was a joyous, pensive ceremony, with many nervous smiles, and worries about backsliding. Ben was thrilled to receive his framed graduation certificate and his blue ribbon for being the most cooperative of the bunch. Janine was thrilled too. She was proud of Ben. She was aware of just how hard it is to change something that has been done chronically for so many years that it's become completely ingrained behavior. She was aware of Ben's pain, and could understand him drinking a little more over time until he developed an issue with alcohol.

After the celebration, Ben walked with Janine back to his room to get his things. He could feel his heart pounding in his chest more than usual, "So, we should be meeting three days per week? Like Monday, Wednesday, Friday?"

Janine said, "Sounds like a plan. We can adjust it later as needed, but you still need more positive support until your addiction is completely overcome. I've taken the liberty of reserving the hours of 8 a.m. to 12 p.m. on those days for now. I'd like to spend at least four hours or so with you each time I see you until we both feel comfortable adjusting it to less time, okay?"

Ben was surprised by the amount of time Janine felt that she needed to spend with him initially, but he wasn't going to argue about having to spend twelve hours a week with someone as pretty and fun to be with as her. "Sure, that sounds just fine. Will you have any issues with going out on the water with me? I plan on doing some lobstering or line fishing so I'd like it if you could come along, and we can have our time together that way, if you don't mind?"

"I was hoping you'd ask." Janine smiled wide, "How fun! I can't wait." She nodded several times before continuing, "Okay then, meet you Monday at the dock at 8 a.m. at which wharf?"

"Union Wharf, right off of Commercial Street in Portland proper, one slip down from ABC Lobster."

"See ya then. Thanks."

Janine started to leave, then stopped, leaned in closer, and gave Ben another quick kiss on the cheek while gently squeezing his shoulder. Afterwards, she turned and walked towards the door, pausing briefly to glance back at him with her beautiful smile once more before stepping into the hallway.

6

DEAFENING SILENCE

The next day, about 5 a.m., Ben woke up suddenly, not sure why. After using the bathroom, he climbed back in bed to listen to the silence and gather his thoughts. After being gone for the last month, he was really glad to be home again, but it seemed a little strange to him this time, a little foreign. Like staying in a hotel in a different city, and the bed and pillows are different. Like he was a stranger in his own house. It made him feel anxious. It was so big, so quiet, and for Ben, it was scariest at night.

Ben knew that some of his feelings about being home, alone in this big house, were completely about not having anything to distract him or soothe those feelings for him the way alcohol did. He was changed. He'd made a clean break from alcohol, and had no plans to go back to it.

He was so grateful for the way things turned out, and being able to get the help he needed to stop drinking, even if it did cost him the tip of one of his fingers. It had been a gift, and he knew it. Now, every time he looked at his missing fingertip, he reminded himself that it was the beginning of the end of his alcohol dependence, and it was also what caused him to meet Janine. Ben already had the feeling that she was going to become more than just his sponsor.

The feelings that he was already starting to develop for her were utterly undeniable, but he didn't want to say or do anything that would upset her and cause her to go away. He acknowledged that he was lonely and he had been missing Bessie, and also knew that Janine being there with him while he withdrew, had only promoted and intensified his feelings for her. He couldn't imagine anyone else as his sponsor after all that they had shared. However, rather than risk alienating her by sharing his feelings with her, he kept them to himself. Thinking about Janine made him anxious to see her again.

Ben got up and started his day. This morning, both the silence, and the warm water were welcome while he stood in front of the mirror shaving. He thought about Andrew and Celia, and felt glad that they both liked their lives. Ben's stomach started growling loudly. He was grateful that Andrew had thoughtfully stocked the refrigerator the day before, because he was starved.

With plenty of time still to spare, he cooked himself some bacon and eggs and toast, then put together a picnic basket for Janine and him for lunch. He packed some plastic plates with a half-inch lip, and put them into the bottom of the picnic basket right next to a bottle of sparkling water. He rolled up the silverware into cloth napkins. He added all the ingredients that they needed to make complex salads, including fresh lobster meat. He packed cocktail sauce spiced with garlic, and put some fresh lemon wedges in a baggie. He added a small selection of cheeses, some green grapes, crackers, a cork screw for a bottle of non-alcoholic sparkling wine, a small pack of wet ones, and two large pieces of New York cheesecake.

Ben put his hat and coat on, grabbed the basket and his keys, and headed out to meet Janine at the docks for their first half-day together.

When Ben arrived at the docks, the only other people around were a handful of workers from ABC Lobster, standing just outside the side door to the processing plant, taking a smoke break. He was glad that most of them were inside working. Ben was well known on this, and other nearby docks, and he didn't feel like answering a bunch of questions about why he hadn't been around in a while.

Once on board Bessie, he was horrified to see how dirty and unkempt things were. The day he lost his fingertip, he had been barely able to get docked. Blood from the stub, having already soaked through his gauze wrapped finger, had dripped everywhere and things were just as he had left them that day, including all the small puddles of, now dried, blood.

Ben started by clearing and dispensing with all of the garbage: an empty whiskey bottle, beer cans in the corner of the deck, and all of the spoiled and rotten food in the galley fridge.

He found the smell of stale beer utterly revolting, and he almost vomited from the faint fumes coming from the whiskey bottle. He finished consolidating the trash into one big bag, pulled it topside, and was dragging it to the dock when he spotted Janine walking towards him from the main dock gate. He smiled and waved, and she returned both back to him.

She waited for him to return from the trash bin in the back of ABC Lobster, "Hi, how are you?" she asked when Ben was close enough to hear her.

"Doing really well, thanks. Got up a little early this morning, and I'm feeling a bit energized for a change. I did breakfast and packed us a nice picnic lunch, so if you brought something, you can put it in the refrigerator down below in the galley."

Janine smiled and said, "Perfect. Show me?"

"Follow me," Ben said with a smile. He escorted Janine onboard Bessie and gave her the grand tour. "It's not much, but it's been my home away from home for a little over thirty years now."

Janine was amused and touched that Ben wanted to make sure that she knew some basic safety rules, such as wearing a life vest when topside while the ship is out to sea. Ben also showed her where the fire extinguishers were, and where the flare gun and flares were located, and how to use them. He showed her where he put the new .357 magnum, and the four boxes of shells he'd just bought to replace the one he'd thrown into the ocean. After becoming sober, he didn't feel suicidal and knew that he wouldn't be drinking anymore, but he still felt the need to have some protection while out on the bay. There had been erratic periods, over the last 30 years, of lobster pirates that have attempted to steal the entire haul from various vessels. Ben knew that he would want to at least be able to offer them some kind of deterrent to go elsewhere if, and when that should happen. He also showed Janine where he stowed a shotgun in a low locker that doubled as his bed in the captain's quarters. His mattress covered the locker door, and there was no need for a lock on it because it was well hidden.

Janine grew quiet, listening and observing Ben carefully. She was very concerned that he'd brought up so many safety-related things that could potentially happen, things that she'd never thought about before, but was glad that he seemed to have it all well in hand, and seemed to have a plan for how to deal with almost every situation.

"I wouldn't have taken the time to share all of this with you if you were only going to be visiting this one time." Ben said. "However, since we're planning on meeting here regularly, then it became necessary, as well as making a good faith effort at being compliant with numerous marine passenger safety ordinances."

Janine looked intently at Ben, "Really? I would think that the safety protocols would only be shared with passengers when the boat is for hire for public use."

Ben answered, "Yeah, that's how it used to be, but about ten years ago a family sued one of the local lobsterman for negligence on behalf of their family members. Apparently, he took a couple out privately to fish. He tried to leave before the storm got too close, but the man who hired him got angry and wanted to stay longer, saying that he wasn't going to be ripped off by paying all that money for such a short time."

Janine looked a little horrified, anticipating the rest, "So, what happened?" she exclaimed.

Ben looked at her, knowing that she knew the likely outcome, but gave her ears what they were stretching out to hear. "The storm caught up with them. The captain was trying to turn the ship around and caught a huge wave. It hit them sideways, and the boat capsized. Everyone ended up in the water. Luckily, the captain had contacted the Coast Guard before the capsize, and they were already on their way. However, both passengers were never seen again. The captain held onto a piece of floating wreckage long enough to be rescued, but was later sued by the family of the deceased couple. The couple's family lost their case, the captain went back to sea, and that was the end of it."

Janine looked down at the deck, "Wow. How sad. How lucky for the captain . . . I guess."

"Yeah, not sure about that," Ben added. "A few of my friends that know him say that he still feels guilty that he didn't exert his authority as Captain, instead of placating the stupid idiot who was willing to risk his life, and his wife's life, just so he could feel a fish pulling on the end of a fiberglass rod."

Janine was surprised, and flattered when Ben had her start the motor. He gave her a crash course on steering the ship, then let her slowly pull away, and wind them through the marina and then out into Casco Bay. Once they cleared the safety buoys, and were officially out in the bay, Ben told Janine to give it some serious throttle, which she did. Instantly, they were skimming along the water, creating a major wake behind them. "This is great!" Janine shouted through her big smile. Ben smiled back. He was feeling pleased and relaxed for the first time in a long time.

Once Janine had some time at the helm and they were farther out on the ocean, Ben took over, and navigated them to an area where he had some traps anchored.

Janine marveled at some of the lobsters they pulled up that first day. She quickly saw that lobstering, like any other job, has its good parts, and its bad ones. She told Ben that being out on the water was amazing, and loved that she was getting exercise from pulling up heavy traps and nets, as well as from controlling their descent when lowering them into the sea. She said, "I can see how this would keep someone in pretty good shape, and it helps explain to me why you're so strong and fit."

Ben looked at her while raising both eyebrows, "But having to work in inclement weather, or having to do it when it is cold, or dark, or both, and the dangers involved while doing it solo, are things that offset the good things pretty much one to one for me. I have lived long enough to have experienced both the yin, and the yang around lobstering many times.

At lunchtime, Janine opted to eat what Ben had brought over her peanut butter and jelly sandwich and small bag of potato chips. She was impressed with the salad fixings and the entire gourmet preparation that Ben had put together for their lunch.

"Ben, you can cook for me anytime. My goodness, this is amazing. Thank you very much."

"No problem. It wasn't anything, really. I just did it while cooking breakfast, and it seemed to come together quickly, and easily. I'm very grateful to my son, Andrew, for getting rid of the spoiled food that was in the refrigerator, and for going shopping for me before I got home so I'd have some supplies, and not have to go to the store first thing in the morning."

"That's really great. How nice of him, indeed." Janine ate her salad without saying a word for a few minutes, as if contemplating many things. Without warning, she suddenly looked up from her plate right at him, "So, this is your first, real love? The ocean? Lobstering? Both?"

Ben paused for a long time before finally answering. When he did, he didn't look at her, but out at the sea. "Bessie, was my first real love and always will be," Ben answered, trying to not sound tense or upset. "But the sea is my true home. It is where my soul longs to be more often than not. Love is something I reserve for only the most special people in my life, if that makes any sense."

"Completely. I get it." Janine said. Her eyes met Ben's and they briefly locked. Now, they both quietly looked into each other's souls for a really long minute, before finally looking away at the same time, and then laughing nervously. She added, "Mind if I spend the rest of the day with you? I don't have anywhere else to be today, so I can hang out longer if you're okay with that?"

Without any hesitation Ben answered, "Absolutely. I'd love for you to stick around. Hey, have you ever fished? You know, with a fishing pole?" His eyes were dancing a jig while he looked at her, just like a little kid on Christmas morning.

Janine's eyes grew wide, "Of course I have," she said through laughter. "I wasn't born yesterday, you know."

"What do you say? Line fishing with a pole for a while?"

"Sounds perfect. I haven't fished since I was forty-two or so, when my husband took me out on our former boat for the last time, the day before selling it. He bought it after getting a nice Christmas bonus from Bank of America that year. Then only two months later, he told me that he wasn't making commissions on new client business like he used to, and he'd really over- estimated his commission income, and had to sell the boat so we could pay the mortgage that month! It was awful. Something I'll never forget.

Ben just sat and listened, noticing her sincerity, and her beauty.

Janine continued, "I was always scared about running out of money when I was with him, because most of the time we were already out of money, and I could never figure out why and where it all went, and I hated it. Then I found out that it wasn't really him not getting enough new clientele commissions at all. Nope. It was my husband's gambling addiction. He was always giving up almost his entire pay to these thugs that he played high-stakes poker with, and he kept losing. Well, that's enough about my past. Let's time travel back to the present and get to work a little bit, okay?"

Ben nodded affirmatively. He could use a break anyway. "Let's go down to the galley for a while. I'll put on some coffee."

Ben turned and headed downstairs, Janine followed closely. Ben pulled a chair out for her and began putting the coffee together.

"Ben, you appear to be in a really good place. Is that a correct assumption?"

"Yes," he answered enthusiastically, "As a matter of fact, despite my continued aging, I haven't felt this good physically in at least 15 or 20 years, and mentally I feel sharp. Emotionally, I'm better than I was, but still healing. I feel grateful for having had this very serendipitous experience and for having met you. You're amazing, Janine. You really are."

Janine felt herself blushing a little, but responded coolly, "I'm so glad to hear this, Ben, and I'm very happy for you. You really have come a long way in a very short period of time, and have some success to celebrate. It's important that you share with me the things that come along that you find difficult and struggle with, both mentally and emotionally. Things will be coming to the surface that will tempt you to backslide and drink. That's when it will be critical for you to have a toolkit handy to help you get through those times without relapsing. I'm here, and I will continue being here for you, Ben. Anything that comes up, call me, text me. I'll be there for you as fast as I can. I promise. Okay?"

Ben felt warm inside. "Okay. Thank you. I'm very grateful to you, Janine."

"You're welcome, Ben. So it's been a whole day outside of the rehab ward. You've had some time alone. Any issues or temptations?"

"Not for alcohol" he said, getting back up to get the pot and pour the coffee. "Well, last night I was a little out of sorts with being in that big house alone. It's creepy at night to me now. I guess alcohol was keeping me from noticing as much as I am now." Janine could see the smile even from behind him as he turned away to go to the coffee pot. She smiled too.

Ben continued, "I think I was really ready to stop the drinking, that's why I planned what I did. I didn't know at the time that I could've died from withdrawal, which would have been especially awful while out at sea alone. I don't know what I was thinking of pulling that stunt. Ultimately, that was really stupid for me to do. I obviously didn't have all of the information that I needed."

"Ben, don't beat yourself up about it now. It's over. It worked out. You're okay, you're not drinking, your boat is intact, and I'm here now to help you stay clean."

"Honestly, facing the silence of that big house for the first time in years, without drinking, was the first difficulty, but it passed. The silence in the house can be deafening, but quiet is so rare in today's world, I endure it on purpose just to give my senses a mini-vacation."

Janine moved a little closer and put her hand on top of Ben's and looked into his eyes, "How did you handle the silence this time?"

"I endured it again. It seemed different. It was better. I started enjoying it. After Bessie passed, I was terrified of it, then I was self-medicating all the time, and adjusted to it, and often didn't notice it.

This morning when I woke up, the silence was profound, and I noticed it just long enough for the old fear to come back into my thoughts and try to start the cycle of fear all over again. I imagined that in that silence and in that darkness, the walls were simultaneously sliding in silence towards me, and would soon be crushing me like a car in the crusher at the junkyard.

After about thirty seconds of letting those thoughts run through my mind, I sat up and turned on the light. The walls were where they were supposed to be. Thank Goodness!"

Janine wasn't sure what to say other than, "Ben, I'm so proud of you for not caving in and drinking when you felt that fear. Thank you for being strong like that. Keep it up. You can do this, I know you can. I'm rooting for you."

Ben wasn't sure about what he had just heard. It was so different from the way other people talked to him. It was encouraging for sure. He felt good inside after hearing all of that, and he liked it.

They finally went topside. Janine was much better at fishing than Ben imagined. She bordered on being a sport fishing expert from what he could tell. She started explaining to him why she preferred one lure over another and why, all in a technically detailed way that Ben could never have delivered. He was impressed.

When the sun got lower, the clouds began rolling in pretty quickly, and the wind began picking up, so they decided to call it a day and return home. When they pulled in, Janine climbed up onto the dock and tied the ship to the cleat with Ben's coaching, then waited for him to join her.

Ben walked Janine to her car a couple of blocks away and thanked her for a lovely time and for being such a good counselor, making her blush a little this time. Once she was all buckled in, Janine turned and looked deeply into his eyes at point blank range and softly said, "Bye Ben. See you on Wednesday, and thank you." She slowly drove away, waving and smiling at him while looking at him in her rearview mirror.

Ben watched her drive off, and waved back. He also had a big smile on his face, and he felt like a young man who was just beginning to date. He couldn't wait to see her on Wednesday.

7

REVELATIONS

Ben turned and began walking back to where Bessie was docked so he could finish cleaning and then lock up. As he crossed to the other side of the pier to go down the ramp, he noticed a black SUV parked about a half block down on the same side of the street as the boat slips, facing him. He couldn't tell if there were more than just the driver because of the black out glass in all windows except the front driver's and passenger's windows, and the windshield, but he assumed there were, just to add for error.

Rather than walk down the ramp, Ben decided to see what, if anything would happen if he simply stood there on the pier looking at the SUV. He sensed that he might be asking for trouble for no good reason, but this activity was very unusual, and he was curious. Besides, he hadn't done anything wrong. He'd only given up drinking.

Let me guess, he thought, now that I no longer drink, it's the thugs from the whiskey factory here to help me rethink my decision.

Suddenly, the SUV pulled out a little from the edge of the pier and drove past Ben while accelerating. The only thing Ben could see was that the driver had dark hair, dark sunglasses, and wore a white shirt and a dark gray suit. As the vehicle passed him, he could see two people's silhouettes in the backseat, just as he had assumed. The SUV quickly drove to the end of the pier, turned left onto Commercial Street, and disappeared. *Hmmm. That was strange,* Ben thought. He decided to mentally log it, then let it go. He flashed on Hernandez and thought, *It can't be him, not after all this time.*

He boarded Bessie and got things tidied up for his meeting on Wednesday with Janine. He had made his mind up on the walk back from her car that he was going to take tomorrow and just be home. He wanted to take stock of the place and, perhaps, identify more clearly what changes he felt that he needed to make regarding staying in that big house alone.

Being with other people while in rehab had made him realize just how isolated he'd become since Bessie's passing. At first, he had been somewhat overwhelmed by so many others, but after a while he found himself enjoying their company, especially when the group had intimately shared their addiction details, which had brought everyone closer together in spirit.

Ben had only been home for about fourteen hours, eight of which he'd slept, but during that time he felt the silence transform itself from a welcome break, to a crushing weight that could barely be endured. He could eliminate it temporarily with television noise, or the radio, or by playing opera records on his turntable, but in the end, all of it would become nearly as unbearable as the silence. He yearned for a balance between silence, alone time, and being with others, especially now that he was thinking clearly. He could see how that was what he really wanted and needed. A simple, sober coexistence with others, who are also simple, sober, and conventional.

When Ben arrived home, it was almost dinner time. He saw Andrew's car in the driveway. He was glad he was finally going to see him face to face for the first time in over a month. He opened the door and threw his keys into the key bowl by the coat rack, took off his boots and slid his feet into his wool lined muck-lucks that he always kept by the front door, and went looking for Andrew.

Ben found him out on the back patio grilling a couple of nice steaks. But before letting Andrew know that he was there, Ben stood for a moment taking stock of his son. He loved how Andrew had grown up. He had matured into a tall, fit, good looking, very successful young man. He felt pride swell in his heart when he realized that he was essentially looking at himself 40 years ago, except Andrew was taller, at six feet two inches, and had thick red hair that he kept immaculately trimmed.

He'd always admired Andrew's attention to detail, a gift that he seemed to have been born with, but Ben could never imagine shaving everyday like his son. Today he noticed that Andrew was staring into the BBQ flames wearing blue jeans, dark blue Converse All Stars®, and his gray University of Maine sweatshirt. For Ben, it was a little strange to see Andrew letting himself engage in that level of relaxation. While growing up, it was something Ben rarely saw him do.

"Andrew!" Ben quickly walked over to Andrew, threw his arms around him and gave him a kiss on his cheek.

"Hey, Dad. Good to see you. You look great."

"So do you, son. Grilling some meat, I see."

"Yup. I thought you might be tired after your meeting with, what did you call her? Junie or . . ."

"Janine. Her name is Janine."

"Yeah, that's it. Anyway, I figured you'd be tired after a long day with her, and since you said in your text that you'd be home for dinner, well, I stopped at the Old Beef Store and got us a couple of ribeyes. I hope you don't mind?"

"No, not at all. They smell really good. I haven't had a steak since, well, over a month, more like two months. I'm sure my doctor would love that bit of news, too." Ben laughed.

Andrew looked at Ben seriously now and said, "So, Dad, what's the deal? What, where, I . . . I don't even know where to begin."

"I quit drinking Andrew. I went out to sea to do it alone, and I had an accident. I almost didn't make it back to shore, but when I did, I drove myself to the hospital. While there, I met a nurse, who is also a counselor at the hospital rehab facility that I ultimately went into. She knew I was going through alcohol withdrawal and became my personal guide, angel, counselor, and support buddy. Now I'm seeing her three times per week as a recovering alcoholic. She's my counselor and guide until I no longer need that level of support, and can finally resist alcohol on my own no matter what happens or life throws at me."

"That's amazing, Dad! So, you did it? You don't drink now?"

Ben looked at Andrew seriously, "No. I don't."

Andrew flipped both steaks over and closed the lid down on the grill. He gave Ben another hug, this time patting him on the back repeatedly, while saying "Good job, Dad. I really mean it. That must have been incredibly hard."

"Well, it's not a once and done you know. You can't do something regularly for that long and then not miss it when you stop doing it. I still think about drinking, particularly when I feel stressed about something. And, by the way, thank you for not having a cold six pack or some mixed drinks ready or, for that matter, you didn't ask me if I wanted a drink when I came in. It wouldn't have been that big of a deal, but I am grateful for not having to be confronted with that type of decision right now. I don't know why, but I cannot stand the smell of alcohol at all anymore. Even rubbing alcohol rubs me the wrong way. Pun intended," Ben said with a big smile on his face.

Andrew nodded, "So you're not messing around! This is for real and now you're really changing and are going to be healthier for doing it. Congratulations! This is really great news and I, for one, am very happy with your decision. Ironic how the smell bothers you now, but I imagine that not liking the smell can help eliminate the temptation to want to drink."

"Definitely!" Ben said.

Andrew added, "I've heard the same thing often happens with smokers who quit, and then can't stand the smell of burning tobacco afterwards."

They ate their steaks while making small talk: Andrew let Ben know that Celia was coming over in the morning for a visit, then gave him an update on his own life. Finally, he recommended that Ben try to just ease into life a little more. "Perhaps not push so hard, Dad. Maybe slow down just a little to minimize chances of a relapse."

Ben listened and nodded while he devoured his meal. After dinner they did the cleanup together, then retired to the front porch. "Now that I think about it," Ben said, "Sitting out here after dinner demands a cigar but, I know as sure as I'm sitting here that if I smoke one, it will be a trigger for me to drink alcohol. Maybe we'd better take ourselves into the den and watch some sports on television or something."

Andrew nodded profusely, and was already getting up, "Sure thing, Dad, I'm sorry. I wasn't thinking."

"No big deal, son. I wasn't either, at first, but then it hit me that I'd better not."

Once in the den and comfortable, Ben tried to watch the game, but had so much going on mentally that, even though he was looking right at the screen, he wasn't noticing anything in particular.

"Dad, what are you thinking about? You're obviously not watching the game."

"What? Oh, sorry, I'm just thinking about how big this house is, and the size of the lot we still own. I'm thinking it might be time to make some changes."

"Like what?" Andrew sat up straight in his chair now that Ben was talking about selling the house and the property that had been the family rock for decades.

Ben answered, "Oh, I don't know. I can't really see myself paying people to take care of this huge property forever, nor can I imagine myself walking an extra five miles per day just going to all the places that I need to inside this huge house. It's a lot to keep clean. It's a lot to go up and down all of these stairs all the time, and it's getting ridiculous how much time, effort, and money it takes to keep the grounds tended, the plants happy, and to pay the taxes on this place."

Andrew said, "I sometimes get tired while I'm here too, so I understand how you're feeling, at least about some of it, especially those damn stairs! I have often wondered how you and mom were still managing them multiple times per day."

Ben looked directly into Andrew's eyes, "Getting old is harder than I thought it would be, for sure."

Andrew was Ben's attorney, and he had just finished redoing Ben's trust, health care proxy, and other final documents only a couple of years prior. He thought he had done an excellent job. Doing a trust can be a fairly simple process, but his father's estate had a lot going on with special bequests, historic clauses regulating the property to a certain extent, as well as Ben's business and other assets related to his fishing and lobstering operation. He always did this work for his dad free of charge, but he was dreading the thought of having to change everything again.

Ben said, "I have a couple of ideas, but haven't decided anything yet. I'll let you know when I do. I am seriously contemplating some major changes, though, and I just wanted you to have a heads up about it. Oh! And, thanks again for taking care of the place and collecting my mail while I was gone. I can't tell you what a load off it was knowing that you were taking care of everything."

"No problem, really. Anytime, Dad. That's one benefit of family."

Ben could always see the little boy in Andrew, and had to pinch himself once in a while to remind himself that the man sitting across the room was his son, and not some stranger, or a buddy.

"You said you had a sponsor from rehab coming to spend four hours per day for three days per week until you can be solo with no issues. Can you tell me a little more about that? About her?"

Ben didn't hesitate. "Her name is Janine Thompson. She's 63, pretty as heck, widowed for about twelve years now. She works as a registered nurse in the surgical recovery ward, and other parts of the hospital as they need her to, part time, but she spends most of her time in the hospital's alcohol rehabilitation center as a one-on-one counselor. That's where I met her. Apparently, she's been working there for almost twenty years. I really like spending time with her. She makes me laugh, and I feel happy when she is near me."

Ben's eyes grew wider, and he could feel his cheeks getting warm from intense blushing when he said that. He avoided looking over at Andrew, but he could see Andrew staring at him out of the corner of his eye. Not able to stand it, Andrew said, "Dad, did you just hear yourself?"

"What? It's nothing. I'm just describing—" Andrew cut him off abruptly,

"—You're just describing your feelings for Janine, and it sounds like you're falling in love with her. Is that the truth?"

"Nah! I think I just have warm and fuzzy feelings for her a bit right now because I am so needy for some female companionship, and because she was there for me every minute of my withdrawal while I learned how to abstain from drinking. She taught me how, but held my hand while I puked, and eventually I learned how to do what she was teaching me. I will never forget what she did for me as a total stranger.

She is an Angel sent to help me recover from booze, help me recover from losing your mother, and to help me recover my own sense of self-mastery over my life. She is special, Andrew. Very special. Love? Yes, but not romantic . . . wait . . . no . . . You know, I just might be falling in love with her after all. It can't be though, I barely know her, but there is this good energy I feel when she's with me. Maybe because I associate my healing journey with her kind presence. I don't know." Ben abruptly stopped talking, looking shocked, while he analyzed this new revelation a bit more.

With his eyes still wide, Ben looked over at Andrew, who met his gaze, but remained motionless. "I am smitten with her, and she makes my heart do somersaults in my chest just from seeing her walk towards me. When I look into those dancing candle lights flickering in her eyes, I lose myself in them. They're downright mesmerizing." Suddenly, Ben stopped mid-sentence, finally snapping out of his romantic trance. "Oh gosh. I'm so sorry, Andrew, to be talking this way about someone other than your mother in this way. I apologize."

"Dad. It's okay. Really. Again, I'm thrilled for you. This is so amazing. Rather than have one good offset something bad, it seems like you've had the privilege of having one good thing, giving up drinking, immediately pay dividends, and bringing you another good thing—a personal healing Angel."

Ben lit up and became even more animated. He smiled and laughed a lot while talking about Janine, completely unaware that his words were gradually filling the room with an intense, warm, invisible, electrical fog of loving energy.

Watching Ben happily going on and on about this new woman in his life, with so much intense, positive energy, was something Andrew couldn't remember seeing with his dad before. He enjoyed seeing his father happy like this and now no longer drinking anymore, and it made him want to cry from joy. Andrew gave Ben a big smile, nodding occasionally as he continued listening to his father, with no doubt that he was witnessing real love take its course.

The next morning Ben awoke to the smell of cooking bacon which immediately made him realize how hungry he was. He got up, quickly dressed, and went downstairs. As he rounded the corner from the stairwell exit to the kitchen, Celia gave out a little squeal of delight seeing him appear. "Daddy! It's so good to see you again." She stopped cooking, wiping her hands on her apron. "You look amazing . . . well, except for the whiskers," she said laughing.

Ben gave her a big bear hug and a kiss, and sat down at the counter to watch her finish cooking them breakfast.

"So, babygirl, how's everything going with you? How's school been?"

"Oh, school is school. I love seeing all the children in the morning. They're all so unique in their own special way. I've been surprised by just how much poverty there is, even way up here in Maine. Most people here are from families that got rich from timber, rich from fishing the sea, or are already wealthy and are now coming here to retire. Heck, Wall Street types are coming here all the time now, building big vacation homes, or at least that's what I used to think. Now I know better."

She set a plate of fried eggs, thick sliced hickory smoked bacon, toast, and a squeeze bottle with organic clover honey in it down in front of him. Everything looked delicious. Ben nodded in appreciation and began eating in earnest.

Celia continued, "Anyway, the kids are great and so is the rest of the staff, but the principal is a jerk and I think he has the hots for me." Celia looked at Ben with one of those, if he ever touches me or tries anything looks, finishing with, "If he is ever untoward with me, I'll call the cops, file a report, haul him in front of the education board, and sue him for sexual harassment."

"That's my girl!" Ben added.

"And, there are these two kids, one is a boy, the other a girl. I'm not sure why, but the girl went to the principal about three months ago and said that I was really mean to her all the time in class. That's when my own trips to the principal's office began for me. The boy did the exact same thing, then they both met with the principal. He then called me in to meet with them and hear their complaints. I was shocked. Now, I have to look at these two kids, and it's hard for me to not feel like I want to come up with a way to get even with them, but they're kids. I can't do that. Other than that, I'm all set, Dad! What about you? Andrew told me that you've been through a lot recently but didn't say what it was about. I thought you took a vacation. Where'd you go?"

Ben finished the last bite of toast with honey, which he always saved for last. It was like finishing the meal with a breakfast dessert. He stood and walked his plate over to the dishwasher. "Where have I been?

I group texted you and Andrew that I went to the hospital after my accident at sea, remember? I've been in the alcohol rehabilitation center at Maine Medical Center for approximately the last month."

"What? How did I miss that text? My God! I feel so bad, Dad. I'm sorry. Why? You've never had any issue with alcohol that I could see, Dad. What the hell? When did all this happen?"

"It's been happening over a long period of time, but started when your mom, God rest her soul, got sick. I was so worried, and I felt so stressed. Out on the water, whiskey became my best friend." Tears were welling up in his eyes. "The good news is, I've completely stopped drinking alcohol for good. It's a new behavior for me, but it's already getting a little easier as time goes on. It was pretty rough for a while, though. Luckily, they minimized my pain and prevented me from having hallucinations while withdrawing from the alcohol."

"I had no idea. Wow! How did it come to be?"

"I was pretty sure that I'd developed a problem, then one day I ran out of booze on board Bessie. I went about 14 hours without anything, but when I awoke in the morning, I couldn't stop the shaking. Not just my hands, but my whole body was shivering, and I wasn't cold. That's when I was sure. When I got another bottle, I opened it right away, drank almost a third of it, and the shaking stopped like magic."

"Oh, Dad." Celia began rubbing his back. He was looking down at the counter while recanting the story, trying not to cry as the emotions welled up inside, eventually filling his entire being, forcing him to pause before continuing, so he could regain enough control over them to be able to finish the story.

"So, I made a pact with myself, then packed a bunch of supplies and took Bessie out. I anchored off shore and intended to stay there for at least two weeks, alone, no booze. Just me, the sea, and the salt air. Always the best medicine."

"Did it work? Are you . . . wait, sorry, you already said that you were no longer drinking."

"No. Not the way I intended. A short time after getting started, I drank my final bottle, and decided to line fish. As luck would have it, I nailed a pretty big one and, like a true blue drunk, instead of using my reel and adjusting the drag, I just reached up and grabbed the line trying to slow it down."

"No! You did not." Celia was totally shocked by this. She knew her dad was one of the best, most knowledgeable fishing figures on all the piers in Portland Harbor.

"Yes, I did. Look." Ben held up his hand and Celia instantly spotted the missing tip. "Yeah, small price to pay considering that my sponsor, Janine, told me that I likely would've died going through detox alone while at sea. Guess that wasn't the best idea either. I think your Mom made sure I got in safely, maybe even helped cause the accident knowing it would ultimately save my life." Ben gave Celia a big smile now. "You, come here again."

Celia immediately gave him a long hug, then a kiss on his cheek, "I'm so glad that you're okay, and even happier that you came to what you did about drinking, and decided to do something about it. That's fantastic, father."

Andrew came bounding into the kitchen from upstairs. "Morning all. I smell the food, but don't see anything. Is it all gone?"

Both Ben and Celia greeted him.

"No worries, brother, I'll make you some fresh cooked eggs right now. Fried? Scrambled?"

"Scrambled would be fine, if you don't mind. Thanks, sis."

"You're welcome," she said, giving him a quick look of affection.

"Dad was just telling me how he stopped drinking. Isn't that incredible?"

"Yes. It is the best news I've heard about anything in a long time, definitely," he said, smiling at no one in particular. "Did he tell you about Janine?"

Ben looked at Andrew as if he had been betrayed.

"What? You told me about her, and you didn't say it needed to be kept a secret or anything."

"No, I didn't, but I didn't think I'd also need to tell you to please be discreet and leave the telling about new things happening in my life to me, thank you very much."

"I'm sorry, Dad. You're right."

Celia listened to this while pulling raw bacon from its package. Without missing a beat she said, "Yes, he mentioned Janine, but now it sounds like there is more to her than what I've been told so far, which is absolutely nothing, only that she is your sponsor."

Ben said, "Janine is my sponsor from the alcohol rehab center. She is sixty three years old and, yes, she is good looking, and personable, and intelligent, and kind, and pretty darned caring. There is nothing wrong with any of it."

Both Celia and Andrew kept looking first at each other, and then at Ben, back and forth, finding it harder by the second to not crack up laughing while watching their father try to explain his pretty new sponsor to them.

Celia chuckled, "You're so cute, Dad."

"Cute? What does cute have to do with anything? My focus is on getting as healthy as I can, then learning how to keep myself that way. Janine has already helped me enormously, and she is scheduled to spend at least four hours per day, three days per week with me to help keep me on the straight and narrow. So far, so good. I will admit that I do find her attractive. We'll see. I have no expectations or fantasies, and I haven't been looking for anyone to replace your mom since she passed away either."

Andrew said, "Dad, I told you last night that I'm very happy for you and have no issues with you doing anything you want to do that might also include Janine. You're a grown man and my father, not my son. I'm not going to get in your way about a potential new romance. No way. I love that this is happening, coincidentally, with stopping alcohol and getting healthier. It's been more than four years since Mom's death. You deserve this, Dad."

"I second all of that," said Celia. "Andrew's right. You are more than overdue for some good stuff and some love, and the right kind, if you know what I mean, and I'm thrilled about it too. For a minute there, I could feel a knot growing in my stomach, but then when Andrew added the part at the end about it being more than four years since mom's passing . . . well, that's when it hit me that you must be really lonely."

"I only felt that way for short periods of time, here and there, over the last couple of years. I think the booze kept me so medicated that I was able to mask my pain and my loneliness behind it. It never stops amazing me how the habit grew without me noticing until I was in trouble, and then without any warning, I had an issue on my hands. My next meeting with Janine is tomorrow morning at Bessie. We have a standing date on Mondays, Wednesdays, and Fridays, from 8am to noon ish. So far, so good."

"I like your choice of words, Dad."

"What choice of words, I mean what words are you talking about?"

"'We have a standing date.' You used *a date* instead of an appointment."

"Oh, come on." Ben began laughing now. "I can't believe you're that attuned to what I'm saying that you make a deal about something like a play on words."

Before Celia could answer, Andrew chimed in with, "The subconscious is a slippery animal, Dad." He smiled extra wide for emphasis.

"Hey, Dad, do you still get the paper, or a newspaper? I know we used to get the Portland Press Herald."

"Yes, I haven't cancelled the subscription, although I should because I just never seem to have the time to read it."

Celia anxiously said, "Well, today is your lucky day, Dad. I'm going to go out and fetch the paper. When I get back, how about we all go into the den, divide the paper up into sections, and read the paper and drink some more coffee?"

Ben nodded, "Hey, that actually sounds great. Thanks for cooking, and thanks for getting the paper."

Ben put a fresh pot of coffee on. He left Celia's mug next to the machine, and he and Andrew went into the den. After a couple of minutes, Ben looked at his watch and said, "It's been a bit of time, I wonder what's taking Celia so long to come back with the paper?"

"You're right. Good question, Dad. I'll go and check it out."

Andrew began walking through the kitchen and was just getting ready to head into the living room towards the foyer, when he heard the front door slam shut. Celia appeared with the newspaper, out of breath and looking concerned.

"Everything all right?" Andrew asked her.

Celia kept walking past him with the paper, and mumbled "I'm not sure."

Once inside the den, she quickly put the paper down on the coffee table and looked at Ben intensely.

Ben knew something was going on. "What?"

"If we lived anywhere else I'd just overlook it, Dad. But when I went out to get the paper, there was this black SUV parked the equivalent of a couple of blocks away, but facing our house. It was just sitting there, but I could see two people sitting in the front seats.”

“Shit!” Ben said. “Okay, now I know that something is up. Damn it. I think I know who, and what this is about. Sounds like an old acquaintance of mine has come back to pay me a visit, and likely wants a favor. He’s likely sent his assistants to see if I’m still living here. If they want to talk to me, they’ll come to me when they’re ready. They’re a strange lot.”

Andrew and Celia looked at one another a bit alarmed. Ben noticed them and tried to reassure them that it was nothing, “Trust me. I’ve dealt with these guys several times in the past and all is going to be okay. Are they of a questionable nature? Yes. Are they dangerous? Again, yes. Will they hurt me or us? No, not likely. I’ve always accommodated them, and it was always lucrative to do so in the past. Never had any issues with them, although I’m aware that others, who are no longer here, used to. Luckily for me, I’ve always had something they needed and were willing to pay handsomely for, so they never had much motive to harm me and, again, they pay really well.”

Andrew and Celia stared at him for a long time, then they both let him know that they were nervous about what they had just heard, beginning with Celia. “Dad, why are we just hearing about this now? You need to call the police.

Andrew took a deep breath and let it out slowly, “Okay, Dad, Celia’s right. You should at least notify the authorities, that way they know that something is amiss, and will send patrol units around more often to check on things.”

Ben answered, "I assure you, everything's going to be fine. I'm just a little concerned because they've never come near the house before, they always met me down at the docks. When I do speak with them, I'm going to let them know that the old days are over, and that I'm fully retired and not running cargo for other people any longer. I'm pretty sure that's what they want. I'm going to let them know that our house is off limits, and they should contact me the way that they always have in the past: by paying me a visit where Bessie is berthed after 4 p.m."

Andrew asked, "And I'm with Celia, how come you've never mentioned any of this stuff before Dad?"

"Why? Because it didn't concern you, and it still doesn't. I'm still here. I've done fine in the past dealing with these guys, and I'm more confident now, than ever, that I'll be able to handle things fine. You were both too young to be hearing about anything that might be scary or potentially harmful to you guys, or your mom, and it was all business involving my boat for hire, something that I never really shared with any of you. I just went to work on the water, made money, paid the bills and raised you guys, and never looked back. I never asked what I was hauling, but I'm certain the cargo was illegal to possess. I can't simply call the police. I'd have too many questions to answer. I'm not certain I could explain enough to still walk away a free man."

"Well, I'm glad we know about it now, Dad. Anything I can do or that we can do?"

"No, I'm going to tell them to buzz off and it'll be over. No worries, okay?"

Andrew looked like he was concentrating hard on a potential solution, "Okay, Dad, but if things get even a little weird, promise you'll tell me so we can help you figure out what to do next."

Celia said, "Yes, I agree. I don't like the sound of this at all. Promise?"

Ben looked at them both, "I promise I'll keep you in the loop if things get weird."

"How about calling the police, Dad?" Celia added.

"That's the last thing that needs to happen right now. If I feel the situation warrants it, I'll certainly notify them about what's going on."

The answer seemed to satisfy both Andrew and Celia, although the incident had changed the dynamic of the morning. Afterwards, no one wanted to go into the den to read the paper. They all sat in the kitchen for a while longer, sipping coffee, staring off into space, making small talk. Each one of them imagined different outcomes from this strange event, and, because of that, they were all getting nervous about what might come next.

8

SEÑOR JUAN SANTIAGO HERNANDEZ

Ben and Janine continued meeting for the rest of the week. He was feeling better about living without alcohol. Janine, whether she knew it or not, seemed to have added the spark needed to get him beyond just surviving alcohol addiction. He looked forward to each day now, and couldn't wait to see her on their meeting days. She brought him out of himself, and he loved
how he felt inside when that happened. It was all new, and very exciting. Sometimes, he almost felt young again.

Friday came and Janine bade him farewell until Monday. She was taking some advanced training classes at the hospital on Wednesdays and Fridays in the evenings, so she needed to head out right away to make the class on time.

Ben thanked her and watched her walk down the dock before turning to finish tidying up. Once done, he locked Bessie up and started walking up the ramp to the pier. An icy wind out of the north picked up speed as it swirled past him. Ben zipped his jacket up a little tighter and put his hands in his pockets. He reached the top of the ramp and opened the gate to the pier. As soon as he closed the gate, a big, black SUV raced up next to him on the pier, screeching to a halt. Two men jumped out. The man who exited the front passenger side door cut Ben off in front, and the second man who exited the rear

93

passenger door got behind Ben to keep him from getting any ideas about running in another direction.

Ben stopped walking and looked at the man in front of him. "What do you want?" he asked.

"Mr. Hernandez needs a word."

Ben raised his voice a notch, "Please tell Mr. Hernandez that, while I'm sure his offer for what he wants me to do for him is more than generous, that I'm in the middle of a personal recovery from a couple of things, and I am also retired. I no longer do much except some light lobstering and I take a couple of folks out line fishing here and there, but I no longer take commercial work of any kind. I'm too old, and I don't need any more money. Hell, it's a part- -time job just managing what I already have. Please tell Mr. Hernandez thank you all the same."

The man facing Ben seemed unaffected and said, "Mr. Hernandez wants to talk to you. Get in."

Ben knew that this was a non-negotiable command, and that any further resistance would likely result in physical injury and pain, so he got into the SUV, and was promptly blindfolded.
Ben wasn't sure where they took him, until he heard hundreds of seagulls screeching overhead and the foul odor of the landfill fully engulfed his nostrils, overloading them with the stench of monumental rotting.

Once out of the vehicle, someone pulled his blindfold off. Ben could see another black vehicle coming towards him. It was a limousine, and it was in no hurry as it slowly glided past the mountains of buried, throw-away treasures that the seagulls seemed determined to excavate. The long, black, low profile, and quiet engine of the vehicle seemed to emanate evil, adding to Ben's uncertainty. He suddenly felt a sinister energy grate coarsely against him, like monstrous tentacles reaching out from somewhere unseen, finding its prey and holding it in place until the mouth can get close enough to consume it. Despite the bright sun, darkness increased by the second as the limousine slowly cruised closer, finally coming to a stop a mere two feet in front of him. The driver, dressed in formal limousine driver attire, and wearing a captain's hat with a shiny black brim, got out and walked over to the passenger side rear door and opened it for the rear passenger, then stepped aside and stood at attention facing Ben.

After a long minute, Ben's old business acquaintance, Mr. Juan Santiago Hernandez, stepped out of the limousine, quickly pulling his coat tails down and adjusting his shiny, dark gray cape where it snapped together at his neckline. He looked at Ben seriously, then leaned over and mumbled something to the driver, before taking a few steps in Ben's direction, his gaze locked and fixed on Ben's eyes as he moved closer.

"Mr. Scot. Good to see you. How long has it been anyway? A long time my friend, no?"

Ben bristled a little. "Hello, Señor Hernandez. Que Pasa?"

"No mucho. Gracias."

"I won't bother to waste our time, my friend. I will get to why I'm here without hesitation."

"I know why," Ben answered instantly, "You want me to move some bags of drugs or money for you like I did a few times before, correct?"

"Almost, my friend, almost. Sì, I want you to move some stuff for me, but this time it's different. No drugs, no money. In fact, let's just leave it at, you don't really have a need to know what I'm wanting to move, so let's leave that part a mystery. I will say this, Señor Scot, my cargo isn't alive, and won't hurt you, or should I say, it can't hurt you."

"With all due respect, I'm retired. I don't do commercial jobs anymore. I don't need the work, and I don't want your job or anyone else's."

"Oh, I see. Hmmm . . . well then, I guess apologies are in order. I had no idea that you were retired. Well, I did hear a little rumor, but decided that I'd come and check with you myself. I want to make absolutely sure that you would actually turn down a job that will pay you $2 million."

The huge amount surprised Ben. That was more money than he'd made over his entire lifetime fishing and lobstering. He really didn't need the money, but it sure would allow him to pay off all debts once and for all, sell his big house and buy another, smaller seaside cottage nearby.

Ben imagined himself standing his ground and letting them know that he couldn't be bought. He pictured himself saying, Well, that certainly is a lot of money but, like I said, I don't do commercial work of any kind any longer, Señor Hernandez.

Not only did he fear for his life, but he was really having a hard time believing that he was, once again, faced with having to deal with these guys. He'd really thought that, when he did the last job, almost ten years ago now, that it would be the last. After a decade of no contact, he was convinced it was finally over, and he'd actually stopped thinking about the cartel, and mostly forgotten about all of his past encounters and business ventures with them. On top of that, he already knew that doing business with Hernandez, or anyone else like him, was a slippery slope.

Do one job for them well, and they want another one done, and another. They don't care about the agenda, or the schedule, or what the rules are of the person they're asking. They only want to hear you say yes. Ben could hear his own voice as if he were listening to someone else. "Okay, you've got yourself a deal, but only for this one time. I will do it for $2 million, in cash, small bills, unmarked. The usual criteria."

"Excellent, Señor! I thought the amount might persuade you.

"The only undone item is the cargo. What is it that you're having me move for you. If I'm going to be on the same boat as your cargo, I need to know what I'm moving in order to better protect it and myself."

Juan stood looking at Ben, but Ben could see his mind working overtime trying to process all the potential variables that might come up and interfere with his plan. Finally, he said, "Human transplant organs. Our friends in the north have a great need for certain organs.

That has made every part of the organ transplant industry extremely lucrative."

"Obviously, if you can pay me what you're offering me, it must be. Where do they come from?"

"That doesn't concern you. I've answered your questions, and offered you a very handsome sum of money to do a simple job for me. You said we had a deal. My associates will be in touch with you soon to arrange the loading of the cargo in your hold, which needs to be kept very cold, but not so cold that it would freeze the organs. Can you ensure that?"

"I don't necessarily feel right about this. Yeah, the money is fantastic, but the whole thing feels wrong to me. I know of someone else that I'm sure will be fine working with you."

"Mr. Scot, that would mean involving others. Since you have been utilized in the past with no issues, you are the person we want for this job. You are still going out on the water, so you can do this for me, and you cannot change your mind on me now."

"Yes, I can, and I am. I have all the money I need, so it isn't all that big of an incentive for me."

"So, you're turning me down, Señor Scot? Think carefully about your real, final answer. Remember, I have friends and connections here in the States that you wouldn't believe. Aside from me simply having you killed or maimed, I can still make your life a living hell as the inspectors, and fishing regulators, and U.S. government IRS agents all decide to start combing through your records, tax filings, and your fishing vessel."

Ben was really getting annoyed now. "No, you listen! Apparently you're hard of hearing. You still keep asking me to help you even though I've said no three times now. As far as your threats, well, certainly all that bureaucracy raining down on my head would definitely be an inconvenience, but they will all go away in the end, with their collective tails between their legs, because my attorney, my accountant, and me, have all been honest, and legal, and the regulators won't be able to find anything."

"That's what you think, Señor Scot. Apparently you aren't that creative and don't think outside of the box too often. Myself, well, I have to do that a lot, and I have already thought of half a dozen things I can do on your behalf that would ruin your existence for the rest of your natural life. How are your children doing, Señor Scot? Andrew and Sissy, no, Celia, yes, Andrew and Celia? How are they doing?" Hernandez stood there looking at Ben with a sinister, half grin on this face, waiting for an answer.

"Go for it. Do what you have to do, Hernandez." Ben said icily, purposely dropping his title. "But if you hurt either one of my children, I will hunt you down and kill you with my bare hands. You'll wake up just in time to take your last breath while you watch me choke the last of your miserable life out of you. Got it?"

Hernandez motioned to the driver who instantly came to life again, like a remote controlled toy, and opened the door for his boss.

Before the driver closed the door, Hernandez leaned out of the opening giving Ben a dead serious look, adding, "Think about our meeting today, Señor Scot. I will give you until Sunday afternoon. My driver will leave you with a phone to use to contact me. Do not smash the phone and throw it away after calling me. You have until Sunday afternoon at 5pm. If you call and say no, or don't call, then be prepared to deal with the consequences, which I will leave up to your imagination to decide what they might include.

Hernandez grabbed the handle of the door and pulled hard, slamming it closed. The driver was so surprised he jumped an inch or so from the percussion of the slam.

Ben watched them drive away, then noticed a small object left behind lying on the ground. It was the phone Hernandez said to use. Ben grabbed the phone, smashed it down on the pavement with all his might, and stomped on the remnants before walking away more determined than ever to not do Hernandez's bidding.

9

THE PLAN PART I

Ben headed home trying to control his anger long enough to come up with a plan. His mind kept racing, I can't believe that after ten long years, an entire decade, these guys are showing up again? Damn it! I have to figure this out. I will figure this out. I damn sure don't need trouble, or illness, or injury, or more death, or jail. Have these guys ever thought about just going legal for a change? Probably less trouble and less costly in the long run. What a bunch of idiots. Really, more like the worst kind, dangerous idiots.

Ben texted Andrew and Celia right away and told them to meet him as soon as possible at the house. Celia, leave work now, Andrew, same for you. Come to the house right away. You're both in danger.

Ben never kept much in the way of armaments, but he did have a .357 magnum, a double-barreled shotgun, and a deer hunting rifle with a scope. Some of his friends belonged to various gun clubs and kept far more dangerous arms, but Ben always felt that he was adequately protected with what he owned and, in reality, he was.

Ben decided he'd better do something with Bessie to better protect her, as well. He wanted a fail-safe mechanism of some kind that he could use in a pinch should he suddenly find himself hijacked at sea loaded with Hernandez's black market body parts, or being told after he's done the job that, either they are going to pay him a much smaller amount, or pay him no money at all as a punishment for him resisting and saying no. Ben knew what he wanted to do for the most part, and he knew Andrew was just the person to help him figure it out and get it all implemented.

The sky was darkening fast from a massive Nor'easter moving in, pushing all reasonable weather aside like a monster kicking and batting aside anything, and everything getting in its way. Even before Ben could finish the ten-mile trek home, the wind gusts were pushing his truck around quite a bit, and massive snowflakes began falling in earnest. Luckily, for now, it was melting as soon as it hit the pavement. The weather forecast called for more overnight, but along with a warmup, so the rest of the storm would be all rain, albeit heavy at times. Basically, fall getting warmed up for winter.

Once home, Ben went to the gun closet and loaded all of his weapons. He nervously checked, and rechecked the windows like a caged animal. First in the kitchen, through the living room, into the foyer, and through the side door back into the kitchen. So far, everything was normal.

His phone rang and startled him so much that the hand he had resting on top of his .357 magnum inadvertently squeezed the trigger! Thanks to good practices, the safety was still on, preventing him from blowing his own foot apart. He looked at his phone. It was Janine.

"Hi, Ben. Terrible weather we're having, eh?"

"Yes, indeed we are. So you're cancelling tomorrow?"

"Yes."

Ben hesitated a few seconds before saying, "Well, I can understand that. See you Friday?"

"No, well, Ben, I'm not really sure how to say this, but I'm going to reduce our sessions to once per week and not do the three times per week after all. You're doing really well, and I think that three times per week might be a little too much. Besides, remember how bad off you were when we met at the hospital? Ben paused, then conceded, "Yes."

"Well, there are many more coming in right behind you all the time, and they need me too. You have a great rest of the week, keep up the good work, and I'll be anxious to hear all about it next Monday at 8 a.m. down at the dock."

Ben was really surprised, and more than a little confused. First, the crazy encounter with Hernandez after a decade, and now, after only a very short time out of rehab, Janine was unexpectedly scaling back on their sessions by more than half.

"Wait a minute, Janine, I'm doing really well because of your help. It's you. You bring out the best in me and make me want to stay straight. Well, I want that for me too, but you've been so good to me, and so good for me, that I don't want to let you down, or myself down. I feel like I need a nearly constant cheerleader, otherwise I know that, over time, I'm going to say to hell with it, and go and get drunk again because I'll be weary, and getting really sick and tired of the battle."

Janine hesitated, then said, "That's what I've been noticing. I'm not saying it's bad, it's just that I feel you becoming romantically attached to me and, as much as I'd like that too, I cannot let that happen. I need to give us more space. We can still work together, but I think it's important for us to be more focused on our work when we are together. You're a really amazing man, Ben. I can see why you and your wife were together for so long. You're a great catch, as my friends and I used to say about the men that really were a great catch. However, I'm primarily your counselor, and you're my client. It's just not allowed, and for good reason."

"I understand. Can we still do twice per week as a compromise? How about Tuesdays and Fridays, at least for a while?"

Janine stayed silent for what seemed like a really long time. Finally she said, "Ben, I'm sorry. It's just that . . . that, well, I think I have feelings for you too, and I'm afraid of it because, I don't know, I just am. I don't want to end up married again and find out that I married another lifeless dweeb, or someone who would rather jerk off all the time than have sex with me. Oh, what am I saying? I apologize. Yes, Tuesdays and Fridays will work."

Ben could picture Janine's beautiful face looking at him while giving him one of her gorgeous smiles. He smiled as he held that image in his head. "See you Tuesday then. And, . . . thank you."

"Sure thing. See you Tuesday, Ben."

After he hung up the phone, he saw headlights approaching. He carefully rested his hand back onto the handle of his gun as he watched the car come closer. Once the car turned into the driveway and pulled forward more, he saw that it was Andrew.

Before Andrew could make it into the house, Ben felt his phone buzz him. It was Celia texting him that she wasn't coming due to the weather, but wanted to know about the danger. Ben replied just stay home. Do not go out anywhere. Lock your windows and doors, and your car doors, and make sure you have a charged phone for 911. Call 911 and report an intruder if any strange vehicles come to your house and park and just sit there.

Celia texted that she would lock up and wait to hear from him.

Andrew walked into the kitchen, locking eyes with his Father. Ben looked back at him, "I turned him down, Andrew. I told him I wasn't interested in hauling his cargo, and he won't take no for an answer. He gave me until Sunday to say yes . . . or else."

"Dad, you have to go to the police or the FBI or someone about this. He's not going to let you say no and live to talk about it."

"I can't go to the police. Bottom line is he isn't going to take any answer but yes. He said he'd leave it up to my imagination as to what he'll do if I turn him down again. He had his driver give me a burner phone to use to call him by late Sunday. Now I can't because I already smashed it in anger, even though he'd just told me not to do that. You know how I feel about others dictating how things are going to be around me."

Ben could feel himself coming apart inside after realizing what he had done. He knew that the cartel doesn't take being told no from anyone. Chances were good now that, unless Hernandez died naturally, or was killed, or arrested and thrown in jail forever, that he would likely see Ben killed for saying no to him.

"They'll kill me now, Andrew, even if I do what they want, just for saying no to them."

"Your only recourse is to involve law enforcement now, Dad."

Ben acted like he hadn't heard a thing Andrew had just said. "I have another idea, but I don't know how to make it happen. Can you help, son?"

"What do you have in mind?" Andrew said, sounding defeated. "I want to set up Bessie to explode if I send a code to a transceiver or something along those lines, like I've seen in so many action shows and movies."

Andrew's eyes grew wide, "Holy shit, are you serious?" Andrew couldn't believe what he was hearing. His otherwise peace-loving, lobstering father wanted to rig his beloved lobster boat, named after the now-deceased love of his life, to be able to blow up simply by making a phone call and entering a code?

"I'm as serious as a heart attack, son. This has got to stop once and for all. For Christ's sake, I turned down $2 million in cash, that's how bad I don't want to move anything for that bastard, or any other asshole. I thought my involvement with these cartel assholes was finally over, and this time I want to make sure that it finally is."

"Dad, I'm not sure. When do you need this done?"

"Yesterday."

"What makes you think that they won't come after you when you've taken their guy out?"

"The explosion needs to look like an accident. I wonder if we couldn't rig it so that a fuel leak causes a fire, eventually leading to the whole boat exploding. Everyone dies including me. That's the way it will look. Hopefully Hernandez will think I died too, especially if there is an obituary in the paper saying I died on my boat when it exploded while at sea from a fuel fire."

"You want to fake your own death?"

"If it makes them leave me alone for the rest of my life—yes."

Andrew could see that Ben wasn't kidding in the least, but tried talking him out of it once more. "We could both end up in jail if they find evidence that the explosion was purposeful. In addition, I'll be disbarred and lose my ability to earn a living. It's just not worth it, Dad."

Ben said, "No one is going to ever find any evidence because it'll be scattered all over the bottom of the sea. No, I'm sorry, but this, unfortunately, has to happen, son.

"Let me see what I can come up with, Dad. I'll do a little research and make a few phone calls. Can I use the den?"

"Absolutely."

Andrew excused himself and adjourned to the den to figure out how to make his father's boat a self-destructing weapon. Ben made some coffee. After taking some to Andrew, he came back to the kitchen and sat in silence, contemplating all the changes in such a short time frame. Throughout his life, he was always amazed at how quickly something good can turn into something bad, and vice-versa. He thought about Bessie, and how she would be terrified. He'd never shared this part of his life with her.

She'd always simply believed him when he said that he was having a bumper year fishing and lobstering. It made sense to her. But remodeling their house into a rustic mansion required significant funds. Back then, Ben was doing various cargo jobs for a much younger Hernandez, moving kilos of cocaine, and duffel bags of cash for laundering.

Hernandez was a lot easier to deal with back then, and Ben actually thought they had become friends of some sort, and he'd thought they would likely do business for a really long time. Then, one day Hernandez just vanished. In the end, Ben was glad. As time went on, he came to realize just how dangerous his work with Hernandez had been, and felt lucky to have come out of it alive, intact, and very rich.

Ben looked at the window over the kitchen sink. The rain pounded the other side of the glass desperately trying to get in. Occasionally, a long, hot-white bolt of lightning would illuminate the dark, ominous clouds, and seemed like the perfect metaphor for his mental state. He wasn't prepared for being swept back into an old role like it had never ended. It was simply bizarre. He had no desire to do any cargo hauling, no matter the amount of money offered. Ben had more money than he could ever spend already, and he likely only had another 15 or so years left to live. The risk of losing all of that security for another big chunk of money that he didn't need seemed like doubling down, putting all of his chips on a single number at the roulette wheel, and absolutely not worth it. No need for unnecessary risk.

Ben had always been shocked by the look on Hernandez's face. His cold, calculating, dark, shark-like eyes that flashed when he was certain that he had you where he wanted you. Ben had never expected

Hernandez to treat him this way after an entire decade of non-communication, and now the constant threat of violence, or of being killed simply for telling him no, seemed excessive, and almost beyond belief.

Thinking everything over again, Ben realized that he'd been stupid to prematurely smash the phone, and he hated the thought of having to destroy Bessie. He knew doing that would hurt him in so many ways, and it was almost beyond belief that he could, or would, do something so dramatic and permanent, but it might be worth it if somehow, he and Janine could start a new life together, and then live their lives together safe and sound. If the cartel thought they were killed by the boat explosion, no one would come and ask for this type of favor ever again. Yet, he wished there was a way to do this without destroying Bessie.

Ben's phone rang. It was Janine. He picked up the call. "Hello."

"Hi, Ben. I just wanted to say again, that I'm sorry for how I was earlier. I'm really glad we finally settled some things and figured out a way to move forward in a way amicable to both of us."

"I am too, Janine. Hey, while I have you, something has come up, and I'm not sure that we're going to be able to get together next week. It looks like it will depend on so many things that, right now, I don't dare to try and figure it out, let alone explain it to someone else."

"Wow, that sounds daunting, Ben. Care to share?"

"Not yet. For now, I think the less you know the better for both of us. I wish I could word it better, but that's it, straight up."

"Okay, well, I'm curious as hell now, but I'll honor your request and not badger you about it. I do hope, however, that you'll share anything that you can with me. I like to have an idea of how my clients are living in real time to help me gauge their level of stress, and better understand their personal strengths and weaknesses. In other words, whether or not they ultimately choose to begin drinking again from what they would describe as having to bear stress, or too much stress."

Ben said, "Fair enough. Thanks."

"Okay. Please let me know on Monday if Tuesday still works?"

"Definitely. Take care, Janine. Talk to you then."

"Bye, Ben. And, please be careful, okay?"

"I will. Don't worry. I have help too, so it'll be fine. Talk to you Monday."

"Bye, Ben."

Ben went to see what Andrew had found out. He was still in the den sitting at Ben's desk. His face glowed from the glare of the computer screen, the flickering light changes hitting his face made him look like someone welding without a protective face shield on. He looked up when Ben opened the door.

"Anything?" Ben asked, sitting down in front of the desk. Now that he was even closer to the floor, the glowing top of Andrew's head was the only remaining part still visible to him.

"Actually, yes. Check this out." Andrew swiveled the monitor around so Ben could see what he was looking at.

Ben saw that it was some type of twin fuel pump solenoid switch. Apparently, it was capable of electrically closing one supply side while simultaneously opening the other one, instantly, and with no leaks. All heavy duty stainless steel, 12-volt DC, simple. Ben looked at Andrew with a big smile on his face. I see. Are you thinking the same thing I am?"

"I don't know, Pop, maybe. What are you seeing, or thinking?"

"We can install this inline with the existing fuel supply line. One side connects to the fuel tank and continues to the engine as usual. The other side connects to an open discharge hose that extends down to the floor behind the engine, so that, at a glance, it looks official, like it's actually feeding something on the engine. You see?"

"Yes. I do."

"Then we hook the electrical wiring up to a transceiver that has a 50-mile range. Once the boat is far enough out, say 20 miles, a simple phone call to the transceiver will send a signal to the valve, opening the hose behind the engine. I think I can rig a simple ignition module to a timer that starts at the same time as the fuel leak, so that after 10 or 20 seconds, the spark plug hooked up to the ignition module will fire, igniting the fumes, causing a widespread fire, ending with an explosion."

Andrew was speechless. He had never known that his father could be so brilliant. Since his birth, he had been in the nearly constant spotlight as the smart one, the genius, or the brilliant one. He thought of his father as an intelligent man, but mainly saw him as a simple lobsterman, who enjoyed a simple life. Nothing wrong with it, but usually not the chosen occupation of an intellectual tower, or someone who can quickly look at a bunch of technical parts and drawings and make total sense of it, neither of which he thought his father capable of.

"Dad, that's absolutely brilliant. Have you figured out how you are going to get out ahead of the explosion? I'm not clear on the logistics involved."

"Oh, right. This is the tricky part. Actually, I was hoping you, the brilliant young man that you are, would come up with a solution."

Ben looked at Andrew with a dead serious look on his face. He could see the wheels in Andrew's head turning. Finally Andrew said, "How good of a swimmer are you?"

"Pretty good, but the water is so cold, hypothermia will set in instantly or give me a heart attack as soon as I hit the water. I haven't been in these icy waters in a couple of decades. It's doable, but it can't be done with street clothes and shoes on, even with several layers."

"I was thinking that we could use your small inflatable boat, but tow it out with you. I could stowaway on it under a canvas tarp and be there to assist you if anything goes south."

Ben had begun shaking his head back and forth as soon as he heard Andrew say the part beginning with I could stowaway. "Absolutely not, Andrew. It's too risky. If any of the cartel guys check that dingy and you're in it, both you and the dingy will be shot and left to sink. I won't let you risk it. It's unnecessary. I know these guys, they know me. I like your idea, just minus you being there."

"Okay, so off you go with a rigged boat and the dingy tied to the back. Now what?"

Ben was getting a little excited now. I'll start a small fire in the most forward part of the engine compartment. I'll light a few oily rags that will burn and produce a lot of smoke, and it will smell like an engine issue. I'll go topside and scream fire to get the three or four guys to go down to tend to it. When they do, I'll make my move toward the aft part of the boat as fast as I can. I'll get in the dingy and, once I'm fifty yards or so away, I'll make the phone call to the transceiver. When the timer finishes causing the ignitor to spark, I should be about a hundred yards out when the explosion occurs. Meanwhile, you'll be in my smaller speed boat waiting for me at coordinates that we've both agreed on, and then I'll follow you back to the harbor.

Andrew looked impressed. "Do you think that this will ultimately be enough to end this once and for all?"

"I think so, but I'll never know for sure until they contact me again, if they ever do. I think the odds of that happening after this explosion will be minimal."

"Dad, I hate to think we really need to fake your death to end this."

"Christ, Andrew, at my age I'm not going to go through all that faking one's death involves. If I were still in my twenties, I might consider it. At 68? No. Hernandez will likely assume I'm dead. He may not even bother to check for an obituary. Why? Once the explosion occurs, my boat is gone, so now he'll have to find another lobsterman to pick on for a change, and I cannot see that it would matter to him one way or another if I'm alive or dead."

Andrew smiled and nodded, but had to fight to control another yawn. "How about we get some shut eye for now, Dad? Last I heard this was going to be a fairly fast-moving Nor'easter. I'm grateful for the warmup, though, and that means it will stay all rain."

Ben said, "I am too. We definitely dodged a potential unforeseen complication. What do you say we get our plan implemented right after breakfast. We'll head into Portland and get everything we need, then over to Bessie and get things set up."

"Sounds like a plan. Goodnight, Dad."

"Good night, son." Ben felt a lot more settled about things now. It seemed like they had put together a pretty good plan, and they still had tomorrow to get things in place ahead of the Sunday deadline or ultimatum that Hernandez had given him. He felt exhausted, and could see the fatigue in Andrew's eyes, so they both turned in for the night.

10

THE PLAN PART II—BROMLEY AND DECKER

The storm finished just before dawn leaving behind 4 inches of rain, a razor sharp blue sky, a bright sun, and stiff northwest winds that made the 46 degree morning feel like 26.

Ben and Andrew had a quick breakfast, then headed out to get the supplies they needed to rig the boat before the five o'clock deadline. Ben wondered how long after 5:00 p.m. Hernandez would wait before any consequences for non-compliance would become known. He was determined to end this situation permanently, and hoped that whatever Hernandez came up with wouldn't prevent him from implementing the plan that he and Andrew had just devised. He had to fight to keep fearful thoughts from interfering with clear, rational choice making. This time, there wouldn't be any margin for error. A mistake could easily cost him his life, and he felt that truth in every fiber of his being.

They decided to go to Ben's favorite one stop store, the Portland Marine Mega-Mart, and found everything they needed to make the plan a reality. Ben pretended to be fiddling with something in his wallet so he could avoid the checkout clerk's eyes when paying. He thought about what it might look like: two men shopping together with dead serious looks on their faces, coming to the checkout with a spark plug, a transceiver, two electronic relay timers, a small container of lighter fluid, a box of rags, and two burner phones—but there

115

wasn't time for online ordering, or driving to another place out of town.

As soon as they finished loading all the stuff into the back of Ben's truck, Ben said, "Let's make haste. I'm worried that the clerk might call the authorities just to put them on notice about what he saw us buying just now."

Andrew chuckled a little, "Come on, Dad, don't be so paranoid. This is Maine. Lobstermen and fishermen need those very same things, and lots of other things that might be construed as instruments of destruction, mayhem, or violence, but not too many folks around here make such assumptions. I think we're fine. Just try to relax a little."

"That's easy for you to say, I'm the one that has to be on board the boat with these assholes. If we get to where we need to be before I have a chance to implement our plan, well, they may very well decide that, since I was such a pain in their asses this time around, that there won't be a next time and just kill me once we get there."

"Dad, I hadn't even thought of that one. You can't do this."

"I don't have a choice, son. I'm going to do this, with or without your help."

"Of course I'll still help you. It's just that I hadn't thought of that possibility and, now that I have, I'm worried for your safety even more than I was before."

"It's going to be okay, Andrew." Ben looked over at his son trying hard to give him a reassuring look.

Minutes later, they arrived at the dock where Bessie was moored. Ben constantly scanned the street on both sides for any sign of Hernandez's men, or anything else that seemed off. So far, everything looked normal.

They parked right in front of Bessie, and quickly unloaded the equipment. Once they got it all downstairs, they laid it out on the galley table. Andrew powered up his laptop, then opened the checklist file he'd made on the transceiver and equipment setup.

Ben worked with Andrew. Together, they managed to get everything hooked up, and completed two successful dry runs. Each time, Andrew dialed the number, the transceiver received the call, then sent signals to both the timer, and the solenoid valve to flood the floor with fuel behind the engine. The timer initialized and counted twenty seconds, then sent power to a spark plug that would ignite the fuel on the floor, and eventually cause a fatal explosion. When they finished, everything worked perfectly. One final check, and all was ready. The equipment had been installed and now worked successfully, and they had managed to hide everything well. The lobster and fish hold was empty and clean, and the fuel tank was topped off. It was now 3 p.m.

Ben and Andrew headed back to Ben's house to wait for the phone call from Hernandez. They grabbed some burgers and fries and ate them in silence, watching the local afternoon news while trying hard to control their nerves. The closer the time got to 5:00 p.m., the more anxiety both of them felt and had to control. Ben's mind raced, wondering what Hernandez's revenge would be.

When 5 p.m. finally came, it was so quiet in Ben's house he could hear the faint sound of the refrigerator fan running all the way in the den. 5:15 p.m. Still nothing but deafening silence. Finally, at 5:36 p.m. Ben's phone rang. It was Hernandez.

"So, Señor Scot, you have chosen to go down this path with me, eh? I don't know what it is that I could offer you to perform such a small favor for me, especially such a lucrative one. Would you not agree, Señor, that it is a lucrative offer?"

Ben really didn't want to talk with this guy at all. It was pointless. You either went along with what he wanted all the time, or you didn't. If you chose not to go along, then you had to risk being killed. It was quite simple. Stupid, barbaric, and limiting over the long run, but simple.

"Yes, it's lucrative, but as I already told you, I'm not poor. I don't need any more money. I don't want to earn money per se, and I certainly don't want to earn it illegally when I have so much life that I still want to enjoy. I'm unwilling to risk going to prison for the life I have left."

"I understand, Señor. I thought you might say these things. Hold on, I have a little surprise for you."

Ben could hear rustling sounds and muffled voices for a few seconds, and then Janine came on the line in a panic, "Ben! Ben! Don't do it Ben! Don't!" Ben could hear her struggling to stay on the phone as someone was trying to pull it away from her already.

Hernandez came back on the phone, "Surprise, Señor Scot. So, let us not mince our words any longer now, eh? I have your friend here.

She is very pretty, no? Here is how this is going to go, Señor. You will be at your boat at the marina by 4 a.m. tomorrow morning. My men will arrive promptly at that time to load your boat. Once the boat is loaded with the cargo and the ice that we will bring, your friend Janine will be accompanying you to deliver the cargo to our friends from the north. Once that is complete, I will wire the two million dollars into your account, and that will conclude our business. Understand?"

"Nice try, Hernandez. Are you forgetting who owns the boat? You're going to have to wire me half the money upfront or we won't do business."

"You are in no position to be bargaining with me, Señor. 4 a.m., as I said. No tricks. No cops. No FBI. Just you being dropped off, and just you at the helm, with your friend by your side. That way, if you were planning to do anything tricky, her life will also be on the line, no?" Hernandez really seemed to be enjoying himself. Ben could almost hear his smile.

Ben clicked the phone off, then pounded it into the couch pillow next to him. Now that Hernandez had kidnapped Janine, he wanted to hurt Hernandez in the worst way. His heart kept pounding from the extra adrenaline now in his system, and he was a little worried that he might have a heart attack from all the stress this was causing him. He was ready to end this situation, for sure, and only wanted to be able to continue nurturing his new life with Janine.

Ben looked at Andrew and said, "Damn it. We're sunk, now." Ben pounded his fist into the pillow a few more times. "That son-of-a-bitch has kidnapped Janine!"

Andrew's mouth dropped open hearing this. "That kind of blows apart our whole plan, Dad. We can't risk having Janine getting shot or, worse, getting blown up or badly burned. We can't do our plan with her on board."

"Agreed. But, I think I have a solution. I'll let Janine in on our plan once we're both on board and under way. We'll do everything the exact same way, just as we planned, but when I'm supposed to get to the aft part of the boat as quickly as possible and get into the inflatable, instead it'll be both of us getting to the inflatable as fast as possible."

Andrew thought for a few seconds, then made eye contact with Ben, nodded, and said, "I think it'll work, Dad. Ha!" As the idea sank in, Andrew's excitement grew and, after walking around the den in circles saying, "It's still going to work," a few times, he threw both arms up in the air as if he were a referee at a pro-football game indicating a touchdown, then rushed back over to his father and hugged him, still giddy from his mental revelation of victory.

Ben smiled back and embraced his son, but inside he felt terrified. He knew this was it. His personal last stand against something he hated. He knew that a lot could go wrong and, just like his father used to always say to him, Hey, Ben, your plan about XYZ sounds great, but have you planned for Murphy's Law? You know Murphy's Law, right?

Ben would always answer yes, but his father would always finish it by re-educating him about it anyway. Murphy's law basically says that if something can go wrong, it will, and at the worst possible moment.

Murphy's Law is precisely what worried Ben now. Janine coming along left him thinking that the plan he and Andrew came up with was far too risky, or they overlooked something, or even worse, completely forgot about something critical. If they had, Ben wouldn't be coming home from this trip out on the water.

Ben looked at Andrew even more seriously now, "I think all we can do at this point is just go with what we've managed to put together already. The only variable that's been added, so far, is Janine coming along and her being there when all the action goes down. I know she is up to this though. She's pretty fit, and five years younger than me. I think we'll be fine. I am going to remain very optimistic and say all will go as planned."

Andrew said, "I sure hope you're right, Dad. No, I know you're right. This is a good plan that we've managed to come up with. It's going to be dark, and everyone is going to be tired, but temporarily on alert because of the circumstances. Reactions will prevail. We can use that to our advantage, and our plan even exploits it. Think about it. The fire will scare the hell out of these guys. Most thugs are from big cities, and don't even know how to swim. And, just like everyone else, they are terrified of sharks and other unknowns down below. You scream fire? Haha! They're going to freak out for sure. That's when you guys make your move, and in the end, the fireworks will cinch the whole deal permanently."

"That's it." Ben smiled and clapped his hands a few times for emphasis. They both decided to turn in extra early knowing how early 3am would come. Ben managed to sleep for only a couple of hours when his phone woke him up, buzzing like crazy right next to his head. He looked at the number and didn't recognize it. Normally, he would let any unrecognized call go straight to voicemail, but under the circumstances he knew it could be Hernandez, so he answered it immediately, "Hello?"

"Mr. Scot? Mr. Benjamin Scot?"

"Who wants to know?" Ben asked.

"Mr. Scot, I'm agent Bromley out of the Boston Massachusetts office of the Federal Bureau of Investigation. Mind if my colleague, agent Decker, and I come inside for a quick visit? I know it's late, but we're on your front porch. I think you'll agree that the circumstances are urgent. I've been ringing the bell, but I guess you didn't hear it."

"Ah, okay. Hang tight. I'll be out in a minute. I was already asleep." Ben shuffled to the bathroom and peed. *What the hell is the FBI doing on my fucking front porch? Gee, I wonder if it's Hernandez? Of course it is. See, this is what I mean. As soon as that son of a bitch comes back into my life—poof—trouble.*

Ben threw on some jeans and t-shirt and stepped into his wool-lined moccasins. He wrapped his terrycloth robe around himself, and went to the front door. Before flipping on the inside entryway light and opening the door, he stood still for a minute holding his .357 magnum with his finger on the trigger, carefully observing the front door. He saw two faceless figures standing perfectly still on the front porch. The backlighting from the porch light compounded their already dramatic, ominous appearance, while the marbled glass privacy doors totally eliminated all of their details.

Ben decided to take the chance that they were legitimate, and slowly opened the door. Both agents had their badges out and they looked real, so Ben didn't waste any time having them step inside and follow him to the kitchen table. The snow boots they both wore made odd squeaking noises as they shuffled behind Ben into the kitchen, scanning as much of the rest of the house as they could, enroute. Ben could tell by the looks on their faces that neither of them had ever been in a residential house this big that wasn't a hotel.

Bromley stood 6'3" in a dark gray suit, white shirt and black tie, covered by a full length black, fleece lined rain coat. His steely, blue-gray eyes and military haircut meant business, just like his demeanor. His partner, agent Decker, looked like a carbon copy of him, except Ben found Decker's shocking red hair to be a nearly constant distraction.

"Can I get either of you something to drink? Water? Coffee?" Ben said on his way over to the refrigerator to get the filtered water pitcher out. Both agents stood there like apparitions who came to warn him of impending doom and destruction. "Drink, fellas? Anything?"

"No thank you, Mr. Scot."

"Ben. Please, just call me Ben. I never liked hearing Mister."

Bromley cleared his throat, "Okay, Mr., I mean Ben. No thank you, Ben."

Agent Decker came right to the point. "Mr. Scot, I mean, Ben, have you seen this man lately?" he said, handing Ben a picture of Hernandez.

Ben looked at the picture, and with a perfectly calm, normal voice said, "Uh, no, can't say that I have. Although, he does look somewhat familiar." Ben took his time, and looked at the picture for another minute before handing it back.

Both agents exchanged quick glances and nods as if they communicated in an alien language consisting entirely of body language and facial expressions. The few small facial gestures just made, somehow had communicated everything each of them wanted the other to know. "Ben, we know that you know this man. We've been watching him for a long time now. We know that he is a captain in the El Rey cartel, and that his full name is Juan Santiago Hernandez. We also know that you used to haul cargo for him between 2000 and 2010, and we know that you just met with him a couple of days ago. Shall I show you the video?"

"That won't be necessary, guys. What do you want from me?"

"Honesty, and transparency for starters Ben."

"What do you want to know?"

"Are you planning to haul for him again soon?"

"No, well, yes, sort of." Ben struggled to find the words and could feel himself swelling with frustration inside.

"Take your time, Mr. Scot. No rush. So, you admit that you met with him, correct?" Ben nodded. "And, what did Mr. Hernandez want with you?"

Ben looked at Bromley, then Decker with an annoyed look on his face. "He wanted to know how many boxes of Girl Scout Cookies he could put me down for, what do you think he wanted with me?"

Both agents formerly had their gaze fixed on him, but after being scolded they were staring at the top of the kitchen counter. Ben continued, "He wanted me to haul some cargo for him again. I told him no. I told him that I had completely stopped hauling after he ditched me ten years ago. I used to haul cargo for him, but I never knew what it was, and I didn't want to know. He always paid me well, so back then I was always game when he and his men came around.

I got used to hauling for them a couple of times per year, and then it just stopped. Didn't know. I speculated a little, but that's all it was. I thought maybe his family had been in a gun battle over some cargo and maybe so many of them died that their enterprise folded. Either that, or they closed shop on purpose before they were caught and arrested. I also thought maybe they already made enough money and decided that continued risk would no longer be worth it. But I had no real idea, and zero information. It pissed me off. I missed the money almost immediately. I was compensated handsomely while working with Hernandez, but I vowed to myself that I would tell him to go piss off if he ever showed up here again. After ten years, I thought I would never see him again."

"Any idea what he wants you to move this time?" Hearing this, Ben almost decided to lie. But, somehow, just talking about all of this out loud, especially with a powerful law enforcement team listening, made him feel stronger, safer, and very relieved. Since first laying eyes on Hernandez, his stomach had tied itself into knots when he realized what he was likely going to have to go through all over again.

"Yes, I do, and it's unusual. It's not the kind of cargo you might expect him to be moving. Nothing I would have ever guessed anyway." He looked at both agents intensely, and then leaned closer to them, "He wants me to move human transplant organs for him."

Decker looked hard at Bromley, then back at Ben, explaining, "We're coming across this new commodity a lot more frequently. Currently, human organs are the product of choice to smuggle. The cartel has devised plausible, believable stories to tell the Coast Guard, or the equivalent of the Coast Guard at other locations around the world, to have an explanation as to why they are in possession of body organs if they are stopped and boarded. Apparently, the market is quite lucrative, with the world's richest, and perhaps also shadiest characters engaging in bidding wars in order to secure the organs they need to replace the failing ones in their, often self-abused, bodies." Ben looked astonished.

"I had no idea. Who would've ever thought? What do you mean by self-abused bodies?"

"Heavy drinking, smoking, cocaine use, heroin or other drug use, those types of things." Bromley said, sounding sympathetic, "Welcome to the 21st century, Mr. Scot, where medical technology has advanced to the point where we can now safely, and successfully transplant nearly every part of the human body. The list of people needing everything from corneas to kidneys, new lungs to a new heart, nothing is off limits any longer, and that has opened up one of the most lucrative sales opportunities in history. Money truly is the driver of most, if not all, criminal activity."

Ben asked, "How much are we talking about here? Let's say I need a new stomach because mine is all eaten up with cancer?"

Bromley answered, "Hard to say, but it is fair to say that if they are whole organs or high demand organs that someone's life depends on, well . . . $100,000 would be ground zero for a starting point, with some wealthy folks paying over $1 million for a new liver, delivered fast, no questions asked. No waiting line. Money talks!"

"So, where are you with Hernandez on the cargo haul?" Decker asked.

"We're scheduled to be at my boat at the docks at 4 a.m."

Hearing this, Decker slammed his fist down hard on the counter, "That fucker knows how to play us. I knew he knew we were watching him the other day. That bastard."

Bromley glared at Decker, "Take it easy, man. We have vast resources. We'll get this figured out. Not an issue."

Ben's thoughts raced through his mind like lightning, activating nearly every synapse in his brain, trying to figure out how he was going to negotiate having these guys stay out of it.

Decker looked at Ben intently, "We're going to need your help, Mr. Scot." Bromley jumped in with the handoff, not missing a beat, "That's correct, and here's the deal: we've been planning a sting on this guy for years, but he always manages to get away or disappear on us, only to resurface again somewhere in the U.S.—anywhere from six months to a couple of years later."

"Why are you telling me about this sting?" Ben said with a cautious voice.

"Because you inadvertently just volunteered as our boat captain, the missing puzzle piece."

Ben looked at them sternly and said indignantly, "I'll be goddamned if I'm going to be your boat captain doing anything with Hernandez. I'm not going to be your patsy or the middle man between the U.S. Government and a cartel captain. No way."

Bromley fired back, "So you'd rather haul cargo for Mr. Hernandez on your own, and without all the resources that the FBI can offer you? Are you nuts, or dumber than we ever thought possible?"

Ben was pissed off now. He shouted, "Hey! Don't get started with the insults. I'm no genius, but maybe you don't know all the facts, and if you did, you'd change your tune a bit, or at least have a bit of understanding about where I'm coming from." As soon as he said that, he regretted it. Both agents exchanged glances again and, somehow, came to the conclusion that Ben wasn't telling them everything.

Decker whispered, "Is there something or some things that you haven't shared with us yet, Mr. Scot?"

The room became silent. Outside, the north winds could be heard, first rising to a crescendo, then diminishing to barely audible again. Some of the window screens rattled from the bigger wind gusts. Then, another voice broke the silence, "Hey, what's everybody doing in here?" Everyone jumped. It was Andrew. "I heard some shouting and got worried, so I came down to check it out. Everything okay, Dad?"

"Yes, and no, but grab something to drink and have a seat. We have a lot to discuss." Having said that, Ben rose to a stand, groaning as he did, then stretched and looked at Andrew seriously, "First, can I have a quick word in private?"

"Sure thing, Dad." Andrew followed Ben back into the den.

"I'll let them tell you again what they told me, but the bottom line is, they know about Hernandez, who he is, and what he does. They know that I've worked for him in the past, and they believe that I didn't know what I was hauling at the time. I've filled them in about our plan to haul the body organs for Hernandez at 4 a.m., but they don't know about Janine, and I don't know if I want to tell them about her yet. Also, I won't, and I'm asking you, to not tell them at all about our explosive plans. As far as they know, it's just me hauling for Hernandez just like I used to."

"I can't believe this, Dad. My God! Twelve hours ago I was Andrew Morse Scot, Attorney at Law. Now, I'm Andrew Morse Scot, saboteur, and co-conspirator in withholding information from the FBI, which is 'obstruction of justice.' Great. If they find out about any of the lies, then I could be disbarred and go to jail.

"I'm sorry, Andrew. None of this is my doing, at least directly anyway. Indirectly, yes, but only in the sense that I've done work for the cartel in the past, and I have proven to be reliable and trustworthy, so they're merely trying to minimize their own risk. In retrospect, I can see just how stupid it is for them to think that no one has caught on to them after all these years."

"Not really, Dad. They're counting on the fact that, even if people have caught on about who they are and what they are doing in

Maine, that they'll be too afraid to say anything to law enforcement for fear of retribution."

"So, make sure you don't mention Janine or the explosive part of our plan, okay?"

"I think we should tell them about Janine, Dad, but not about the explosives. If they are going to be involved, then they are going to need to know about her being kidnapped, especially when she's going to be on board with you and the other cartel crew members. If the FBI does anything that causes them to be exposed, then all hell could break loose, and both you and Janine could be caught in the crossfire. What if Janine is there but hasn't been mentioned before, and the FBI thinks she's part of Hernandez's crew and shoots her inadvertently?"

"Good point, Andrew. I think you're right. Let's do it, and then have them help us figure out a modified plan. Besides, they are already doing a sting and will be arresting everyone on board, and repossessing the illegally obtained, black market transplant organs that might be on board." Andrew agreed and they both returned to the kitchen.

The four of them stood facing one another. Andrew in a robe that was the same color as Ben's, looking like a clone of his father on one side of the kitchen island, Bromley and Decker, looking like two cloned government suits on the other side. Both facing off like they were all starring in an old western shootout, each side trying to decide if they should draw first or not.

Ben broke the ice, "Gentlemen, we have one small additional issue."

Decker immediately responded, "What's that?"

"I just finished going through an alcohol rehabilitation treatment and my counselor sees me several times per week to help me stay sober. When I told Hernandez I wanted no part of working with him again or hauling his mystery cargo, he gave me a couple of days to change my mind. I didn't, and he kidnapped my counselor, Janine. I thought he would target my kids, and I spent all my time trying to protect them. I don't know why I didn't think to warn Janine. I had her on the phone on Saturday, and we made plans to start meeting on Tuesdays and Fridays beginning next week. The next thing I knew, Hernandez phoned to let me know that he'd taken her as an insurance policy."

Bromley looked at Decker and said, "This is definitely going to complicate things. Better notify the folks upstairs about this development." Decker nodded. Bromley looked at Ben and said, "Don't worry, Mr. Scot/Ben, everything's going to be fine. We'll figure this out together."

Ben's heart felt like it was being stretched downward like a rubber band inside his chest. He was worried about how things might turn out, and he was upset about having his chance at love taken away from him so abruptly. He wasn't prepared for any of this, or the sheer danger that lurked, especially since it all happened so fast, landing in their lap without any warning.

Ben looked at both agents and said, "Like hell. You're not going to figure anything out. I know who I'm dealing with, and my son and I have already devised a plan that I think might actually work." Ben said, looking at Andrew with pride. "However, I think I can modify my plan, and work it out so that you guys can arrest the crew that will be on board, while we get away. Interested in the details?"

Bromley said, "We're all ears."

11

THE PLAN PART III

Ben met Bromley's eyes and said, "We're planning to start a fire on Bessie, my boat, as a distraction, then escape to my inflatable boat tied to the aft end of her, and get far enough away before she blows up from leaking fuel."

Bromley and Decker's eyes were just about popping out of their heads after hearing this. Decker couldn't contain himself. He pushed himself past Bromley, leaning in close to Ben's face, so much so, that Ben backed away a little. "What's the matter, worried I might hurt you?" Decker hissed.

"No. Just backing away from that graveyard in your mouth spewing death gas in all directions while you talk. Pop a mint!" Ben spat into the sink for emphasis.

"You're already looking at twenty years for attempted murder, conspiracy to commit murder, and a whole host of other charges that are related to those, so you might want to wise up, old man, and get serious before the judicial system shows you a thing or two.

Andrew stepped closer, and with the most authoritarian voice he could muster said, "Alright, that's enough. We're all on the same team here."

Decker cut him off, "Not quite. Your father here just admitted to planning a murder."

Andrew shot back, "Of a captain in the El Rey cartel."

Decker added, "And to hauling illegal cargo for him."

Andrew pointed out, "Completely against his will. He said no. They won't take no for an answer."

Bromley said, "You were really going to blow up your own lobster boat?"

Ben paused for only a second then answered, "Yes, and I still want to."

"Why?" Bromley asked, looking truly puzzled.

Ben stated matter of factly, "I want the cartel to think I'm dead. I will go so far as changing my name and not lobstering any longer to make that a reality. Besides, I'm tired. I want to go out on the water for fun now, not for work. This way it will make it look like an accident. They'll have lost their precious cargo and a few men. But when they see that my boat blew up, knowing that I was on board when it happened, they'll more than likely think that I'm dead, and will finally stop coming around asking me to haul cargo for them."

Both Bromley and Decker nodded. Bromley said, "Understood. I get it."

"So, now I'm wondering if there is a way to still make this all work with the government's help. Any ideas, agents?" Ben looked at both of them waiting for some sort of intelligent answer.

Bromley finally took the challenge, "Mr. Scot, Ben, I believe we can help you, I'm just not sure if I'll get authorization in time to facilitate the manpower and equipment I'll need by 4 a.m."

Ben looked at his watch, it was already 10 p.m. and he still had not slept, and his entire plan was in limbo.

Andrew cut in, "Well, gentlemen, let's just say for the sake of argument that you can get everything in time, what is your plan?"

Decker answered, "We can be your distraction, we can start with engaging the crewmen with heavy gunfire while you get away. Then, with the assistance of the Coast

Guard, we'll surround, then board your boat, and arrest anyone left standing. In the process, we'll recover the illegal cargo, and preserve your boat." He looked at Ben, giving him a quick nod and smile.

Ben seemed pleased. "Now we're talking, gentlemen!"

"Only one small remaining item, Mr. Scot." Bromley looked at Ben dead serious again.

"What's that?"

"Earlier you alluded to a plurality in your plan. You began with the term we're planning to start a fire on my boat. Who is the other person? Not him, I hope," Bromley said, pointing at Andrew.

"No, absolutely not. I would never ask my son to risk his life with these people."

Ben chose not to add anything else in the hope that neither agent would pursue any further questions about it.

"Then who were you referring to?" Bromley persisted.

Ben looked right at him, "No one. I was just saying or using we're because it was Andrew and I that devised our plan. Therefore, *we're* simply means Andrew and I, the ones who devised the plan.

Bromley looked slightly puzzled, but seemed to accept Ben's explanation at face value. "Anything you need to tell me about this mission that you haven't told me already, Mr. Scot?" he added looking into Ben's eyes.

"No. But I have my own question for you. Why not just hide ahead of time at the docks, and bust them while they are loading the cargo onto Bessie, rather than wait for me to get twenty miles off the coast?"

Bromley smiled, "I was wondering if you were going to think of that. Now that you've confirmed to us that Mr. Hernandez is, in fact, moving illegal cargo again, and inside twenty five miles, the Coast Guard can board any vessel suspected of moving illicit cargo. However, there is an overlap zone where the Canadian Coast Guard can do the same, as they have similar laws. By taking your boat all the way to the rendezvous point, both you and the pickup vessel will be able to be legally boarded and the crew members subject to arrest. We'll wait for the crews of both vessels to begin unloading the cargo off your boat onto theirs. Our goal will be to shut down the east coast arm of the multi-armed pipeline for organ smuggling."

Ben looked horrified, "How does that afford me a chance to get away and not be shot once you start the raid on both vessels?" Silence.

"That's what I fucking thought. Oops! You forgot that I'd still be on board and the first person to get blamed for any law enforcement interventions. Oops!" Ben sat back down shaking his head. It was his life at risk, and they didn't even know about Janine being held hostage, which added its own particular set of variables. How was he going to explain that away?

"Will you have eyes on the docks while we're loading the cargo or will you just be at the rendezvous point when both vessels meet up for the exchange?"

Decker said, "Less risky if we put a tracking device on your vessel so we can monitor your precise location at all times. We have the same thing in place happening on the Canadian side. We'll be able to stay close by, but must remain completely out of sight and unable to be heard. When the time arrives, we can swoop in and pounce down on that location with so many boats, loudspeakers, helicopters, and a couple of drones, that the situation will get chaotic very fast."

"Can you set it up with all law enforcement on the scene to not fire on the old man from Maine running to the aft of the boat and getting into the inflatable boat to escape?"

Again, the room grew silent for a few seconds, then Bromley and Decker busted out laughing. But when the agents saw the looks on both Ben's and Andrew's faces, they stopped laughing instantly.

"Sorry, it's just that . . ."

Ben cut him off, "I know, it is a pretty funny scene to imagine, and it sounds funny, but when the shit hits the fan, the situation is going to be as serious as a heart attack. Don't forget, it's me. I'm the old man who's doing the running in that scene that you find so hilarious."

Andrew and the two agents nodded in agreement without saying a word.

Ben continued, "That's when we'll make our break for an escape, with both of us heading for the inflatable as fast as possible."

Ben stopped talking, trying to figure out what the stares in his direction meant. Then he realized why, "Okay, damn it. I better tell you now." Ben looked down for a moment, as if reflecting on his decision to confess, or just to gather his thoughts. He finally looked up and said, "As I already told you, my alcohol rehab counselor, Janine Johnson, from the Maine Hospital Alcohol Rehabilitation Center is being held hostage by Juan Hernandez. What I didn't tell you is that she will also be on board Bessie with us, adding to what's at stake for involving any law enforcement agencies." Both agents rolled their heads.

Decker groaned, "God damn it, Ben! We asked you if you had anything more to tell us and you said no."

"I know. I wasn't sure what to do about that. Taking her was his way of convincing me to move his fucking cargo for him. The asshole just wouldn't take no for an answer. I tried to convince him that I knew other people who wouldn't ask any questions and would keep their mouths shut, but he didn't want to risk trusting any new people whatsoever. He called me shortly after 5 p.m. today to let me know that he had her, and said he would harm or kill her, if needed, to keep me in line until this job was over.

Bromley injected, "And do you know he has her? You believe him?"

Ben looked at Bromley directly and kept talking as if he hadn't heard the question, "He also informed me that she will accompany me on Bessie to the rendezvous point, because that way, as he put it, I am better assured of having no funny business interfering with this transfer.

Overall, I think our plan will still work. I'll have Janine start heading to the aft of the boat as we're getting close to the rendezvous point and get into the boat as discreetly as possible once we stop moving. Once we've moored together with the other boat for the transfer, I'll slip out from behind the helm, make haste to get to the inflatable, jump in and Janine and I will get as far away from there as quickly as we can, assuming that's when you guys will pop in for a visit?"

Bromley and Decker both assured Ben that they would be showing up as soon as they saw the cargo being transferred. They would be watching silently in the dark using night vision equipment.

Both agents seemed satisfied with the plan.

Andrew was speechless and Ben could see his wheels still turning. Andrew's eyes told Ben he was worried sick, but Ben knew this was going to be the most logical solution. He felt glad that he finally told the truth to the FBI, because now he also had their assistance and resources on his side.

Six hours earlier, a driver in a dark SUV had backed into a little dirt access road behind some trees, catty-corner from Ben's place. As Bromley and Decker left Ben's house, he photographed them as they drove by.

12

HURRY UP AND WAIT

Ben woke up disoriented and in a cold sweat. In his lucid dream, he was stranded in icy ocean water with no land in sight, trying to fend off a group of hungry sharks taking turns coming at him from all directions. He could feel his fear rapidly growing inside himself. As the dream continued, the energy inside him coming from that fear is the only source of light, and warmth, and is actually goodness itself. It is also the only thing keeping him alive against the dark, penetrating cold that seems just as determined to kill him as the sharks.

Wanting to clear his mind of the nightmare, Ben sat up and turned on the light. It was 2:55 a.m. He realized that in only a couple of short hours he would be at sea with Janine, a bunch of cartel henchmen, and some human organs. He got up and got dressed. He felt tired, confused, hungry, and sick to his stomach all at the same time. He could already feel his mood getting dark, and he wanted closure in the worst way.

When Ben finally went to sleep after the meeting with Bromley and Decker, he had felt confident, and even a little happy. Now he was worried, and had a strong feeling that something wasn't right. Something was being overlooked or not being said. He quickly went over the plan in his head again, and couldn't find any real flaw. A couple of minor things that may, or may not happen, but nothing that would cause the plan to not succeed.

Andrew was already up, sitting in the kitchen drinking coffee. He looked terrible. Ben couldn't ever remember seeing him look this white, drawn, frail, and worried. Ben silently went to the cupboard, found a mug, then poured himself some coffee. He turned around and faced Andrew. Their eyes met, and Ben tried like hell to convey that everything was going to be okay to him telepathically, but Andrew broke his gaze after only a couple of seconds. He stood up and strode past Ben, heading out to the garage for something without saying a word. When he came back, he set the box of marine flares down, and looked at his father.

"You might need these, and before you say anything, I want to say that I don't want you to do this Dad. It's too dangerous."

Ben looked back at him, "I don't want to do this either, Andrew, but I can't risk having them harm Janine or anyone else because I am refusing to do something or go along."

Andrew grew more insistent, "I just don't get why they offer so much money for you to do this. Why not just rent a boat and use it? Why not buy a boat and use that with your own in-house crew and captain? There are so many other options that kind of money can buy, it doesn't make sense to me that Hernandez is so insistent about having my nearly 70-year-old father be the one to captain the boat."

Ben stopped him, "I think I know why, Andrew. I never told anyone this before because I've been so ashamed of it, and I've been afraid that if it ever became known, that something like this, or worse, could come out of it. I was naive."

"What are you talking about, Dad? More Hernandez ghosts?"

"Kind of. You see, when he and I were running cargo, we had an incident on one of the trips where a crewman thought he could kill both me, and Hernandez, and take the illegal cargo and my boat. Well, without getting into all the details, the crewman thought he had Hernandez alone down in the engine room. He didn't realize that I was still in the very back of the room when he came in and confronted Hernandez. The crewman finished saying that he was taking over, and that Hernandez would no longer be needed. He raised his gun to shoot, and that's when I hit a home run on the right side of his skull with a long piece of inch and a half rigid pipe. Some of his brains hit the deck before his body did.

Andrew said, "Whoa. No way. You didn't."

Ben continued as if not hearing him, "After that, Hernandez and I dragged his body up the stairs and, with the help of two other crewmen, threw his body overboard. I saved his life and he knows it. He trusts me. It's that simple. Money is nothing to this guy Andrew. $1 million, $2 million, or $8 million, it doesn't really matter because he's swimming in it.

Andrew responded, "Okay, that makes more sense to me, but it doesn't completely dissipate my doubts about this weird offer and situation."

"I know, son. I have my own weird feelings going on about today. I don't think he was counting on me turning him down. He didn't realize how much I'd already earned with him in the past. A lot of money that I stashed away, invested, and built this house up with. I think he thought an offer of $2 million would have me on board in an instant, complete with a big smile on my face. He probably thought the poor fisherman would never turn down that much money. That would be like turning down a big lottery win. The thing is, Andrew, the cartel culture of torture and terror is very effective. It usually works instantly, and with very little effort when used against average, everyday people who have never before been in those circles. The cartel doesn't take kindly to being told no about anything."

Both Ben and Andrew finished their coffees, gathered up their stuff, and left to go meet Hernandez and his crew at the docks.

This morning, there were many other lobsterman determined to get a head start on the day, and the docks were humming with activity. Ben parked his truck in his usual spot, and he and Andrew slowly walked over to where Bessie was moored. Ben looked up and down the dock for any sign of Hernandez and his crew. He wasn't sure how Hernandez was going to show up and load his cargo without being noticed. Everything about him was dark brown or black. Clothing colors, hair colors, vehicles used, and choices of words. Dark, like a black hole that sucks the life out of everything around it, including light, and along with it, goodness itself.

Ben and Andrew turned on the lights for their mooring, got Bessie warming at idle, and opened the fish compartment doors to prepare for the cargo and ice. The weather today wasn't going to be an issue. It was supposed to be windy later, but they would be long gone and back by then.

Ben checked his watch. It was now 4:10 a.m. The activity level at the docks had reached peak, and was already beginning to wane. One by one, all the lobster boats left their moors to head out into the glorious Gulf of Maine, to see what the great Atlantic ocean god would bless them with today.

5:45 a.m. came and went with no showing up as planned. Ben and Andrew were getting extremely anxious. Ben was pacing back and forth across the deck. His mind raced, trying to figure out what the hell was going on. Andrew finally broke the silence, "What the hell? Why aren't they here yet?"

"I don't know, but something is definitely wrong with this picture. I don't like it. I have no way to call anyone. I have no idea what this will mean for the operation that is set for today either.

Ben's phone rang. It was Hernandez. "Señor Scot, you have been up to no good, no?"

"I don't know what you're talking about. Here we go again with the riddles and puzzles. How about you just speak straight for a fucking change so we can finally get on with this dog and pony show?"

"Okay, Señor, you want to hear it straight. Then hear this!" Ben could hear Janine in the background struggling,

"What are you doing? No! No, you're not going to, No, no, please, no!

"God damn it, Hernandez! What are you doing to her? You hurt her and I will kill you so help me God!"

"You are not really in a position to pose a danger to me now, are you? Why did you involve the authorities, Señor? I thought we had established the rules of our encounters long ago. I don't know what you're thinking or planning, but we are going to reset our rendezvous for another time, and if I see any contact with the authorities again, well, let's just say your friend here will become shark food after we cut her up into little pieces, beginning with the tip of her little finger on her right hand, which was almost just snipped into a bucket."

"You bastard. She has nothing to do with anything that we did in the past, and she still doesn't. Let her go. You have my word. I'll do what you want, just let her go, now!"

"You will never retire, Señor. I had my men watch you for quite some time to see what had become of you before making contact with you again. I knew that we've both grown older, but I was sure you would still be here, still doing what you do, because I saw how much the water was your passion all those years ago. I saw how skilled you were on the water, with everything, and then I trusted you, and together we became wealthy, together, you and me, no?"

Ben was still pacing, silent now, trying desperately to come up with something he could say to change Hernandez's mind about the whole thing. It was too late. There was too much invested on both sides and too much in play already.

"Señor, are you still there?"

"I'm still here. Look, just let Janine go and please just find someone else to work with.

"Señor Scot, it is you, and only you that I want for this job. You will be here tomorrow morning at the same time. This time, you will leave your fish holds unlocked and we will put the ice and the cargo in before you or anyone else arrives. Tomorrow morning, Señor. My men will come and pick you up and bring you to your boat. All you will need to do is get onto the boat and pilot it to the designated transfer point. I'm not asking, Señor, and there will be no more contact with the police, FBI, DEA, CIA, or anyone else. Understand?"

"I understand."

"Good to have understanding, no? Be ready. 3:45 a.m. and this is only you. You can leave your son behind. He isn't wanted or needed."

Ben hung the phone up and looked at Andrew briefly, then with his head hung low, closed the cargo hatches, but left them unlocked, and turned off the lights.

"Dad, what's going on?"

"Nothing good, son. They somehow figured out that we had a conversation with the FBI. They almost cut the tip of Janine's little right finger off as retribution, and said that if we contact any law enforcement again, they will cut it off, and turn the rest of her into fish chum as well."

"Jesus Christ! These guys are despicable."

"Yes. Despicable and murderous, and everything dark and bad."

"So, what now?"

Ben looked at Andrew. His expression was semi-crazed, and very frustrated. "Hernandez is sending some men to pick me up at 3:45 a.m. tomorrow, and we've been put on notice that any more law enforcement, Janine will be killed, and her body will be chopped into chunks and used for shark chum. Also, he told me to leave you behind."

"Son of a bitch. Coward." Andrew hissed.

On the way home, Ben stopped and went into a convenience store and bought several cheap, disposable burner phones. He went into the restroom, activated one of them and immediately called the FBI and left messages for both Bromley and Decker letting them know that the same deal was on for the next day, and gave them the time. He also told them about Hernandez almost cutting the tip of Janine's finger off, and their threat to chop her up if Hernandez thought that Ben was still in contact with either of them.

The wait for the rest of the day seemed like an eternity. All Ben could think about was Janine. He hoped nothing else would go wrong. He was beginning to realize that his feelings for her ran deeper than he originally thought. She meant the world to him now, and he knew deep in his heart that he didn't want to spend any more of his life without her in it.

He felt helpless in his ability to help her, and wanted more than anything to be able to find her and free her. He also realized for the first time that he was capable of, and willing, to kill anyone who got in his way.

13

THE UNLIKELY RENDEZVOUS

The next morning came quickly. As soon as his alarm went off, Ben jumped out of bed. His adrenaline began coursing through his body almost immediately, and his mind began racing while thinking about all of the possibilities that might manifest today. His heart rate and blood pressure were already sky high from fear. He quickly dressed, grabbed a bite, and was just finishing up when he saw the icy blue headlamps of the SUV coming down the long driveway towards the house.

Ben put on his coat, and stepped out into the early morning. The remote location muffled all lingering sound almost instantly, making the whole world seem like it was housed inside a special sound proof room. The SUV pulled up and stopped. Ben opened the right, rear passenger door to get in. Janine sat on the other side of the bench seat. She looked at him, trying to pull a smile into place, but never made it.

Before Ben was allowed to get in, the driver came around to the passenger side and patted him down. Finding one of the burner phones Ben had just bought the day before, he threw it on the ground, breaking it into a couple of pieces, then finished the job by stomping on it until there we so many pieces that Ben wasn't sure if he would be able to identify what it was before its destruction.

The driver gave him a very pointed *you don't know who you're messing with look* after he finished motioning Ben to get in. Ben slid inside and sat down in silence. The driver slammed the door shut. Ben gave Janine his best try at a reassuring look, and then reached over, took her hand and gently held it. She gently, and swiftly pulled her hand back away, then looked at him with pleading eyes. Ben decided to sit quietly for the rest of the short trip to the docks. Once there, he would likely be busy, and need to stay that way.

Ben noticed that Janine had tears welled up in her eyes. He imagined that her life had been a scary, living hell for the last day or so. He would get revenge on Hernandez if given the chance, but his main objective was to get both of them to the rendezvous point safely, then get them off and away from Bessie before all of the fireworks started.

The SUV reached the docks faster than Ben could believe, and pulled up in front of Bessie. There was a large truck from ABC Lobster parked alongside his boat, and three men were finishing loading bags of ice and distributing the ice over the cargo stowed inside. The boxes of human organs Ben thought. Janine and Ben got out, The driver said, "Señor Scot, Señor Hernandez has instructions for you."

"Yeah, I'm sure he does," Ben said with as much sarcasm as he could muster.

"You are to board the boat, start the engine and get ready to get underway. We will give you the coordinates when we tell you to get under way."

Ben and Janine exchanged quick glances and then proceeded up the ramp over to Bessie's top deck. Janine went first.

Just when Ben took his last step onto Bessie, he heard his name being shouted. "Ben. Hey, Ben."

Ben glanced over his shoulder in the direction of the ABC Lobster building, and saw Christian Grumman, the manager, running to catch him before he left.

Ben stopped short and turned to go back to the dock. He did it quickly so there could be no objection to his decision by any of Hernandez's men.

Ben ran-walked the last 10 feet and held his hand out to Christian, who latched onto it and pumped it like someone who had just made a huge sale and was profusely thanking the customer.

"Hello, Christian. It's been quite some time, how are you?"

"Could be better, actually. Got a minute?" Christian looked frazzled standing there out of breath with his thick, dirty blond hair torqued backwards from the run over, his huge belly thrust outward, pushing his black, brown, and red stained apron towards Ben from over a foot away.

"Can it wait? I've got an urgent, one-time project enroute here with a picky customer that is paying well, but gets pissed off really easily."

"Well, picky is one way to describe them, I guess, but pissed off fits much better." Ben looked over at the driver that brought them. He nodded sideways at Ben, motioning him to get on his boat. Ben looked back at Christian, who just kept right on going, obviously shook up about something. "That guy that you just looked at."

"The driver that brought us?" Ben asked.

"Yep, that guy. I opened at 2 a.m. to get things ready. You know, I get my first customers, the ones that are going way out or all the way up to the Bay of Fundy the earliest. They like to get started early enough that they'll still have most of the day to latch onto something worth bringing home."

Ben was getting nervous as hell now, but was determined to act normally and not start anything. "Anyway, that driver guy came in with two others to get a bunch of ice. Too much. They wanted all that I had. I told them that I couldn't sell all the ice I had stockpiled just for them. When I said that, he pulled a gun on me and told me to stand aside. I almost shit myself! He had his two buffoons take about 80 percent of the ice I had on hand and . . ."

"Señor Scot, it's time to go!"

"Oh, geez. You'd better go. He was going to shoot me if I called the cops. I didn't. But I had to call Polar for an emergency delivery, so the others would have enough for their holds as well." Ben apologized as he began walking away, saying he would make it up to him when he got back, then turned and quickly walked up the ramp to get under way.

Ben had Janine stay in the galley while he went up to the helm and started the engine. The boat rumbled to life, the deep bass sounds of the idling engine emanated from below like a monster waking from a long sleep. Adding to the symphony, a trillion tiny bubbles quickly rose up from around the entire circumference of the boat, popping at the surface, giving the engine noise a slight gurgling and hissing quality.

The sound helped soothe Ben's nerves a little. He began to feel calmer now that he was surrounded by his usual world, like arriving home after a long trip. He was at odds with not being able to talk with Janine without prying ears always present and ready to remember or even record what they might say to one another. Indeed, it seemed that every time Ben became involved in illicit cargo moving, there were always listening ears.

Everyone involved, even law enforcement people that can come into play, are all paranoid, and they're all listening to the whispers of criminality being reported from witnesses, from cohorts, from bosses, from tapped phones, from snitches.

Hernandez's crew never said a word unless they needed you to move, or they needed further clarification about something. After a while, this lack of communication, this silence, made them seem like another piece of furniture in the room, like wax museum statues. They stayed so still and quiet, they slowly faded into the background, making it very easy to forget about them, and also real easy to inadvertently say something that you wouldn't want heard by others, or want repeated to Hernandez.

Ben had no idea how to relay the coordinates to the FBI, and it worried him. He needed to get Janine and himself away from the boat in time before the Coast Guard and the FBI intervened in the transfer, otherwise they would both be at high risk of being killed.

Salvador, the head of the four-person onboard crew, came up to the helm. He gave Ben the coordinates to the meeting with the Canadian lobster boat, and ordered him underway. Ben looked out and saw the last rope being tossed aside and slowly pulled away from the dock. Salvador stayed with Ben. From the helm, he was high enough to oversee the boat, his crew, and the rest of the surroundings. Ben piloted the boat through the marina first, followed by the area inside the breakwater jetty, finally exiting out into the open waters of the Gulf of Maine.

Ben then watched in utter horror as Salvador made his way down to the main deck, then all the way back to the aft of the boat, and promptly cut the rope tying Ben's emergency inflatable boat to Bessie! Ben saw it almost stop in the water, then begin to get smaller as they continued moving away from it. Twenty-five yards later, Salvador pulled out his 9mm pistol and fired multiple rounds into it. The inflatable collapsed almost instantly.

The last thing Ben saw while he was still able to, was the current moving the inflatable around in a circle, causing it to coil around itself into a huge floating mass as flat as a pancake, and as lifeless as a bloated corpse.

Ben's heart sank. Now, they were going to have to stay on board and take their chances at the transfer point. He didn't see any other way. They would need to stay on this heading for at least another hour, so he engaged the autopilot, then went to the galley for a coffee and to see Janine.

When he entered the galley, Janine was sitting alone with her clasped hands in front of her, both on top of the table. There was a strange object sitting next to her coffee mug on the table. There was only one person stationed to guard her, and he was facing the inside of the galley, right next to the exit hatch, standing motionless. He looked like a no neck, military trained, wax museum statue, ready to kick some ass and looking for anyone to give him a reason.

Ben quickly walked over to Janine, "Are you okay?" Ben asked, sounding truly concerned.

Janine met his eyes, "No," and immediately began crying. At first it was a gentle release of emotion, but once that gate opened the crying quickly became uncontrolled sobbing. She laid her head down on her arms and cried hard, just like she had when she'd learned that her father had been killed in a car accident.

Ben sat quietly, comforting her. He gently rubbed her back, whispering, "Let it out. That's it. That's right. Yes, just let it happen." He periodically looked over at the wax statue standing by the exit hatch, proudly wearing a strong look of disapproval on his face. So far, it was beginning to look like he was going to be able to have a conversation with Janine after all. Maybe, he thought, looking over at the statue again. Luckily, the rumble of the engine would mask any conversation with a lower volume, and Ben was grateful for that.

As he continued comforting Janine, he directed his gaze onto the strange object on the table. He picked it up with his free hand and turned it around a bit to examine it.

Janine said, "It's a tracking device that was found on the side of your boat at the aft end, near the engine discharge ports.

Ben felt a massive wave of hopelessness come across him and almost bowl him over with the shock of that revelation. No inflatable, no tracking for Bromley and Decker, no phone. Hernandez had covered all the bases. Ben realized that he and Janine would have no choice but to figure it out on their own as the situation unfolded in real time. There really wasn't any choice. He felt sad, and he was beginning to get the feeling this might end up being his last voyage.

None of the possibilities and scenarios marching through his head at that moment ended with a positive outcome for either one of them. It was almost as if he could feel the icy hand of death reaching out and touching his shoulder for a second, putting him on notice, trying to convey to him that his time was short.

He was glad that, if today was his day to die, then he would die near or with Janine. Sadly, he no longer had any plans left to discuss with her because all of their options had just been eliminated, and the circumstances were too stressful and bizarre to make small talk, so they both sat in silence for the time being.

Finally, Janine spoke, "Ben, what's going to happen to us? Are they going to kill us?"

"I'm not sure, but it's starting to look likely."

"I didn't know anything when they interrogated me, and they almost cut off my fingertip! Now, you're doing everything they want, and they're going to kill us? I don't get it. What if they need you again? It doesn't make sense that they would leave you alone for ten years, show up, use you for your boat, and then kill you."

Ben thought briefly, "It's been too much trouble this time I think."

"What do you mean?"

"Well, before we were on the same page. We both wanted to make a bunch of money. Now, Hernandez still does, and I don't. I've made this whole trip a pain in his ass, and he's even had to resort to kidnapping to get his way. I think once the job is done and the transfer is made, one of these guys will shoot us, then throw our bodies overboard so the blood will attract the sharks. Once our bodies are eaten, there won't be any evidence to prove that Hernandez or his crew men had anything to do with our disappearance or deaths. If anyone asks why I'm not with my boat, all these guys have to say is that I agreed to rent it to them."

Janine looked truly horrified, and on the edge of coming apart mentally. Her hair was frazzled and greasy, she had huge, ugly, dark bags under her eyes. She looked like she hadn't slept beyond an hour here, and a fifteen-minute cat nap there, in several days.

"Well, if that's what is planned for us, who the hell is going to pilot the boat back?" Janine asked, her voice wavering.

"I watched the head guy, Salvador, when he came up into the pilot house. He gave me the coordinates, and watched very carefully how I input the information into the navigational controls. Then, he kept watching me to see how I navigated us through the marina, and the breakwater cove, and how I did everything. Damn. Now I'm certain they're going to kill us."

Janine began quietly crying again. Ben put his forefinger to his pursed lips for a split second to silently ask her to stop, if possible.

"Don't worry," Ben said, his voice trailing off. He remembered Bessie saying to him many times over the years, I'm sure you'll figure something out, honey, you always do. He looked back at Janine, "I'll figure something out," then gave her a quick smile for good measure. The fear in Janine's eyes seemed magnified by her tears. She tried to compose herself a bit, then sat up taller and looked at Ben and, with a little enthusiasm said, "You know, if they're planning to kill us, then maybe we should kill them first."

Ben was taken aback by this, but he liked her spirit. "There you go! That's what I'm talking about."

Janine continued, "We can try to off them one at a time and try to make it look like accidents."

"There is only one glaring problem that I can see." Ben said. "The trip is in broad daylight and it's only going to take about three hours to get to the coordinates at our current speed."

Janine hung her head a bit and mumbled, "Well, it was a fun idea while it lasted."

Suddenly the hatch to the top deck opened up. "Señor Scot! You are wanted by Salvador in the pilot house."

Ben told Janine he would be back as soon as he could, and went up to see what Salvador wanted. When he opened the door to the pilot house, Salvador looked pissed. "Are you trying to sabotage this journey, Señor?" Without waiting for Ben to answer he continued, "What are you doing leaving this helm? The ship could be heading straight for another boat or an island and you wouldn't know it because you're not here! I expect you to pilot this vessel properly at all times, clear?"

"Absolutely, my friend. I am piloting this vessel, just not in the way you think I should be. There are no islands this far out. When vessels move to within several hundred yards of one another, the captain will adjust course to prevent collision. That is far more likely than having an actual collision with another boat and, furthermore, I have us at a safe speed, and on automatic pilot, which is something that I've been doing out here for thirty plus years, so just calm the fuck down! Oh, and one more thing, the auto pilot would have sounded an alarm to let me know that my attention was needed. That's the way autopilot is set up." Ben was so annoyed with these assholes that he didn't much give a damn what they thought about him talking to them with a little truth and anger for a change.

"From now on, why not leave the piloting up to me? After all, that's why your boss wanted me in the first place. Understand?"

To Ben's surprise, after hearing that Salvador nodded, "Sì, Señor," and walked out without any resistance. He went down the stairs to the top deck, and resumed his position at the stern. He stood there, holding his automatic rifle with both hands across his chest like a warrior staring straight ahead to ensure that, if anything came along not to his liking, he would be ready to strike, and take it out immediately.

Ben stayed in the pilot house for at least another twenty minutes to appease Salvador. Now alone, with only the throbbing noise of the engine and the sound of the wind whipping past the pilot house windows for companions, he suddenly felt exhausted. He leaned back in the captain's chair and closed his eyes for a minute, trying to calm his mind. His entire being was fighting the side effects of too much adrenaline. At his age, he felt the effects of stress more than ever.

Ben let his body relax all the way and get heavy. He let his mind turn to mush and started to fall asleep.

Not sure if he had actually fallen asleep or not, Ben opened his eyes with a sudden start. He had it! He knew how he and Janine would deal with this. It was going to be risky for sure, but this whole excursion was life and death. That much was apparent. Time to get proactive, he thought.

Ben left the pilot house and made his way back down to the galley. Janine was still where Ben had left her, but now she was fast asleep, with her head lying on her folded arms on top of the galley table. Ben sat down next to her. Sensing his presence, Janine opened her eyes and sat up when she saw it was him.

"Everything okay?" she asked.

"Yes, and I think I've figured out a way out of this situation."

Janine's eyes lit up. She straightened her posture then said, "Tell me."

Ben looked over at the wax statue, who, much to Ben's glee, wasn't even paying attention to them any longer. He was reading some hispanic newspaper he'd brought along, and only looked up at them periodically.

"I'll make this short. My son, Andrew, and I bought some stuff and rigged up a system to blow this boat up before yesterday's deadline. Then the FBI showed up unexpectedly, and changed everything, as did Hernandez, by kidnapping you. Anyway, I had already come to the conclusion that we wouldn't be able to go through with our plan. A short while ago, I think I dozed off in the pilot house, and when I awoke, I remembered that Andrew and I had already done all of the work, but we weren't going to use it. Do you see where I'm going with this now?"

"So, the stuff is still here on the boat?"

"Better than that," Ben said, "it's not only onboard, it's already in place and hooked up, waiting for a phone call."

"I don't understand." Ben temporarily lost Janine with that comment.

"You see, the whole set up is rigged so that if you dial the number of the transceiver, it regulates a small three-way valve that supplies fuel to the engine in the normal position, but in the activated position, the fuel pump discharges gasoline all over the engine compartment deck while simultaneously starting a 20-second timer. Once that timer reaches zero, it activates a spark coil that will ignite the gasoline, starting a quick moving, hot-as-hell fire down there. Once the fire reaches the nearby fuel tank, the entire boat will explode."

Janine could see the hope, like tiny torches in Ben's eyes. She watched him mentally search for any flaws, gaps, or holes with his revitalized idea, and was a little shocked. She couldn't believe Ben even knew about such things. He looked at her and, like he had read her mind said, "I'm more than just a simple lobsterman, Janine. I've been around the block more than a few times, and I've picked up quite a bit in the 'how-to' arena over the decades.

She smiled at him for the first time since their unfortunate reunion. He leaned in and kissed her cheek. That's when the wax statue came to life.

"Hey!" He was shaking his head from side to side saying no.

Ben just smiled, and nodded at him.

"Our original plan had me creating another fire in the front of the boat as a distraction, running to the inflatable and then calling the transceiver, and both of us getting as far away as possible before the boat exploded. Now, things have changed considerably.

"That's right," Janine said, "We no longer have that. You're not planning to blow us up with the boat are you?"

"No, I want to live as much as you or anyone else. So, this option is a little more scary, but it's an option that will, hopefully, allow us to escape anyway. Have you ever heard of an immersion suit?"

Janine looked at him unsure of how to respond, "No, and I'm not sure I like 'immersion' in the name of it either. Sounds like something that would be underwater?"

"Not exactly. In the water, rather than under water would be more accurate. And, I have four of them on board."

"What exactly are they?"

"Suits that can keep you alive in the water and prevent hypothermia from setting in. The ones I bought have emergency GPS beacons that will transmit our coordinates via satellite so we can be rescued." Ben was smiling from ear to ear now.

Janine thought about what he said, and didn't hesitate, "I'm in. Tell me what I need to do and I'll do it."

Ben and Janine continued sitting at the table for another 10 minutes or so, and Ben quietly filled her in on the do's and don'ts of the immersion suits. "Shed any large jacket, but layering is fine. Quickly remove the suit from the bag. Step into the suit, zip it all the way up to your neck, place the hood over your head, and close the flap over your face. Put on the life jacket, and enter the water feet first. That's it."

Janine said, "Thanks. I got it. Straight up and easy."

"Okay, I'm going to test our wax statue friend over there."

Janine looked worried, "What are you going to do?"

"I'm going to go to my quarters and grab a couple of mementos, at least that's what I'm going to say if asked."

Janine said, "Somehow, I get the feeling that there is just a little more that you're going to do."

"Yes, I'm going to start a fire and get this show on the road. Unless you can give me a great reason why we should wait. I feel that the longer we wait, the more danger there is to us. Once they make contact with the other vessel, and can see it visually, I'm almost certain they'll shoot us, then throw us overboard before they get too close to the other boat, so their actions aren't seen or heard.

Janine nodded in agreement. "I'm as ready as I'll ever be. Let's do it."

"Okay. I'm not sure how this is going to go. Be prepared to move as fast as you can."

"Okay."

Ben stood up and stretched, looking through his narrowed eyes at the wax statue. He looked up and kept his gaze on Ben. Ben stepped away from the table and said, "Hang on just a second, I think I have some pictures of that trip in my quarters. Let me go and find my photo album and I'll show them to you. Hang on a second."

Without looking at the guard, Ben began walking towards his berthing quarters. He was just about to step around the corner, then run the rest of the way once out of sight, when the guard shouted, "Hey! Señor, where are you going?"

"No worries, Mr. Wax Statue, or whatever your name is, I'll be right back. I'm getting my pictures, my photo album to show her some pictures." Ben could tell that the guard didn't understand him. Ben knew a little Spanish, but he hadn't needed to use it in a long time.

"Fotos. Mi fotos en . . ." Ben looked frustrated and perplexed.

Janine suddenly blurted out, "Va a sacar sus fotos."

Ben stood still waiting for the response. The guard nodded and went back to his reading, but glanced up a couple more times still skeptical.

"What the hell did you say to him?"

"He is going to get his photos," Janine said, managing a smile. "So, go get them!" She gave Ben a wink, then said, "Wait. Will an alarm go off?"

Ben thought for a split second, "I'll take the cover off and disable it. I can't disable the whole system, but I can disable the sensor in my quarters. That way, the rest of the crew won't know what's going on right away, and they won't be coming down the ladder when we're trying to go topside. Also, there are two suits in the closet over by the topside ladder, and two more in the closet at the base of the pilot house on the topside deck. We'll use those. That way, we'll be unencumbered while getting up there.

Janine nodded in agreement. "Hurry, Ben."

Ben headed towards his quarters, but once there, continued past them to the engine room at the end of the short hallway. He quickly slipped inside and closed the door, then went directly to his transceiver and disabled it. He pulled the signal wire from the transceiver to the timer, and left the wires connecting the timer to the three-way valve. He set the timer to manual, selected twenty minutes, then tapped enter. The timer began counting down. In twenty minutes fuel would be leaking everywhere in the midst of a huge fire, eventually causing an explosion once the fire reached the main fuel tanks. Old Bessie would be blown into a million fiery bits and pieces.

Ben left the engine room as quickly as he arrived. He ran the short distance to his berthing compartment and quickly went inside. He quickly disabled the smoke detector over the hatchway. Next, he went over to his bunk and pulled out the wide, low, aluminum, under-the-bed floor locker from underneath, slammed it down on top of his bunk, and opened it up. He grabbed his lighter, and the lighter fluid, and set them aside while he pulled his bedsheets and top blanket up together into a bunch on top of his bunk. Next, he emptied his small trash can on top of the cloth pile to use as kindling, soaked the whole pile in lighter fluid, then lit the pile on fire.

The pile caught fire instantly. Within two seconds, the flames were already licking the underside of the top bunk, which doubled as a cork board, complete with an adjustable light and some sticky notes. The sticky notes ignited instantly and moved onto the cork next to it. Ben shut the hatch door and ran back out to the galley.

"Fire! Fire!" Ben shouted.

The guard jumped up looking alarmed and confused. Janine looked at him and screamed "Fuego! Fuego!" pointing towards Ben's quarters. The guard ran past Ben straight into the already thick smoke that was getting denser by the second. A few seconds later, Ben could hear the guard coughing, then it sounded like he was choking. He ran down the passageway with a fire extinguisher, intending to surprise the guard, and then hit him over the head with it.

Ben took a deep breath and headed into the thicker smoke. When he finally came upon the guard, Ben started to raise the extinguisher to hit him with it, but the guard thought he was trying to hand the extinguisher to him. In the blink of an eye, the guard set his automatic rifle down against the wall, grabbed the extinguisher from Ben, then turned and began using it against the fire.

Having only a few seconds of breath left, Ben didn't hesitate. He grabbed the automatic rifle and immediately swiped the back of the guard's head hard with the butt end of it. The guard fell instantly, and remained lying motionless on the deck. Blood began spreading on the floor fast. It was visible even through the heavy smoke.

Ben ran into the galley and grabbed Janine by the hand. They both ran over to the topside ladder and began their ascent, slowly climbing up, like a couple of homicide detectives trying to quietly tip-toe up to their perp's apartment, guns drawn and ready. Once at the top, Ben slowly opened the hatchway door to see where the others were.

Salvador and the other two guards were all standing at the bow of the boat smoking cigarettes. Ben quickly closed the door and looked at Janine. "Let's grab the suits in the closets down there at the bottom of the ladder on the right. Unfortunately, if we exit now, our movements will be noticed immediately. There is no way of getting to the closet at the base of the pilot house safely that I can see. I'm glad I put two suits down here in the galley."

Janine nodded, "Stay there, I'll grab them." Ben watched in amazement as she descended the stairs two at a time, slammed the closet door open, and grabbed the two immersion suits inside. Ben realized that he wouldn't be able to put his on while standing on a stairwell at an odd angle, so he followed her back down, and now stood next to her. They opened the bags, and put on the suits. They were cumbersome and heavy, but not so much that they wouldn't be able to move or walk the way they were going to need to.

They crept back up the stairs and this time when Ben opened the hatchway a little, only one guard was at the bow. Ben had no idea where the other two might be. If Salvador had returned to the helm at the top of the pilot house, he and Janine would be leaving almost directly under him, making it impossible for him to see them at such a steep angle.

Ben looked at Janine with fear in his eyes, but nodded nevertheless. She nodded back. Ben took a deep breath before opening the hatch about halfway. With no one in sight he stepped all the way out, quickly turned, then held his hand out for Janine. She immediately exited, and they both began hugging the wall of the pilot house while working their way towards the stern.

Ben was perplexed about where the men might be, but grateful to have already made it halfway to the stern undetected. Ben thought Salvador must be at the helm above us and the other two must be on the opposite side of the pilot house. Perfect!

Ben pointed to the starboard side of the boat, then began fast walking, half running towards it when, suddenly, he heard the thundering sound of a weapon being fired, followed by the sound of several bullets whizzing past his head.

"Alto! Stop!" Salvador screamed, firing more rounds at them. They both ran as fast as the immersion suits would let them while staying hunched over at the same time.

When they got to the starboard side railing, Ben shouted at Janine, "Go! Go!" Ben turned to see where Salvador was and felt terror creep into his soul. Salvador was running towards them with his rifle in the firing position. Ben decided that he'd better do something to protect Janine while she finished getting herself over the railing, and safely into the water. He grabbed a life ring and threw it at Salvador as hard as he could like a frisbee, which only slowed him down a little, and he was getting really close now. Finally, Ben decided to charge right back. He ran right towards Salvador screaming at the top of his lungs.

It worked. Salvador stopped and stared at the crazed man coming at him, not knowing what this actually meant to his own safety. Instead of raising his rifle and shooting Ben when he had the chance, Salvador actually took a step back. That hesitation was all that Ben needed. He threw himself at Salvador with all the strength he had.

Salvador ran backward trying to stay upright, but Ben continued running forward, hitting Salvador right in his knees and wrapping his arms around both of Salvador's legs, then pulled them in as hard as he could, tackling Salvador onto the hard deck.

Salvador's rifle fell and slid slightly away from him. Salvador stood back up and swung hard at Ben. Ben ducked just in time, and punched Salvador in his abdomen, below the belt line as hard as he could. Salvador doubled over in pain, and was holding his stomach. Ben grabbed the rifle and pointed it at him..

At first, Salvador just smiled at him while keeping his hands raised. His ultra white teeth in high contrast against his dark skin. Ben motioned for him to go down into the galley. Salvador moved towards the hatchway door and opened it. Smoke came pouring out, causing him to start coughing again almost instantly. Ben quickly pushed him into the hatchway, then slammed the door, spinning the wheel until it tightened up completely, and continued holding onto it tightly. Within five seconds, he felt Salvador trying to open it from the other side. The sound of his coughing was loud enough to penetrate the steel bulkhead and hatchway, and Ben felt bad, but it was Salvador or him. He looked around nervously. He saw two other crewmen appear at the bow and look around. When they saw Ben holding onto the hatchway wheel, they began fast walking over to him.

Ben looked over at Janine, still straddling the stern railing, waiting for Ben. Finally, Salvador's coughing stopped, and Ben felt him stop trying to open the hatch.

Ben ran back over to Janine. He climbed up on the railing, sat down, and turned to face the ocean. He looked right into Janine's eyes and shouted, "Follow me, and do everything I do." He lifted himself up a little off of the railing before jumping feet first into the icy waters of the Gulf of Maine.

The boat was already moving away fairly rapidly, and Ben worried that Janine would stay paralyzed and not make it. He waved to her to jump, shouting, "Come on! Come on! Let go! Janine, let go!"

Almost a hundred yards away, Janine finally let herself go, and was now safely in the water. As soon as she let go, Ben started working his way over to her, as fast as he could. The current was strong, and it seemed that for every three or four strokes forward, the current would take him back two.

As he got closer to her, he noticed the boat was no longer moving. The engine was barely audible, and that told Ben it was at idle. Ben saw Salvador coming out of the pilot house. What? He lived?

Ben grabbed onto Janine, "Are you okay?"

"I think so."

"Salvador somehow made it out of the galley in one piece. I just saw him come out of the pilot house, we need to swim away as fast as possible. This guy is like a terminator or something. I cannot believe that he didn't die from smoke inhalation when I put him in the galley. The smoke was so thick you couldn't see anything farther than two feet away. Come on, Janine. Let's make some tracks. Here, let me turn on your beacon before I forget." He reached over and pulled the beacon cord. Immediately a tiny little green LED light began to flash indicating that it was doing its job.

Ben pulled his own GPS beacon cord and together they slowly began to move away from the boat again. When they reached about 20 yards from the starboard side, one of the other guards appeared at the railing and started firing rounds at them.

Ben struggled to talk while swimming, but managed to belt out, "Come on, Janine. Let's move it. We're not going to be hard to hit. We look like a couple of giant yellow targets out here."

They both managed to pick up their pace a little, swimming as hard and fast as possible away from Bessie, while bullets continued hitting the water all around them. Ben thought I can't believe out of all those bullets, that none of them hit either one of us."

After a few more minutes, and totally exhausted from swimming while wearing bulky immersion suits, they both stopped and held onto one another, resting for a few minutes. They quietly floated, rising with the swells that passed underneath them. A few minutes later, they were both jarred out of their rest by the sound of automatic rifle fire again.

Ben looked over just in time to see Salvador shoot the guard that had been shooting at them and missing. Together, Salvador, and the only other remaining guard, hoisted the dead body over the railing straight into the water. Ben said, "Come on, Janine! Bessie should go up any minute now." Both of them started moving even farther away, as fast as they could.

14

SURVIVAL AT SEA

Ben and Janine stopped swimming when it appeared to Ben that they were a safe distance away. Looking at Bessie from their location, Ben estimated they were about one quarter mile out from her, and counting. He was worried. It seemed like at least twenty minutes already elapsed and nothing had happened. Fortunately, he also knew that, with their beacons turned on, their chances for rescue were better now than when they left Portland Harbor.

Ben said, "I think we're good for now. Let's just float and rest. The Coast Guard will be around within the next 12 hours, but likely even sooner than that. They've come a long way with the GPS rescue network."

Janine started to answer, but she was too exhausted to say anything. She looked at Ben and nodded, then managed to say, "I'm listening."

A low pitched thundering sound could be heard coming from Bessie's direction. The source slowly crept into their reality and their vision while remaining low on the horizon. It was a helicopter.

"Hey, maybe our signal is already being addressed. See that? I believe we're about to be rescued!"

Both Ben and Janine struggled some to hug one another while floating in their immersion suits, but succeeded, even managing a quick kiss. Ben looked deep into Janine's eyes, and said, "I love you, Janine."

Without hesitating Janine enthusiastically replied, "I love you back, Ben Scot."

The medium sized black helicopter flew straight at them at a fairly high speed. Once close enough, it began shooting at them using high powered rotary machine guns that were mounted on both sides of the main fuselage. After the first pass by, the helicopter made a hard turn and came around for another try. Ben pushed away from Janine extra hard, and began swimming in another direction screaming, "Swim away, Janine!" He wanted to force the gunner to have to choose who would be shot first. Neither of them could dive under the water whatsoever while wearing these suits, but without them, they would die from hypothermia.

The helicopter made a maneuver that allowed Ben to catch a brief glimpse of the pilot and a passenger in the back, but he couldn't see well enough from the glare to make out any definite features. This time, it came closer than Ben could believe, but it didn't fire at him. It was almost like the pilot was trying to take Ben's head off using the helicopter. After the chopper flew over his head with maybe a foot to spare, Ben saw Hernandez look back at him from the right side doorway, smiling.

The helicopter flew back towards Bessie, then started a long, wide turn, accelerating as it approached the boat. Ben wasn't sure if it was coming back to shoot at them some more or not.

Just as the chopper passed over Bessie, she blew sky high, sending a ball of fire into the air that looked like a mini-Hiroshima nuclear bomb going off, complete with a nice little mushroom cloud.

The percussion from the blast instantly bent two of the blades on Hernandez's chopper. The bent blades hit the side of the helicopter two to three times before forcing it down. It fell straight down, directly into the sea, landing right next to Bessie, which was now nothing more than a mass of flame, and wreckage.

Ben swam back over to Janine with a smile on his face. It was over. And, they both made it out alive. *After that little fireworks show, the cavalry should be along within two hours tops,* he thought.

Ben felt relieved. All they had to do now was wait to be rescued, and life would finally be able to return to normal again. Only this time, he would be sober, and have Janine in his life. Those two things, along with knowing Hernandez was finally dead, were already giving Ben more hope for a positive future than he'd had in a very long time.

Ben and Janine held onto one another and relaxed a bit. After a while, Ben closed his eyes and drifted off to sleep without even realizing it. He dreamt that he and Janine were thirty years younger and they were newlyweds. When Janine announced to him that she was pregnant with their first child, he felt serene and had so much joy in his heart that it hurt.

Suddenly, Ben woke up on full alert. Janine was thrashing around like crazy and screaming at the top of her lungs. She was hysterical. Then Ben saw the knife-like fin slicing through the water and now it was heading straight for them, and picking up speed. "Get ready to kick it in the nose. You won't see him until the last second.

When you do, kick him right in the nose as hard as you can. It works to deter them. They hate being hit there." Ben offered.

Ben felt Janine's legs moving extra fast back and forth. He scanned the water straight down, but couldn't see much at all from point blank range.

"Janine, I'll go underwater by doing a bobbing movement." Ben kicked hard, and then relaxed, kicked hard, and then relaxed, each time allowing him to go higher in the air, and lower into the water in a vertical, see-saw fashion.

In a matter of five seconds, Ben managed to submerge enough to see underwater just in time to see a huge Great White shark coming up from deeper waters to take a bite of Janine's right leg. Ben swam closer and kicked down, then brought his legs back up to his chest and kicked down again, over and over. The second time, he felt his foot connect with the shark's nose and, luckily, it swam away and disappeared back into the icy darkness.

Ben accidentally swallowed some sea water, and began coughing so hard that he couldn't talk or do anything. Janine was shaking, and had begun crying hysterically. Ben knew that if they weren't rescued soon, both of them were likely going to become shark food. He figured that, barring too much fatigue, they would likely be able to manage until sunset, but once the sun went down, there would be no way to see the sharks to fight them off. For the first time in his life, Ben felt so overwhelmed by his circumstances, he had to fight to keep the panic from growing out of control inside him, and he fought it with all his might.

Ben looked around. At least for now, no other sharks could be seen. He spotted a few piles of debris from Bessie that were close by, and decided to investigate more closely to see if he could find something to help him fend off the sharks. He swam over to the first pile and retrieved a long piece of fiberglass for poking the next shark in the nose, but there was nothing else practical left to use, so he swam over to another pile. This pile seemed to consist mostly of tangled rope used onboard to secure hatches and to tie things down with. He dug into the mass a little, looking for anything that might be useful.

Once Ben pulled some of the pile apart, Salvador's head suddenly bobbed up to the surface from somewhere inside the mass, startling Ben so much that, when he kicked his legs out of fear, his right foot became entangled in something below the surface that he couldn't see. He kept trying to free it by kicking and moving it to get it untangled, only to have his left foot also become entangled. He was still floating, but his feet were now weighed down by a small, semi-heavy mass that completely restricted his ability to use his legs for swimming.

Ben was as close to freaking out as he'd ever been in his life. The fear had kept his heart rate and blood pressure way up, and for too long. So long, that it had given him a potent headache. He was on borrowed time, and so was Janine, and he knew it. He glanced back at Salvador's head, and saw a tangle of tendons, arteries, and connective tissue hanging from the bottom of his neck. Tiny scavenger fish were swimming and hovering just below the mess, taking turns moving in and sucking small pieces of the tissue off for food. He couldn't submerge easily to free himself without great difficulty, and he couldn't swim away until he did exactly that.

"Ben. Are you okay?" Janine shouted. Ben finally managed to turn sideways a little, away from Salvador's head, so that he could try to grab the small tangled mass on his feet without having to submerge in the direction of the head.

"I'll be okay. My feet are tangled in rope and debris, but I have a plan to get free. Stay there unless I ask you to come over and help. I don't want you to suffer the same fate." He plunged forward and went below the surface, first looking down, then back at his feet as soon as his eyes submerged, and he immediately saw the problem. Some of the rope had gathered debris and formed a hoop just large enough for one of his feet to go into it, but almost impossible to pull his foot back out due to the weight of the rest of the debris attached to it.

He righted himself in the water, and tried pulling his feet towards his chest, using his suit's buoyancy to stay above water so he could still breathe. Pulling all the weight of his immersion suit, his clothes, and his shoes, plus the mass attached to his feet upwards, heavily strained his abdominal muscles to the point of going into spasm—twice.

Every time he would pull upward, he would get his legs halfway up to his chest, and feel the beginning of a muscle spasm. Eventually, he had no choice but to give up and wait for the spasm to subside, then try again. While waiting, he looked around at surface level, and saw more debris piles. On the third try, Ben was finally able to grab the side of the loop around his right foot and unhook it. Afterwards, he brought the mass to the surface by raising his left leg up far enough to grab it on that side, and finally unhooking it from that foot.

The debris field was widening fast, and some of the floating human body parts entrained in it were being rummaged through by other sharks. In the short distance between himself and Janine, he saw two more body parts: a hand, and a leg blown off right above the knee. Both were being pushed along by sharks trying to get them inside their mouths. They kept missing the parts because their biting action was so strong that the water being pushed out of their mouths would push the part off to the side at the last second. Ben was horrified. He realized that he was swimming around in debris filled with body parts, actively being fed upon by enormous, hungry sharks.

As Ben got closer to Janine, he could hear her moaning with terrible, agonizing fear. "Janine, try to control your breathing as much as you can. You need to keep your wits about you and fend off the sharks that come towards you. Your life depends on it, Janine."

Janine didn't say a word. Another, even bigger shark made a run at them. Ben saw it closing in from Janine's left side. He tightened his grip on the fiberglass pole, raised it like a javelin, plunged it downward and hit the shark directly on its nose. The shark didn't like it, and Ben saw him submerge, and swim away quickly. As Ben turned his attention back to Janine, he saw the shark's fin emerge out of the corner of his eye. This time, it was even farther away, near one of the floating debris piles.

Ben flashed on Salvador's head in that pile and realized that if the shark found it, he would have it for dinner. He hoped it would be enough for the shark to leave them alone now, and keep him preoccupied for a while. He realized that time was short, and that neither of them would be able to keep this up for too much longer without having more serious consequences. He looked back at Janine. She looked like she wanted to sleep. Ben felt panicked. He screamed, "Janine! Stay awake! Stay awake, Janine! Hey!" He gently slapped her cheek, and she opened her eyes looking at him with disbelief.

Janine wrapped her right arm around Ben and pulled herself tight against him. When he looked at her again, she had passed out. Ben was so full of adrenaline that it would've taken an elephant tranquilizer to put him to sleep. They managed to float unbothered by sharks for another thirty minutes or so, before he had to use the fiberglass rod to thump an aggressor twice to get it to back off. A short while later, another shark that he hadn't seen, also managed to get extra close. Janine had awakened without Ben realizing it, and startled him by pointing it out. Ben had only seconds to react. He hit the shark hard on the snout with the fiberglass rod just in time, and the shark quickly swam away.

It was difficult for Ben to tell how much time had elapsed. There were just enough body parts and blood in the water to keep the sharks coming around semi-regularly. The nearly constant attack kept the stress level sky high. Five minutes seemed like thirty.

Ben was fearful about what they were going to do when nightfall came, if they weren't rescued yet. They would no longer be able to see the sharks to fight them. He tried to shut the thought out of his mind. He'd already experienced so much fear and stress today, already, that he was starting to wonder in the back of his mind which would get him first—the sharks, or a heart attack. He involuntarily drifted off to sleep, until another shark bumped him passing by, before turning around to attack seconds later.

Ben stabbed at him and connected more than once, but this one wouldn't leave. Ben's arm was getting tired moving the pole around and stabbing at the water. He was getting worried that he would lose his grip on the pole, and it would sink and be lost forever. Just in case, he glanced around to see if he would still have a shot at another piece of debris that could be used as a weapon, but felt his heart sink when he saw that all the debris piles had already drifted off, and were no longer in sight.

The sky grew dim, as clouds became dominant in the sky. Ben was exhausted and rapidly running out of fight. He couldn't see anything well anymore, and Janine was getting weaker by the minute. Another shark turned and made a run towards them. Ben only noticed him at the last second when his fin had just started to submerge, and he knew that if he managed to get this one to leave, it would be like winning the lottery, because it was too dark to see anything below the surface now.

He closed his eyes, hoping that the pain of dismemberment wouldn't be as excruciating as he'd imagined. He felt his heart momentarily flutter, while it was already likely beating close to two hundred beats per minute, waiting for those razor sharp teeth to sink into a part of his body. He imagined the shark tearing a chunk of his body away for a meal, leaving him watching his entire life flash before his eyes like a high-speed movie, knowing he was about to die.

Shots rang out. Ben opened his eyes, and saw the Coast Guard cutter off to his side. It had seemed to materialize out of nowhere. It cruised by with a gunner on the top deck sitting at the controls of a high powered machine gun. He looked over to where he last saw the shark he'd just shot at, but all that remained were chunks of the shark's body shrouded in a cloud of his own blood.

Ben passed out.

15

RECOVERY

Ben woke up in a hospital room with a view of the Gulf of Maine and the Portland Maine harbor area. He pulled his gaze away from the beautiful day outside, and looked over at Janine who was still asleep in the only other bed in the room. He smiled. Together, they'd actually made it out alive. He flashed on what they'd just gone through. It seemed odd that the whole experience now seemed a little like waking up from an intense bad dream, or like something that only happens to characters in a fiction novel, not in real life.

In his mind he replayed Bessie blowing up. Watching her blast into a fiery ball, sending debris out in all directions for nearly a hundred yards. He felt sad about losing her. They'd had quite a long history together. In the end of her life, she'd saved his. She'd given him a way to escape his own likely execution, while simultaneously killing his enemies.

It was going to be hard not going out lobstering anymore. Then he realized that he still had his speed boat, and that it would be more than adequate for fishing and recreating on the water, and he would still be able to harvest plenty of lobster for get-togethers. Thinking about it that way, he felt resolved and extra good about how things had ended up, and now he was certain that Hernandez would finally leave him alone since his helicopter went down over Bessie's fiery wreckage. He couldn't believe his good fortune having Hernandez showing up to personally see to it that Ben and Janine paid dearly for saying no to him, and then losing his own life after his helicopter fell straight down into that fiery mess

Just for good measure, Ben looked right, then left, checking to see if there were people in the room that he didn't want seeing what he was about to do. Certain that he wasn't being watched by anyone, he pinched himself. Ouch! he thought.

The nurse came in, "Ah, I see you're awake. How do you feel?"

"Mentally, I feel exhilarated, but physically I feel like a freight train rolled over me."

"I see. You're sore?"

"You could say that, yes." Ben replied.

"Are you feeling well enough to accept guests? I have two gentlemen outside who said not to wake you, but asked to see you if you were awake and feeling well enough."

Ben felt his heart rate increase instantly. "Any chance you got their names?"

"Oh, I'm sorry, Mr. Scot, yes. I believe their names were, um, agent Decker, and the other one said his name was Bromley, agent Bromley." She could tell by Ben's face that he was alarmed. "Are they dangerous? Should I call security, Mr. Scot?"

"No. I thought they might be some other people. These two, I've already spoken with before. They're with the FBI."

"Thank goodness. I'll send them right in then, if that's okay."

"That's fine. Thank you, Ms.?"

"Anderson. Nurse Anderson."

"Thank you, Nurse Anderson." Ben said, smiling.

She smiled back, and went to the door. She opened it halfway, then leaned out a bit and said, "Gentlemen, Mr. Scot will see you."

Bromley and Decker came right in. They looked extremely stressed and very concerned. Bromley blurted, "Ben, we're so sorry that we didn't arrive to help you. How on earth did you manage to survive?"

Being reminded of their ordeal so soon rubbed Ben the wrong way. "Where the fuck were you guys?"

Decker answered, "Going crazy looking for you guys. I thought it would be a fairly simple task to locate you, but first we lost your signal before you left. We figured that the cartel located the tracking device and got rid of it."

Ben cut him off, "Yeah, they located it alright. It was sitting in front of us on my former galley table, already de-energized."

Bromley said, "We figured that's what happened."

Ben fired back, "So, you guys, the famous FBI, didn't have a plan B set up?"

"Yes, we did, but the helicopter portion of that plan didn't materialize. Despite having paid to reserve it in advance from a local operator at the nearby airport, some newly hired, just out of high school newbie got confused, and let someone else take it out—right when we needed it. They were hundreds of miles away, so even when the chopper returned after being recalled, you guys were nowhere to be found once we were finally airborne."

"I cannot believe that the FBI couldn't do better than that. We almost fucking died out there! Don't you get that? Janine almost lost her mind from the fear of being torn apart by sharks because neither of us had the energy to continue fighting them off. She came within a hair's width of losing her life. Goddamn you guys anyway!"

"We're sorry for what happened to you, Mr. Scot, and we're very glad to see you alive and your lady friend alive as well. We seriously tried in earnest to find you once we were finally able to, but you have to realize that the Gulf of Maine is 36,000 square nautical miles with over 7,500 miles of coastline"

"Yeah. Right. Okay. But the Coast Guard found us just fine. Whatever. Is that why you guys showed up? To say you're fucking sorry? Why? So you can feel a little better about yourselves now that you've apologized?"

The two agents looked at one another, then looked back at Ben just in time to have him say, "Get the fuck out of my room and get the fuck out of my life. I regret the day you showed up at my front door. I knew then, in my gut, that letting you guys into this cargo transfer was a huge mistake."

The two agents nodded at him. Bromley set a business card on Ben's bed. "If you need us for anything in the future, Mr. Scot, please don't hesitate to call."

Ben stayed silent until they left the room. He looked over at Janine again, and saw her eyes open. "How long have you been awake?"

Janine looked terrible, but she had life back in her again, and she looked much better. "Only since you started yelling at those guys. I didn't want to deal with them or talk to them about what happened. I just want to get well and move forward, you know?"

Ben said, "I completely understand, and concur."

Ben was discharged the next day, but spent the whole day with Janine at the hospital anyway. Both Andrew and Celia stopped by and met Janine for the first time, and Ben could tell that they both thought she was pretty, and amazing.

During one afternoon visit, Andrew accompanied Ben to the cafeteria, expounding his admiration for her all the way down the hallway, "Dad, wow, Janine is amazing. I can't believe that she can be so charming and fun while lying in a hospital bed healing from such a traumatic experience."

"She is a strong lady, son. Really strong. That's why she's a healer. She has enough strength to absorb the weaknesses of others long enough for them to become strong enough to deal with their demons on their own. She can handle the rough language, and even threats to her physical safety while someone is in the throes of a hard-core withdrawal from alcohol, or heroin." Ben smiled at Andrew adding, "She's a keeper, son."

A week later, Janine was discharged. Before they let her go, she had spent time one on one with a therapist for multiple sessions to help get started with reconciling what happened, and her Post Traumatic Stress Disorder from the ordeal. Ben wondered if she somehow managed to hide her anger and rage about being kidnapped, and fighting off sharks, by screaming and raging about it when no one else was present. Under the circumstances, she seemed almost too happy, but Ben let her be however she needed to be. He knew that healing is different for everyone. He thought time doesn't necessarily heal all wounds, but it can do a fantastic job of moving them way into the background so you can live a relatively normal life.

Ben really didn't want Janine to go home. After what they'd just been through what he really wanted was to help her recover, and he simply wanted to be with her as much as he could. So, instead of asking her if he could drive her home, he took a really deep breath and asked her to come home with him. "Janine, I have a house so big it's like a hotel. You're more than welcome to come and stay for as long as you like. It's really not any trouble, and I would love to have you close by. We will both still be able to help one another, as needed, while you finish recuperating."

Janine was secretly hoping that he would ask her if she wanted to stay with him, and didn't hesitate to accept his offer. "Thank you so much, Ben. Yes. What a generous offer, but I really couldn't."

"Janine, please. Besides, I think it would be better for us to be together to help each other process what happened."

She heard his sincerity, and believed him. He was looking at her with such caring and love in his eyes. "Okay. Now that you put it like that, how can I say no?" She stepped closer and hugged him.

She placed her body against his, and Ben felt the same jolt of loving energy and excitement pass through him that he'd felt when she'd first kissed his cheek at the rehabilitation center.

16

THE NEXT STEP

Janine expressed pleasant surprise at Ben's house. She listened to him talk about it before, but only a little here and there, and never enough for her to get a complete picture of it. Ben happily showed her around, really enjoying watching Janine's eyes light up as they entered a new space or another bathroom.

"Have you thought about turning this into a hotel, or bed and breakfast before?"

"It's crossed my mind, but the truth is, I don't want the hassle. The only thing I'm really interested in as far as money making now, is money making me more money. For instance, I don't have to do anything at all here except maintain the property, upgrading it as needed and, like magic, the value of the property and the price others would pay to own it goes up over time. Ask what you want, and nowadays, someone will come along and add 30 percent to it just to ensure that they are ultimately the new owners."

"I had no idea real estate could be that lucrative."

"It can be. When you end up with a place like this, with a lot of square footage, multiple rooms for family and guests, a gourmet kitchen, and detailed woodwork throughout. All on a huge manicured property that ends at the water's edge and, well . . . it is very lucrative, or at least it has become so. Wine? Tea?"

"Tea, please."

Ben put the kettle on the stove and got the tea selection tray out. He loved tea, and was happy that she had chosen it. He brought out a small tray with two cups, and some little glass containers full of tea and condiments. All the containers were labeled, and secured with airtight lids. Green: *DazHang Mountain*, and *Oolong*. Black: *Earl Grey*, and *Ceylon* teas, and a small container of sugar cubes, and a small creamer.

"Well, you are certainly a man of many surprises today. I didn't know you liked tea."

Ben smiled, "A little something that Bessie got me started on. When I first started drinking tea, I noticed that it would give me a nice lift and it came with a good amount of energy, but in a different way than coffee that's hard to describe."

Janine took a sip of her *Earl Grey*, then set her cup back down and looked up at Ben. "I know exactly what you mean. Less caffeine than coffee, but at least as much, if not more, energy."

"That's it, exactly. There must be other compounds in different teas that stimulate us in more ways than just a simplistic caffeine, intake and response mechanism."

Janine took another sip, "I've read that people who sip green tea off and on all day long have really low Body Mass Index's, and seem to effortlessly keep their weight under control."

Ben said, "Hmmm. That's interesting. I might have to switch, and give that theory my own test. I certainly could use a hand in controlling my weight these days. Hell, if I didn't forget to eat half the time because of being so busy—along with not noticing that lunch time came and went without me even noticing it—I'd likely already be as big as this house, and I would likely already have one foot in the grave."

Janine laughed. She seemed very relaxed and comfortable, and liked Ben's company a lot. "Thank you for having me, Ben. I think this arrangement will be fine. I want to commend you for being so kind and caring to me when I tried to go so clinical on you the last time we spoke on the phone."

"No need to apologize, but thank you for that." Ben said, giving her a nod and smile. "How about I help you stow the stuff you brought, and I'll get started making dinner for us. Tomorrow we can go over to your place and get some more of your things, if you'd like."

"Thank you, Ben. That would be fine."

"Please, follow me then." Ben led her past the den, past the small library, and then across the main entrance lobby, and through the door leading into the first floor guest suite. "This is where I thought it would be easiest for you. Plenty of room and amenities. Privacy as needed or wanted, and no stairs to deal with."

Janine put her things down on the kingsize bed. She was flabbergasted. She had never stayed in a room this nice before in her entire life, even when at nice hotels on vacation.

The room was plainly decorated in pastels, and had a timeless modern look that Janine instantly fell in love with. On one wall there were two doors leading into two huge, walk-in closets that lit up when entered, and had full-length mirrors covering the wall at the far ends of both of them.

At the far end of the bedroom, there was a short corridor leading to an enormous bathroom with double sinks in front of a mirror that covered the entire wall. There was a private commode, with a bidet in its own closet, an ultra modern glass shower stall, and a spa tub with a view of Casco Bay. The bathroom was well stocked with towels, washcloths, and bathrobes. The shower had liquid soap, shampoo, and conditioner already there, but in stylish, self-contained glass vessels that appeared to be built into the wall of the shower stall just to the right of the shower control lever.

"Oh my gosh, Ben. This is amazing, simply amazing. I feel like a queen or a celebrity. This is just so lovely and beautiful. Thank you very much. I feel like I won the grand prize on a gameshow or something. What a view, too."

"I'm glad you like it, Janine. I thought you might. I pictured you here, in this room." Ben's voice trailed off a bit saying that. He felt a little embarrassed and looked down for a second.

Suddenly, Janine went to him. She slid both arms around his waist, turned her head to the side and hugged him tightly. He wrapped his arms around her and held her in silence. He was falling deeply in love with her, and he wanted it to happen. He also hoped with all his might that she felt the same way, and wanted him in her life just as much as he wanted her in his.

Realizing this truth, tears of relief welled up in his eyes, then began slowly leaking out onto his cheeks, until a steady stream of drops quickly formed, then refilled wet lines down his cheeks on both sides, before pausing briefly, before falling off of his jaw and onto Janine's head. He had almost forgotten just how good it felt to care about someone deeply, and hold them close.

Janine must've felt the wet drops working their way through her hair. She looked up at Ben with a serious, concerned look on her face, then pulled back from him a little and gently wiped his tears with her hands. She never said a word. Their eyes connected and locked. Slowly, they moved closer to one another. She reached up and slid her hand behind his neck and gently pulled him towards her lips. She slowed, stopping short, just before their lips were about to touch, savoring their breath exchange for one more second, poised, looking into his hazel eyes, before closing hers and kissing him passionately.

When the kiss ended, they remained standing together in each other's arms. Ben felt exhilarated and light headed, like a schoolboy getting his first kiss all over again. He felt good energy coming from her. It filled him up inside, and stirred him in a way he hadn't felt in years. He smiled and tried to squash his laughter, but began chuckling a little anyway.

Janine looked up at him again with a delicate smile, her eyes sparkling with joy, "What are you chuckling about, Mr. Scot? If it's that thing I feel, I already know all about it." She giggled, adding, "And, it's okay. As a matter of fact, it's fine. It's going to be perfect." She kissed him hard again, this time exploring his mouth with her tongue.

Ben hadn't felt this aroused in years. He couldn't believe the depth of it. He felt powerful feelings of attraction coming over him now. He said, half kidding, "Should I draw us a bath, light some candles, and get the wine now?"

Janine fired right back with a provocative, devilish tone, "You get the wine. I'll get the bath going, and light some candles. When you get back, we'll see where it takes us while it's filling up." Then she gave Ben a what are you waiting for, get going! look.

17

SPARE SAVIOR

Ben loved having Janine home with him. She was pleasant, easy to get along with, and seemed to have an intuitive way about her. At times, it was almost as if she could read his mind.

Within reason, he let her do what she wanted as far as contributing to the household. She loved to cook and presented him with daily surprises, and many different foods and meals than he was used to, but he loved the variety and trying new things out, so it worked. They worked.

Her recovery succeeded. She would continue therapy three times per week, but was told she should attempt to resume her normal life. To Ben, Janine seemed to have nearly boundless energy. She was fit, often taking the stairs two at a time. He constantly found her utterly intoxicating. He wasn't missing his former, solitary life whatsoever. In fact, he didn't want to let her out of his sight. Her beauty and energy often fooled him, but only in positive ways. She seemed so much younger, more youthful, more vibrant than other women he'd met who were in their mid-sixties.

Their first intimate night, Janine had been exceptionally skilled and thoughtful while making love. Once she began working her magic on him, all of his doubts, insecurities, and anxiety rapidly melted away. He was grateful, and reciprocal.

They spent as much time together as they could. Ben was deeply in love with Janine, and felt that Janine also loved him, and that she was just as afraid of losing him, as he was of losing her. He never asked her about it. He didn't need to. It was unspoken, but understood. They enjoyed each other every day for as long as they could. Eventually, her sick time at work ran out, and she had to go back to work.

At first, Ben acted enthusiastic. He praised her for being so strong and courageous during her ordeal at sea, and the long recovery. He loved that she still wanted to be of service to others, even though deep inside himself, he dreaded her leaving to go to work. He felt addicted to her and how she made him feel. He hated being without her, but accepted it.

The first few days he found things to do, but now that Bessie was distributed all over the Gulf of Maine in little pieces, he missed going down to the harbor and taking her out for a half day. When Janine left on the fourth day, he looked around at the big house and, once more, heard the silence echo through thousands of square feet of unoccupied rooms. He couldn't stand it any longer.

Ben's speed boat was moored in Bessie's old spot, right where Andrew texted she would be. It looked odd sitting there now, so small in comparison to Bessie. He suddenly realized that he'd never gotten around to naming this smaller boat. Not only that, the boat seemed more like Andrew's, because Andrew used it more than anyone, and when he wasn't, it just sat tied up. A spare waiting to be used. A just in case boat which he always felt strange about.

Like a spare car that sits on the side of the garage, outside, getting covered with pine needles, just in case it might be needed, while having to watch the shiny, garage-kept car coming and going everyday, always getting driven, refilled, maintained, cleaned, and polished regularly.

Ben looked the boat over carefully, "I hereby name you *Spare Savior*." Ben said it out loud so his ears could hear it spoken. He liked it. It rang true, and didn't sound half bad. He texted the name to Andrew. *Hey, I just named the small speedboat, 'Spare Savior,' I hope you're okay with that. I know it's my boat, but you use it the most.*

Almost immediately, Andrew texted back, *Love it, Dad.*

Ben got in *Spare Savior* and fired up the twin, 80-horsepower Johnson outboard motors. It was a typical Maine morning, crisp, and a marine damp that could give you a chill to your bones if you weren't dressed right. Ben was dressed right, but he decided to zip up the plastic side windows attached to the overhead canopy before idling out into the marina.

Once out on the Bay, Ben cranked both motors wide open and accelerated until he was doing about 60 mph. He kept raising his speed until it felt like he was flying, with the boat suspended only a few inches off the surface of the water. He cruised for half an hour or so, feeling the exhilaration of his speed, while letting his mind wander. He needed some time alone to process all the things he'd been through recently.

He wanted to honor Bessie's memory without any tarnish, and fought to keep from feeling guilty about the recent physical activities that he and Janine had engaged in, even though Bessie was gone and he was a free man.

He didn't like it, but it still felt odd to him that he was older, an older man, a senior, even though there was no denying that reality. Janine was right behind him, trailing him in age by only five years. He'd almost lost his life. He'd had many flashbacks, and quite a few bad dreams since then, but being able to share and talk about it helped. Ben thought, Life is too short to waste any more time waiting to do anything I might want to do.

Since Bessie's passing, little by little, Ben began trying to take life more from a now or never stance, rather than believing, unrealistically, that he still had plenty of time to live before dying. In reality, well, no one ever knows when they're going to die, but he felt that he likely had maybe a few more years before serious medical things would begin to happen, preventing him from traveling the world the way he'd always dreamt of doing. Despite his youthful attitude and approach to life, Ben still has to remind himself, on a regular basis, that he's almost 70 years old now.

Ben slowed Spare Savior to a stop about five miles out, turned the motors off, and let his thoughts drift, along with the boat. He considered plunking a fishing line into the water, but held back. He felt conflicted inside in the biggest way. He loved Janine, that was something that he knew in his heart was a completely true statement, and he knew his feelings and intentions towards her were honorable. Then why do I feel so anxious and unsettled? What am I supposed to figure out here?

Being brutally honest with himself was the key, but what was the truth? Ben was going to keep asking himself questions until he found the truth in his heart. He still felt overwhelmed by what happened to him while moving the cargo for Hernandez. He flashed on how lonely and alone he'd felt that morning when Janine had left to go to work, and knew that he wanted to sell his big house, which was really overwhelming him now. The truth was, he felt lonely and isolated a lot while home alone by himself. For decades, that house was like *Grand Central Station* for his family, the kids, and their friends. It hosted all the parties, impromptu gatherings, holidays, birthdays, and wedding events over the last several decades. Bessie was always there when he came home. Not so long ago, so were the kids.

Ben restarted the motors and pulled forward fast and hard, before turning the boat back towards the harbor in a long, high-speed arc. He couldn't wait to get off of the ocean. That had been the most surprising revelation of all today. For the first time in his life, Ben was afraid of what might be below the waterline. Since being in the water, and having to fight so long to stay alive, Ben had been having nightmares regularly. They'd been interfering with his sleep, and beginning to impact almost everything else: his mood, his appetite, his energy levels, and his ability to think clearly at times. Twice, he'd had flashbacks of the near misses with sharks, even while doing minor chores around the house during the day. He was even becoming a little afraid to drive, worried that he might have a flashback while driving.

With the same speed as someone snapping their fingers, he would be there with Janine, in the water, watching the mouth of a huge shark open right before attempting to take a bite of him. The shark's teeth were fully visible from the bright sunlight illuminating them, as he swam just below the surface only feet away from doing serious harm to Ben. Just as the shark would take his final lunge towards Ben, Ben would snap back to the present.

Randomly, he would flash on the image of the shark coming up from below that almost bit Janine's leg off, and he remembered how terrified he felt watching shark, after shark, come at them while they were waiting to be rescued. He remembered mentally coming to terms with the fact that his life was about to end soon, and that he'd felt like he could no longer continue, physically. The terror he'd felt while watching the sunset turn into dusk, then the beginning of nightfall, knowing that the darkness left them unable to see the sharks that would continue coming. Perhaps it was better that way. Adding to his anxiety, Ben also remembered, vividly, the intense fear he felt wondering if Salvador was going to put a bullet in both of their heads, and then throw their bodies overboard.

As soon as Ben got back to the pier, he quickly moored Spare Savior and headed home, feeling almost driven to get there, as he had felt while wanting to get out of the house earlier that same morning. Right now, he felt frazzled, unsure, stressed, and, for the first time since choosing to become sober, his mouth watered for a whiskey.

Once that thought entered his mind, he didn't even hesitate to reactively pull up in front of a liquor store. He sat in his truck for a few minutes thinking, *just this once as a reward for enduring all that I have.* Ben finally got out and went in.

He felt like he was having an out-of-body experience, like he was floating to the door. He heard the bell attached to the inside of the liquor store door jingle, and a voice welcomed him. He took a few steps into the store, and noticed all the neat rows of different sized bottles of poison lining the shelves. The almost sickening, yet oddly familiar stench of old, stale, beer, residual whiskey, and cheap wine all blended together, wafting through the store from the bottle recycling room in the back. A gloved worker wearing a medical mask angrily sorted all the returned bottles and cans brought in for their return deposit value. The nearly constant rummaging came and went in high decibel noise waves that sounded to Ben like a bulldozer pushing loud white noise in his direction that came in tight pulses, with silence in between them.

Ben raced back outside and ran straight to a nearby trash can, managing to get to it just before upchucking his breakfast, and the snacks he had eaten while out on the water.

He was shocked by his revulsion to the smell of alcohol, and his physical reaction to it. He felt grateful that he'd vomited. It was serendipitous and, for Ben, nothing short of miraculous. A divine intervention, a guiding hand, pushing him back onto the road after he accidentally drove onto the shoulder.

Ben got back in his truck feeling completely cured of his craving for a drink. He decided he would share the incident with Janine. He thought she would enjoy hearing about it, if not simply for the entertainment value. Feeling better now, he decided to put together a special surprise for her.

He checked his calendar. Today, Janine would be home no later than 5:30 p.m. He shaved and showered, and began preparing them a nice meal of steaks topped with sautéed onions and baby mushrooms, baked potatoes with the works, and broccoli with cheese sauce. He looked over at the luscious cherry pie he'd bought, now sitting proudly on the counter, and hoped Janine liked that kind of pie. He was excited, almost giddy. He couldn't wait to tell her about his day, and then give her the surprise that he had spent the afternoon finalizing.

Finally, he heard the garage door opener, then her car door closing in the garage. As soon as she walked into the kitchen, Janine knew that there was something going on. Ben seemed nervous and really energized. "Everything okay?" she asked with a semi-serious look on her face.

"Everything is as close to perfect as it can be," Ben answered. "I've taken the liberty of preparing this evening's meal. Would you like to unwind a bit before eating, or are you hungry?"

"Thank you. Actually, I'm starved. I'll change into my lounging clothes, wash up, and I'll be right in." She said heading for her room.

"Dinner at the dining room table tonight, if you don't mind. I wanted to have a more romantic setting, and have already set the table up with flowers and candles."

"Oh, okay. What's the occasion?"

Ben smiled at her, "I have you in my life." Janine blushed and looked down for a second, then walked back to him, and looked deeply into his eyes.

"Yes, you do," She said. She closed her eyes and passionately kissed him for several minutes, then walked away. She felt his eyes on her as she walked to her bedroom. She paused, looked over her shoulder, smiled at him and said, "I'll be back shortly," in a sexy, provocative tone.

Ben was excited. He returned to the kitchen to get ready for dinner. He turned the heat off on the remaining pots, then went to see what, if anything was still needed on the dining room table. He lit the candles, and poured the non-alcoholic sparkling wine into two champagne glasses, leaving the bottle submerged in the ice bucket that Bessie gave him for Christmas one year. He put it near his chair so he could reach it without issue.

He put the rest of the food on the table, served her, and covered her plate with a thermal dome. Finally, he dimmed the chandelier lights, and took his seat. He sipped the sparkling wine, it tasted okay, but he was never that big of a fan of any kind of wine. He hoped she would like it.

He was nervous as hell, but happy about the choices that he'd made earlier while out on the water and, now that he'd made them, he wasn't going to change them for anyone, not even Janine.

Ben heard Janine coming out of her room. From his chair, he couldn't see her door because the bottom one-third of the stairwell finished curving down in front of it. He fixed his eyes on that part of the room, and then saw her slowly move into his line of sight. Once she became fully visible, he felt speechless, and was mesmerized by her beauty.

Her long, thick, hair was all the way down. Her shiny waves cascaded past her shoulders, nipping at the middle of her back. She wore a black, short-sleeved, see-through negligee, bordered in white lace along the bottom of each sleeve, the bottom skirt cuff, and along the edge of the long neckline that showed off her magnificent cleavage.

Ben was stunned by her attractive, modern, pre-sex attire, and couldn't take his eyes off of her curvaceous, silky, body sleeved only in the bare minimum. She had tastefully accessorized with a platinum and diamond necklace, and matching waterfall earrings, leaving her looking stunning and extremely sexy.

Janine gracefully slid past him, motioning for him to stay seated, then gently touched his back for a second, before silently taking her seat. Ben found her movement, and her alluring appearance both exotic and stimulating. Between the dimmed lights, the candles, the erotic dress, and the alluring, mysterious scent, Ben felt himself begin to deeply relax now. He decided to wait on his surprise until after dinner. He'd know when the time was right.

Ben tried hard to read all that he was seeing and getting telepathically from her eyes. Love, lust, passion, gratitude, hunger, and . . . something that he'd felt or gotten from her before, but could never unlock or figure out what it was. Something still unidentifiable, unnamed.

Ben raised his glass to her, "Your beauty leaves me speechless tonight, my love."

"Thank you." She smiled at him, her diamonds sparkling brightly. She took a small sip of her sparkling wine. Ben reached over and lifted up her thermal dome.

"Your dinner, Madame."

"Ben, thank you. That looks even better than it smells."

"Awesome. Eat. Enjoy. Tell me about your day."

Janine really was starved. She ate fast, happily talking with food in her mouth, even licking her fingers afterwards.

Ben enjoyed her energy. He loved that she felt so relaxed with him that she could really be herself. She was so sexy sitting there in her silky, revealing underthings, eating and chatting away at him like a cowboy sitting at a campfire. Just a starved, extremely sexy human being deciding to put etiquette aside for a change, and eat like a pig with complete abandon.

Ben listened carefully, and with great interest at all the things she expounded about her day, while carefully watching all of her unique mannerisms, and listening carefully to her tonal changes and laughter. She seemed to have an endless supply of things to say or talk about. On and on she went, and then, like a fast car driven at high speed that suddenly runs out of gas, she put her fork down and simultaneously stopped talking. After a few seconds of staring straight ahead, she looked at him and said, "So, what about you? Anything new?"

Ben was caught completely off guard. He had prepared, and even rehearsed in his mind how he wanted this evening to go, but aside from the naughty nightie, and her astounding physical beauty, she really took the wind out of his sails with the endless chatter and the cowboy eating. For the first time since meeting her, he saw a bawdy aspect to her that he wasn't sure he liked. She had become, at least temporarily, what he always imagined a tavern wench would be like. The beauty and sophistication he normally witnessed and admired so much in Janine, had somehow transformed into a rough sawn version of her that he'd enjoyed for a while, until it struck him that the cowboy at the campfire, eating like a pig, could be the real Janine.

He finally answered, "Um, yeah, not too much. I took a drive down to the harbor. I've been missing my boat some, and took the small speedboat out. I finally named that boat today. I've had it for years, and just never got around to doing it. I named her the "Spare Savior"

Janine looked pleasantly surprised, "What a perfect name. I love it."

"Yeah, I thought it was appropriate. It has a nice ring to it. I ran it by Andrew, he thought it was perfect too." Ben said, shifting in his chair a little, and feeling uncomfortable about what he was going to say next. "I felt really stressed out earlier today for some reason. I guess from all the things that have happened to me, and you," and us as a couple he thought.

"That's normal and completely understandable, Ben. Try not to be so hard on yourself right now. Just try to relax and process what happened organically, letting time take care of buffing the memory hazy, and moving it to the back of your mind."

Ben looked at her seriously and said, "I went into a liquor store today."

Janine quickly sat up tall in her chair, her breasts distracting him as they visibly collided, ricocheting off each other momentarily while she shifted, before settling back down again, "and?" she said with a razor sharp tone.

"And, nothing. It was horrible. I walked in, and I felt like I was going to pass out from my fear of backsliding. I saw all those rows of bottled poison, and I got a massive whiff of the overwhelming and disgusting odor of stale whiskey, beer, and wine from the bottle return in the back of the store. It was all I could do to make it to the trash can out front where I puked my brains out. I stood there, bent over a disgusting trash can, hurling again each time I remembered that smell. This went on until I had nothing left and was dry heaving." Ben felt a little ill in his stomach reliving the awful experience.

"I hate to say this Ben, I really do. But, I'm so glad that it went the way it did. It tells me that A.) you've never cheated and drank since going sober, otherwise you would not have had such a distinct reaction to the alcohol odor the way you did, and B.) that you didn't override your reaction and still drink, and C.) that you're an honest man, who just told me something that many would be too ashamed to share, and that tells me how much you trust me, and how honest and sensitive you are. Thank you for sharing all of that with me, and keep it up.

You're doing an amazing job staying sober, and under extraordinary circumstances."

Ben felt good about telling her now, but he still couldn't get the weirdness of the whole setting out of his head. He wished she had just worn a normal outfit to dinner and eaten like she usually did. He gave her permission to be herself, but didn't realize that what he was about to witness would permanently alter his perception of her in a negative way. He decided to forego his surprise and think about it some more.

When they finished dinner, Janine helped clean up afterwards in her nightie, which in the bright light of the kitchen revealed even more. Unfortunately, the tavern wench image persisted and Ben found it hard to enjoy anything with her now. The entire night was disintegrating right before his eyes, like a train wreck.

"Hey, as sexy as you are right now helping me clean up in your sexy nightie, I suddenly don't feel too well. I'm not sure why."

"Oh?" She said, looking concerned.

"Yeah, I'm sorry Janine. I'm just going to go ahead and turn in early tonight. My stomach feels really unsettled. I hope it's nothing from this meal causing it."

"Well, I hope not, too. I feel fine, and ate twice what you did. Hmmm. I hope you feel better in the morning. Then I'll just go up and get a head start on tomorrow's paperwork before lights out." She latched onto him and gave him a passionate kiss. While kissing him, she reached down to stimulate him by rubbing the head of his knob through his pants, trying to get him to change his mind and come to her room with her. He was stirred, some, but it wasn't enough to sway him. He was too deflated now, and just wanted some privacy.

18

THE PROPOSAL

The next morning, Janine seemed a little icy. Ben tried not to read too much into her behavior, mainly because he was keenly aware of what she did for a living, and knew that she had to take on a lot of the psychic pain of her clients while they went through the initial withdrawal from alcohol.

Sometimes, while walking past her bedroom on his way to the laundry room, Ben heard her talking on the phone, often in Spanish. Janine dealt with many different types of people and she was bilingual. She once told him that it was one of the most valuable skills she ever learned. It enabled her to communicate better with her Spanish-speaking clients and develop a much better understanding of them and their individual circumstances.

Ben never questioned anything about what he heard, or asked who she was talking to, even out of curiosity. He knew that it was none of his business. The last thing in the world he needed to do now was to start poking around and asking a bunch of personal questions about things that were none of his business, like a jealous lover. If he wanted things to continue with Janine in a progressive, honest way, then he wasn't going to do that. Besides, he already knew Janine was a good person.

They ate their breakfast mostly in silence. As she rose from her seat at the breakfast bar to put her dishes in the dishwasher, she glanced at him and said, "I'm not sure how long the training session is, so I'll just grab dinner there tonight."

Ben smiled at her, "Thanks for letting me know. I planned to cook for us again tonight, but now I won't unless I hear from you later that you'll be able to be home for dinner after all." She didn't say anything, but came to him. He kissed her goodbye. "Have a wonderful day."

"You too," she said with a flat tone, then walked into the garage without looking back, closing the door hard for emphasis.

He walked out to get the newspaper and waved to her after she'd finished backing down the driveway. Either she didn't see him or didn't want to look at him, because she just looked straight ahead and drove away. She appeared to be talking to someone on speaker phone, and her face seemed tight and tense.

Ben sat at the breakfast bar for a while trying to read the paper, but his mind kept wandering to Janine, and the strange turn of events between them. Strange, because the entire rift had happened so suddenly, and with such profundity, that he was still reeling from it. It was all unspoken, and this one was all on him. He needed to go for another drive or do something to at least have a temporary escape from all of his thoughts, and the feelings churning inside him. He felt restless, uncomfortable, nervous, and scared. Thoughts about his future with, and without her, floated in and out. Questions about his ultimate safety from Hernandez intermingled with them, as did even more questions around the strange way Bromley and Decker had suddenly swooped into his life. They'd wrapped him up in their illusory veil of the power, and scope of the U.S. Government, and then conveniently excused their inability to find them to other people's incompetence, and mistakes. Mistakes that almost cost them their lives. So many things struck him now as being more than a little off.

The surprise party, with all those people praising him and showering him with gifts for his kindness, caring, and help over the years, marked the apex or the pinnacle of his life. Unfortunately, despite all good intentions, the party celebrating him and his acts of kindness and compassion seemed to have left him cursed, despite him even managing to give up alcohol and not go back to it under extraordinary circumstances. Ben put his coffee mug in the dishwasher and headed to the bathroom feeling heavy and angry.

Why do I not feel happy? he thought. So what, she ate like a pig one time and grossed me out somehow. Yeah, but that was a glimpse of several of the seven deadly sins, and you know it. You saw how she looked. Like she was drunk on the gorging and the flavors, the oral enticements, added to by the promise of a lusty, passionate, physically satisfying end to the evening. Like a happy monster, happy while being fed, and stroked, and gratified. Maybe it was your mindset at the time, and nothing else Ben. Don't blow this. Good luck finding anyone who makes you feel as good as she does, and she does 99 percent of the time. Get a hold of yourself. What the hell is wrong with you? What's still not clear?

Ben pushed the bathroom door open and immediately saw the envelope sitting on the counter between the two sinks. His name was on it, next to a hand drawn heart. He stood and peed, looking at the envelope the whole time. When he finished cleaning up afterwards, he took the envelope to the big outside deck on the left side of the front entryway, sat down, and opened it.

Dear Ben,

I'm not sure what happened at dinner last night. You and I seemed to both be in great moods and the meal was fantastic, and everything was going great. All of a sudden, you changed. I saw this odd look come over your face and I wasn't sure what I had just said or done to cause you to have an issue, but I also knew that you didn't want to disrupt our evening to talk about it. You were still processing, I get it. I thought it might be something to do with your memories connected to Bessie, and something last night triggered uncomfortable feelings along those lines, so I let it go. I want you to know that I love you, and that I'm here for you, now and always. Take as much time and space as you need. I'll be waiting for you on the other side with my arms wide open, ready to take you, once again, into my arms, and hold you tight.

Yours, Truly, Madly, Deeply, Passionately, and Forever,

Janine XXXO

Ben dropped the letter into the sink and stared at himself in the mirror for a long time. The longer he looked, the older he felt. That made him want Janine now, more than ever. He didn't want to be alone anymore. He really loved her. The self-induced, premature pain he felt in his heart from imagining life without her was almost unbearable. He felt foolish to be so sensitive and judgmental. He had been a fool. Ben picked his phone up and texted Janine,

Hi, I just read your nicely written letter. Thank you for doing that. I needed to read what you included in it. No issues, I promise. Can't wait to see you later. Let's forget last night and go for a repeat at the end of the week when we aren't tired or having to get up early the next day. Love, Ben XXO

Ben took a drive to clear his head. Now he felt sure, and there was no more uncertainty. He wanted to marry Janine. No more wondering. No more conflict. No more second guessing himself about his feelings for her. He knew that they were destined to be together.

Finalizing his feelings felt good. He felt lighter inside now.

Janine texted Ben that she was taking a week off beginning next week. *Perfect,* Ben thought. He decided to arrange an impromptu party for Sunday evening, just Janine, Andrew, Celia, and himself. It was important for Ben to have his children present when he proposed to Janine, and he thought a small, intimate gathering would be perfect.

Luckily both of them were onboard for Sunday at 5 p.m.

The rest of the week went without incident, other than Ben having the darnedest time remaining cool and not letting Janine in on any of his plans for Sunday. He thought that she likely sensed that he was up to something, but remained quiet and non-inquisitive, and he was glad.

Celia was the first to arrive on Sunday, and she was in a particularly good mood. Celia and Janine seemed to hit it off right away. Celia said, "I can't remember the last time I felt this unencumbered." She added, "I almost feel like I'm single again." Giggling aloud.

Andrew arrived a short while later. He and Ben sat at the breakfast bar talking and watching Janine and Celia joke with one another while preparing the appetizers. Ben momentarily flashed on a past memory with Andrew, Celia, Bessie, and himself. They were all in the kitchen talking about where they might want to go during the upcoming summer vacation. A loud noise, from the wind knocking over one of the deck chairs on the patio snapped Ben back to the present.

He felt love and gratitude inside, but a piece of his heart still belonged to Bessie, and it would always be that way. He knew it, and he accepted it, knowing that Bessie would like it if he found someone new and was getting married again. He remembered her saying to him more than once over the years, Hey, if I'm gone, I want you to live your life. Find someone new. God knows that you're the type of person that absolutely needs to have someone else in his life. I would hate to think you spent the rest of your years lonely and miserable.

When they all finally gathered around the table, Ben picked up his glass, "I'd like to propose a toast." Everyone picked up their glasses and looked at Ben. "To family," he said, raising his glass higher, then clinking glasses with everyone, starting with Janine. "And now, I'd like your attention, please." Ben stood up and went around to Janine's side of the table. He knelt down before her and looked into her eyes, then brought his other arm around from behind him and said, "Janine, will you please marry me?" with a slight waver in his voice. He opened a little maroon box, and presented her with a gorgeous engagement ring.

Janine, with a tear in her eye, accepted his proposal without hesitation, while pretending to not notice the internally flawless two carat diamond engagement ring flashing and winking at her. She stood and wrapped her arms around him, hugging him as if her life depended on it. Andrew and Celia were smiling, and occasionally stealing glances at one another now that Ben and Janine were locked in a passionate kiss.

Ben finally came up for some air, "Wow." He looked ecstatic and happy. "So, you guys. Are you both good with us getting married? Don't hold back. We both want the truth because we want to be happy and we know that we cannot really have happiness without our marriage being supported by family members."

Celia answered immediately, "I couldn't be happier about this, you guys. I am so relieved that you have someone in your life now to help you grow old gracefully, and peacefully. When's the wedding?"

Before Ben could answer, Andrew chimed in, "Of course, Dad, Janine. Yes, I support your marriage, and I'm happy for both of you." He smiled, "I propose a toast." They all raised their glasses once again, "To Dad and Janine. May your marriage be happier than you ever dreamed possible, and may you only know love, peace, and happiness." Everyone clinked glasses, and then happily ate, drank, talked, and really enjoyed the rest of the night.

Ben had thought about going to Las Vegas to get married, but now that Janine accepted, he asked what her preferences were about a wedding. He was surprised to hear her say, "I actually know a Marriage Officiant licensed to perform marriage ceremonies in the State of

Maine. Her name is Shirley Hotham, and she's right here in the greater Portland area. We could save a lot of money by having our ceremony and reception right here. We can have a party with our friends and family and eat lots of lobsters." She was beaming at him after this, enough that he didn't trust that she wasn't pulling his leg.

"Really?" Ben asked with a surprised look on his face.

"We can go formal if you want to though," she added, getting more serious, but I'm truly fine doing it that way. I've already had my church wedding and So—Did—You," she said, tapping on his chest with her forefinger for emphasis with those last three words.

"Okay. I'm fine with that. Really. I just didn't expect it, but actually I love that idea now. It's perfect."

On Monday, they decided to locate their deceased spouse's death certificates. Ben retrieved Bessie's out of his files, then he and Janine drove over to her place to get the certificate for her deceased husband. Ben had never been to her place before, and wondered how much longer she would want to continue renting it. "Hey, have you given notice to your landlord yet?" He said, half kidding.

"Doing that today, my big hunk. On our way out."

Ben looked around, her place was really nice. Tasteful, modern, filled with expensive furniture known for medically correct back support. Bright and well lit spaces, with just the right amount of decorative objects on the walls, and very quiet. "How long have you lived here?" Ben asked.

"Almost ten years now. It's been a really good place for me. Pretty close to the hospital, and very stable rent. It's only gone up $50 per month since I moved in. Unheard of these days."

She ducked into the bedroom for her files. Ben looked around the living area, then wandered into the kitchen. On his way over to the window facing the shopping mall on the other side of the road, he happened to glance down at Janine's phone. The phone was lit up. At the bottom it showed a text message from someone with the initials JSH. Ben kept walking, not giving it another thought.

He looked out at the shopping mall, shocked to see how many people were there on a Monday morning. He flashed on that text again. JSH? Why just initials? Why not John Steve Haley, or Sandra T. Henderson? Janine was still in her bedroom. Feeling a bit like a criminal about to steal candy at the corner store, Ben went back to her phone and gently tapped the screen. It lit up again, and Ben could read some of the text. *Got your final list for this week. A little shy aren't we? I expect . . .* Ben couldn't read anymore, as it was only a preview or summary of the whole message. Now it was going to bother him, and he knew it. Does she have someone else in her life? he thought.

Janine came out of the bedroom with the death certificate. On their way out, they stopped by the office. Janine introduced Ben to her longtime landlady, Mrs. Hoffstead, who looked so frail, Ben thought she would likely come apart in several pieces from a good blast of wind. "Oh, Janine, NO! You're not leaving, are you? You're one of my best tenants. You're always on time with your rent, and I adore the way you always greet me and give me gifts for my birthday and Christmas. You are just so kind. I will miss you dearly!"

"No worries, Mrs. Hoffstead. The hospital is nearby. I still work there and plan on coming to see you and visiting even after I've moved out, and you can still count on me for birthday and Christmas presents," Janine said, giving her a wink. She moved in close and gave Mrs. Hoffstead a nice long hug, then pulled back and looked at her. "Thank you for being so kind to me as well. I love the way you talk to me and greet me when you see me. You're the best, Mrs. Hoffstead." Janine gave her a big kiss on the cheek.

Ben stood near and watched, feeling the love and warmth of the special moment. "Nice to have met you today, Mrs. Hoffstead."

"You too, Mr. . . . ?"

"Scot, Benjamin Scot."

Mrs. Hoffstead smiled at him, then looked at Janine, "I think you got yourself a keeper here, Janine. I'd marry him too if he'd have me, she giggled. Oh yeah, he's a good-looking chap, that's for sure and, if I were 20 years younger . . . well, I'll tell you what, I'd give you a run for your money trying to reel this one in."

Ben blushed, and thanked her again. "What a nice woman," he said when they got back into the car.

Janine wholeheartedly agreed, "Yes, she really is. She's the real deal. Rare these days." Janine's phone made a noise, Ting-Ting, Ting-Ting. She looked down at her phone and Ben saw her face get really tight.

"What's up?" He asked casually.

Janine seemed extra focused while texting back, "Hang on a sec," she said.

"Not 'JSH' again I hope?" Ben added with a half smile on his face.

Janine immediately stopped texting and stared at him. Ben could see her glaring even as he continued driving and looking straight ahead. "Have you been looking at my private things on my phone?" She asked with ice in her voice.

"Ah, no, yes, I mean . . ."

"Ah, crap. Somehow I knew this whole thing was a little too good to be true. How could I have been so stupid to believe that I actually met a really decent guy, even though he was an alcoholic? How?" She kicked the inside panel of the door really hard, then looked at him while he struggled to get a word in and explain what happened.

"Janine, I was walking over to the window in your apartment when the text came in. The screen lit up, I noticed the summary in the bubble that popped up. I couldn't help it and that's all there is to it, I promise."

"You weren't snooping around or trying to see something on my phone on purpose?"

"I promise, Janine. I would never do that on purpose, but please don't expect me to somehow override my human responses. I mean when something bright lights up in front of our eyes, we can't help but look to see what it is. It's a built-in response designed to protect us from getting hit in the face with an ember from a crackling fire or notice a screen lighting up while we're walking by."

Janine still looked pissed off, but not as much as before. They rode in silence for a while, then Ben said, "Not to start rubbing the wound raw again, but it did perplex me a little as to why someone would text using their initials only. I mean, I've never seen that before, and why not just go by their name? I don't get it."

"To be quite frank about it, neither do I," Janine snapped back, "but if you're worried that it's my secret lover, I can assure you they aren't." Janine knew if she didn't let Ben know who 'JSH' was, that it would drive him a little nuts. She decided to delay telling him and see if he could handle it. She remained quiet, periodically glancing at Ben to gauge his level of discomfort.

To his credit, he continued driving normally, staying silent, and not appearing to be the least bit concerned about it or anything else right now. He finally caught her looking over at him. He smiled at her, and began glancing back and forth between her and the road, "What?" he asked, knowing that she was dying to tell him who 'JSH' was.

"Don't you want to know who 'JSH' is?" she said playfully.

"Doesn't matter to me. I don't want to stick my nose in your private business. I'll listen though if you care to share," he said, this time keeping his eyes on the road.

Janine took a deep breath and let it out slowly. 'JSH' stands for Jackie Shirley Hotham. She is my friend that I told you about. You remember, she is the certified marriage officiant."

"Okay, well, that makes total sense. All but why she goes by JSH and not Jackie."

"I have no idea either. Everyone has their worries and security precautions these days."

"Yep." Ben looked over at her. "No worries, I'm good. I was just curious because I've never seen, or known anyone else who did that. So it stood out, and it still does a bit, but, again, it's none of my business."

19

MR. AND MRS. BENJAMIN MORSE SCOT

Janine's schedule was completely full for the foreseeable future, so they decided to go ahead and have an impromptu wedding that coming Saturday. Both of them agreed, simpler was better. They would put together what they could.

Rather than sending out formal invitations, they had Andrew and Celia help them call and or leave messages with a small group of about twenty people that previously gathered for Ben's surprise party. They were his friends and the people who cared about him the most. They also made sure to let everyone know not to bring any gifts.

Janine invited ten of her friends, with the same request for no gifts. All of them seemed happy for her, and most of them were going to be available. Janine's friend Sarah had said, "Oh how perfect. Now I have something romantic, fun, and completely new and unexpected to look forward to this weekend. So much for my new diet. Oh well. Don't forget to throw the bouquet in my direction, ha-ha."

They both went to *Mainly Events,* over in Biddeford to see about an enclosure and other supplies. Steve, the owner, looked at their list, and had almost everything they needed. Steve agreed to have his small crew arrive Friday afternoon and install a temporary enclosure with lights, set up the tables and chairs with linens, and put up streamers and other decorations. Saturday morning they would bring the ice, soft drinks, and water. Finally, a band called *Unnamed Band* known by their ability to play all different types of music, from Big Band Era to the *Beatles*, and Country, to *Ozzie Osbourne* would be there to play for both the wedding and the reception.

Ben and Janine were thrilled. They were grateful to have found a company that could provide so much for their wedding on such short notice. That, alone, was both a wedding gift and a blessing.

Ben asked, "Is it common to be able to hire your services so easily?"

Steve smiled at him and laughed. Well, the big summer push in June is our busiest time of year, followed by Spring, followed by Fall. Mid-October is hit or miss. This year, you guys managed a hit!"

Ben called his good friend, John Stillman, over at *ABC Lobster*, and ordered fifty pounds of fresh lobsters, 30 pounds of steamed clams, 50 haddock filets, and enough corn on the cob, coleslaw, and baked beans for 50 people. John said he would come and get the food set up in the early afternoon, right before the wedding. Ben tried to sound stern when he told John, "You make sure you bring a change of clothes, and your wife, John. This is the last time I'll ever get married again, and I'd love to have both of you see me do it."

"Sure, thing, Ben. I wouldn't miss it, even in my jeans while wearing an apron." he said, giving Ben a thumbs up and a big smile.

Ben was getting a little nervous. Everything seemed to be coming together effortlessly, and he wasn't used to that. He was having a hard time trusting it. He checked the weather forecast. Friday, and through the weekend, and even into the early part of the following week the weather was supposed to be comfortable and dry, with highs in the fifties, and lows in the thirties, with light breezes out of the west, and partly cloudy, with mostly sunny skies. It was amazing, and a good omen.

The weather in Maine is extremely changeable and can come from any direction. Sunny and warm today, snow tomorrow, it happens all the time. For Maine to know that many days of gorgeous, comfortable weather—back to back—was very unusual. Ben was very grateful, but still remained somewhat skeptical.

He went ahead and scheduled his regular groundskeeping crew for that Thursday to tidy up the landscaping. Later, he and Janine went over to *Cake Elizabeth* in Portland, and paid extra to have a nice, three-tier wedding cake made and delivered to them on Saturday morning.

For clothes, they decided to wear what they already owned. Ben had Janine pick out a suit from the three that still fit him. She selected a dark gray suit, white shirt, and a teal green tie sparsely decorated with tiny lobsters embroidered on it, and black leather, wingtip shoes. She accessorized him with the Rolex watch that had been handed down to him by his father to complete his outfit.

Janine showed Ben her dress collection and told him to choose what he wanted her to wear. He chose a well fitting, collarless, forest green satin dress, with zippered back and short sleeves, and the length ending just above the knee. For jewelry, he chose all pearls. Two long 8mm pearl necklaces, a triple strand 8 mm pearl bracelet, and matching 8 mm pearl stud earrings. For her shoes, he chose her shiny black leather, with medium high heels.

Overall, the wedding preparation felt magical to Ben. He was surprised at how relaxed he'd felt all week and, for the first time in his entire life, nothing fell through or needed rescheduling.

With the sun about to set on October 14, 2023, Ben and Janine exchanged their vows while looking deeply into each other's eyes outside in Ben's backyard, overlooking Casco Bay. Once they were pronounced man and wife, everyone clapped and congratulated the two of them, then proceeded to celebrate their new union until well past midnight. The guests ate almost all the food, and happily drank, sang, and danced to the incredible music provided by *Unnamed Band*. It was one of the happiest days of Ben's life.

The rest of the week went by so fast it seemed like five days were two. When Ben woke up with Janine on Sunday, the entire week, including the wedding, seemed like it had been one, long, vivid dream. After breakfast, they talked a little about taking a trip for a honeymoon, but at a later date, and for a minimum of two full weeks, maybe longer.

"You know, Ben, I wanted to go to Paris when I first got married, but Bill wanted to go to London."

"So, where did you end up going?" he asked.

She looked at him seriously, "London—where else? Our entire marriage was like that."

"Hey, let's focus on us and what plans we'd like to make." Ben reached out and stroked her cheek. Then added, "I get it, though. I'll tell you something that might strike you as a little funny, now that you just shared that story with me."

"What's that?"

Ben continued, "When I first married Bessie, I wanted to go to Paris, just like you, but Bessie wanted to go to London."

Janine cracked up laughing. That's funny. So, where did you end up going?"

Ben looked at her with a little sideways smile, "London—where else?"

"Wow, what a really strange coincidence. It almost sounds to me like Bill would've been happier with Bessie, than he ever was with me."

"Bessie was happy with me . . . I'm pretty certain she was anyway. If she wasn't, she did a damn good job keeping it from me. So, it sounds to me like it's all settled. We'll plan a trip to Paris—together. Why don't you check the calendar at work, and see if you can find a good two-week block that would work best for you so we can plan it soon. Then, we'll have something to look forward to while we do the countdown to our honeymoon."

"Ben, call this spur of the moment, but it really isn't. I'm going to go in and tell them that I am taking off for Christmas this year, and that I won't be coming back afterwards. I'm going to go ahead and retire."

Ben was surprised, but in a good way, "Whew, I didn't see that one coming. My goodness. For sure I'm good with that. It's fantastic. Then there won't be any time constraints on our traveling or having to worry about getting back to work, etc. I'm thrilled. Gosh, the good news just keeps coming this week." Her unexpected announcement both thrilled and excited him. Now, they would be able to be together a lot more, and travel together far more frequently.

During breakfast, Janine said, "Ben, I was looking ahead at my calendar and I forgot to tell you that a week from tomorrow I have to leave for a conference. It's a four-day retreat for the staff, and it's once per year in the Fall."

"Oh? What is the retreat part?"

"A getaway for those that work in the alcohol rehabilitation wing. It's semi-work, away from work. In other words, it's designed to facilitate growth for the staff, including some group therapy around our own inter-dynamics, and brainstorming improvements for us, our workplace, and the patients we serve."

"That sounds interesting . . . sort of," Ben said.

"It can be pretty interesting, but it's usually quite a snooze fest. I always overeat and, even if I don't, I still gain weight from four days of sitting on my butt."

Ben said, "Why not suggest that, weather permitting, you guys take the group for a hike or a long walk as part of the group activity?"

"You know? That's a fantastic idea. I think I will. I can see how that would work based on prior retreats. I can't believe no one, including me, has suggested it in all these years, at least as far as I can recollect."

Janine spooned leftover chunks of fresh fruit from their wedding into her bowl, then added a dollop of plain Greek yogurt on top. She rolled a watermelon ball through the yogurt and popped the whole thing in her mouth, munching away while looking at Ben. She swallowed and said, "Unfortunately, and I hate this, but they make us lock our phones up, and we're only allowed to use them for an absolute emergency.

"Even at night?" Ben asked.

"Yeah, we put them on chargers in a locker, but can only get them at the end of the retreat or for an emergency, like if someone calls saying that a family member of someone at the retreat had been hospitalized or similar.

Ben shrugged his shoulders, "So be it then. I'm fine with it, especially since this is going to be the last one for you, right?"

"Right." Janine agreed.

After getting the place cleaned up from the wedding reception, Ben spent the rest of the day reading, and half watching a football game. Janine came and went all day, checking in with him periodically as she bounced from their bedroom to the laundry, then to the kitchen, and back to the bedroom. He heard her talking to someone a couple of times, and noticed she seemed tense afterwards. He trusted Janine, and knew that if she needed his help in any way, she wouldn't hesitate to ask.

Ben thought a little more about that retreat, and knew that he was going to be in for a stretch alone in his big house again, and was dreading it. Especially, not being able to call, or talk to Janine for four days. It'll be like it was before he met her, but this time without the booze or his beloved lobster boat, Bessie.

Ben made a call to Andrew about having his final documents, his Will, the estate trust, durable power of attorney, health care proxy, and all of that changed to reflect his marriage to Janine, to ensure that she is taken care of when he dies.

Andrew said, "Sure, no problem at all, Dad. But I would recommend waiting six months before you do."

"Why, son?"

"Well, believe it or not, many new marriages end in the first six months. There is a sixty day waiting period before I can draw up a trust document, but I always tell my clients to wait a minimum of ninety days, or six months if there is no real reason to be in a rush."

Ben paused, then said, "I understand. I'll wait ninety days, but not six months. Okay?"

"Okay, sounds good. I'll put in a reminder and get with you when it's time to proceed."

"Thanks, son."

"How are things going so far?" Andrew added.

"Great. We have another week together, then she's going to a work retreat for four days."

"Oh yeah? Week after this one you said?"

"Yes."

"If you'd like some company, I can come and spend a couple of days with you then. Does that sound good?"

"Yes. That would be great, Andrew. I appreciate it. Let me know what you'd like for dinner for a couple of nights and I'll be sure to go shopping for what's needed. I'm really looking forward to it."

"Me too, Dad. Will do. I'll call you next Sunday afternoon to make sure we're still on."

"Perfect. Talk to you then, Andrew." Ben hung up very happy. It was an unexpected but pleasant surprise, and he was already looking forward to his son's visit.

Things were quiet and peaceful for the rest of that week. Both Janine and Ben got along perfectly as a married couple, and they seemed happy, relaxed, and very compatible. Twice that week, they arose early in the morning and made love to one another before having breakfast.

He loved being her support person now. He kept the house clean, and he cooked for them. He did their laundry, and he shopped for what they needed while she was at the rehab center. Ben would fix her some snacks, and some leftovers for lunches, and see her off to work each day. He hadn't been in this type of role before, except both times Bessie had given birth, but even that had been less maternal than his current role, and he hadn't felt this happy and content for many years. For now, he was enjoying being a direct caregiver to his new career wife.

Friday finally came and Ben was glad he'd have Janine all to himself until late Sunday afternoon, when she would start getting her stuff together for the trip. He'd cooked them a nice big pot of spicy chili with beans, and had some small flour tortillas wrapped in cloth being kept warm. He placed three little matching white bowls near their eating areas at the kitchen bar, one with cheese, one with chopped chives, and the other held sour cream for adding as desired to the chili.

Ben was excited when he heard Janine's car pulling into the garage, then silence for a few minutes, followed by the voices of people talking. He had just started toward the door that connected to the garage when it suddenly opened, and Janine stepped into the kitchen, still talking to the two men following her into the house."

The man in the back said, "So, we'll be able to come by and get you on Sunday and take you to where you need to go."

Ben felt goosebumps form on both arms, and crawl from the back of his head right down his backside to his bum in two seconds flat. Decker, and Bromley!

Ben's mind told him to chill out, but his danger radar was now on full alert. Ben couldn't believe he was seeing these two guys again, and why?

"What the heck are you two doing in my house?"

"Hi hon, they were sitting in front when I came home." Janine said, giving him a quick peck on his cheek.

"And what brings you two idiots here today?" Ben said with an icy tone, but still friendly.

"Very funny, Mr. Scot. Just a little follow up, that's all."

"Okay. Let's see, we were told that we were going to be protected and that nothing really bad would happen to us. But bad did happen, and to both of us. We did our end, you guys fell down and didn't do yours. You guys are lucky that I don't sue you both personally, and the FBI as a whole. How's that for some follow up?"

Bromley said, "I understand why you're upset with us, Mr. Scot, but believe it or not, we did the best we could under the circumstances that we were presented with. I know you think we're incompetent, bumbling fools, but we're not. Most of the time we get the job—our jobs, done just fine, and often in an exemplary fashion."

"Fair enough. What do you want?"

"Just wanted to see you, and find out if there have been any further communications or contacts made with anyone since your ordeal?"

"Like who?" Ben asked suspiciously.

"Like any cartel members, like anyone trying to take advantage of you right now. Periods of transition can leave people vulnerable, not knowing what to do, or who they can trust. Feeling like that a little right now, Mr. Scot?"

"You nailed it. Especially seeing you two again, which I never thought I would."

Janine said, "These two have offered to take me to my retreat in a couple of days because they are heading in that same direction. I won't have to leave my car in a public parking lot, I can leave it right here in the garage. Isn't that nice?"

"Sure, I guess. And all that got decided ahead of walking into the kitchen?"

Janine looked at both agents nervously, enough that Ben picked up on it. "Ah, I actually don't remember how, or exactly when that came up. I think I said I was fine, and that I was looking forward to going to a retreat next week, and they asked where, etc."

Ben looked at her without saying a word. He wasn't sure why, but he knew she was lying to him. "If you want to do it that way, then

I'm good with it, too." He looked at the agents, who were both staring at him with disturbing ferocity.

Janine relaxed a little. "Then it's settled." She looked at the agents and smiled. "Well, thanks for checking on us, guys. I'm happy to say that we have nothing to report. I'll be looking for you on Sunday afternoon then at 4 p.m.?"

Bromley said, "We'll be here to get you then. Glad to hear that you folks are both okay and have nothing to report."

Decker nodded, and without a word, followed Bromley back out through the garage. Ben stepped into the garage and watched them leave. He spotted their sedan, just past the thick bushes on the right side of the driveway. He kept his eye on them until they were back in the car, then pressed the control button and closed the garage.

Once back inside, he looked at Janine again, and could tell she was hiding something. "That was weird," he said.

"I'll say. I was driving up thinking, 'I know that car,' but I couldn't place it. I saw them get out as I pulled into the driveway, and they began walking towards the open garage almost immediately. It took me a second to figure out it was them. I was pretty scared, at first."

Ben said, "So, they're coming Sunday, and you're going to let them take you to your retreat instead of me?"

"Yes. Why not? It saves both of us the trouble of driving, using gas, and having to leave one of our cars in a public area for four days."

"Who is going to bring you back home? Them?"

"No, I was going to call Uber or get a ride from one of my coworkers."

"Okay, if you can get a coworker to drop you home, that will work, but forget Uber. Even a one way Uber will cost enough to negate your gas savings. If no coworker can bring you home, then call me immediately, and I'll come and get you. Okay?"

"Okay.

Ben couldn't stop thinking about Bromley and Decker stopping by like that. At the surface, it seemed innocent enough, it even seemed a little like them going the extra yard, but something about these two didn't add up, and he could not figure it out, or put his finger on why he felt that way. But, Hernandez was dead. Ben watched his chopper go down into the flames of Bessie's wreckage into the icy waters in the Gulf of Maine. So, why would these two show up now?

One thing that had always hit him in the face was their lack of professionalism. Ben had always taken issue with people in professional positions who obviously don't step up or live up to their job responsibilities. In Ben's eyes, these two half-assed their jobs, counting on people's respect for their badge and the authority it represents to get their jobs done.

Ben had spent his entire lifetime working around men who effortlessly did their jobs from thousands of hours of practice. He could always tell the difference between real, fully competent professionals, and skaters who always managed to just barely get by, while always doing just the bare minimum necessary to still get paid. To Ben, it was obvious that they lacked the discipline to do the work needed to become a professional or expert at what they did. Ben could tell that neither Bromley nor Decker, would be able to do their jobs from their own expertise, knowledge, or professionalism. As a matter of fact, the more Ben thought about Bromley and Decker, the more they struck Ben as professional low-lifes, and perhaps not even real FBI agents at all.

For the time being, Ben tried to put those two out of his mind, but they persisted while he cooked dinner, more while cleaning up afterwards, and again while he tried to watch a movie with Janine. He couldn't stop thinking dark thoughts about those two. Somewhere between the first hour of the movie, and the pause to make popcorn, he decided that he would call the FBI field office the next day.

All the thinking about the agents got Ben agitated enough that he wasn't feeling ready for bed when the time came. He kissed Janine good night, but decided to watch a little late night comedy first. He pulled out his phone and decided to look up the FBI while it was on his mind. The FBI office in Boston, MA serves the states of Maine, New Hampshire, Massachusetts, and Rhode Island. Ben bookmarked it, and left that tab open so he'd be able to call first thing in the morning. After thinking about it a little more, he realized that he wouldn't have any privacy if he waited until then, so he decided to go ahead and dialed the number. After a brief introduction and some menu options, Ben was able to get to actually get an agent, even at this late hour.

"Agent Davidson here, how may I help you?"

"Hello, agent Davidson, my name is Benjamin Scot. I've had two of your agents helping me off and on for several weeks now, and I'd like some more information about them. If that's possible?"

"Well, sure, but it depends on what you want to know."

"For starters, I'd like to verify that they are in fact FBI agents. Their names are agents Bromley and Decker, who work out of your office, I believe."

Agent Davidson began typing, "Just one second, Mr. Scot. You said, Agents Bromley and Decker, correct?"

"Correct."

"First names?" Ben thought for a minute before realizing that they'd never given him one, or if they did he couldn't remember what their names were, now.

"I'm sorry, I don't recall," Ben answered.

"No worries, Mr. Scot. Still checking. Any other names given to you?"

"No. They just call themselves Bromley and Decker."

"Well, unfortunately, Mr. Scot, our records do not show any agents who go by those last names as currently working for the FBI anywhere in the world."

"Are you sure?" Ben felt his heart rate skyrocket, and his blood pressure right along with it.

"Please tell me that you're messing with me."

"Mr. Scot, I represent the Federal Bureau of Investigation. We don't mess with law abiding citizens. No record of either an agent Bromley or Decker on file. I think perhaps you need to fill me in on your situation right away if you're able to at this time."

"Hang on a second, please."

"Sure thing, Mr. Scot. My shift runs until 8 a.m., so take all the time you need."

Ben took a look around the den and, just for good measure, he got up and tip-toed to the door and peeked out. The small night light in the kitchen cast its happy glow into the foyer, and the night light at the foot of the stairwell was on, but the house was otherwise quiet, and Janine was asleep. Ben decided this would be a great time to have a discussion with agent Davidson.

"Okay, all clear. Listen, agent Davidson, I really don't know where to begin. So much has happened in such a short time period."

"You can call me Chris, and my advice when you feel that way, is to begin at the beginning, not the middle, or the end."

"I like you already, Chris. Great advice. First, if I really begin at the beginning, I may get into trouble with you myself for past transgressions, so I'm not certain what I may need to pass over or leave out."

"How long ago was the last thing that may come into legal question?"

"Well, other than six weeks ago, which you guys knew about, ten years ago."

"Mr. Scot, again, we have no record of those agents, and we have no record of anything involving you on file either."

Ben felt shocked all over again. "My God! How could this happen so easily? How the hell could I have been so stupid as not to be more diligent and checked these bozos out when they first showed up at my door."

Chris said, "Did they show you the proper ID?"

"I remember flip wallets—correction—a flip wallet from Bromley. Decker never showed me his, I was stupid enough to just assume he was what, and whom he claimed to be also."

"What did that ID wallet look like?" Chris asked.

"Black, flip open with a picture ID in the bottom half with his name as agent Bromley FBI, the badge on top."

"Actually, Mr. Scot, normally, it's just the opposite, the named part with the picture would be readable as the top half, with the badge at the bottom. What was the color of the badge?"

"Silver."

"Ours are gold, Mr. Scot."

"Okay, now I'm really freaking out. These guys are supposed to come on Sunday afternoon, pick up my wife, and take her to a work retreat function."

"Start at the beginning now, Mr. Scot. I think it might be the best thing that you could do at this point."

Ben took a deep breath, then another, letting his breath out slowly both times, "It all started almost thirty years ago when I was still actively lobstering in the Gulf of Maine, looking for a way to raise a bunch of cash to expand my house with . . ."

20

THE ORGANS AND WHOLE BODY DATABASE

Ben decided to not tell Janine about his conversation and discovery until Sunday afternoon. He didn't want to scare her unnecessarily, but when she found out that those two agents weren't agents at all, he wasn't sure what to expect from her. He would drive her to the retreat, and he hoped that she hadn't given them the address.

Even though he was exhausted, Ben was too keyed up to even think about sleeping. He paced around in the den trying to figure out what to do next. He went into the kitchen and poured himself a glass of cold water. He kept pacing, thinking about all the things that had transpired since he'd got out of rehab. He realized that Bromley and Decker had been working for Hernandez all along. That totally explains why they never showed up to rescue us, he thought. More exhausted than he realized, he finally went back into the den, laid down on the couch, and promptly fell asleep.

Ben was awakened by the feeling of a warm, moist, tender mouth pressing against his. He opened his eyes to see Janine kissing him with her eyes closed. "Good morning," he said when she pulled away.

"Good morning, sleepy head. What are you doing down here still semi-dressed? I wasn't sure what to think when I woke up and saw that your half of the bed hadn't been slept in."

"Ah, I wasn't ready to go to bed yet, so I stayed up for a while, watched some late night comedy, read a little on my phone, AP news and the stock report."

"Are you hungry? How about I make us some nice fluffy, warm waffles with bacon, maple syrup, and a little powdered sugar this morning. Doesn't that sound great?"

"Sounds perfect. Thank you," Ben replied, trying to hide his discomfort at the thought of eating. His stomach felt sick, and had begun churning during his long conversation with agent Davidson last night.

"I'll go ahead and grab a quick shave and a shower. Make a stack and put them in the oven on warm, please. when I'm through, we'll be able to eat together."

"Okay, sounds good."

Ben texted Andrew while he was in the bathroom. He told him to come over in the early afternoon, instead of calling him in the late afternoon. Hey, please come over tomorrow at 2 p.m. instead of calling. Bring your Glock, park around back by the pool house, and wait for my text. I'll explain tomorrow. You're not going to believe it. I can't.

Andrew texted back almost immediately, Will do!

Ben felt conflicted all day about not telling Janine his discovery about the two so-called agents that had been coming around. He was sure she'd exchanged contact information with them right in front of him yesterday, in case something came up at either end. If he told

Janine now, she would call or text them about not needing a ride, and that might raise some suspicions, so he continued not saying anything.

While showering, Ben wondered why they'd come around again. They both knew Ben lost his boat, that he was no longer in any position to cart body organs around for Hernandez anymore. It didn't make any sense. They also knew that both he and Janine had made a full recovery, and were back to their normal lives again. There were so many little things starting to pile up that didn't make sense, but Ben was determined, for now, to let it go, and just try and have a good rest of the day with Janine. He'd deal with whatever, or whomever he needed to deal with tomorrow.

The rest of Saturday went fine. No one showed up, and to Ben's knowledge, there were no phone calls or texts to worry about either. They spent most of the day together, lounging, making love, eating, and talking about everything but the elephant in the room. Finally, Ben broke the ice, "I'm going to miss you while you're away, Janine."

"I'm going to miss you too, Ben."

"It's only four days, but even one day is too much for me now."

Janine blushed a little, then kissed him.

After dinner that night, they watched *African Queen*, one of Ben's favorite movies. He was shocked to learn that Janine had never seen it before, so he insisted. Janine had loved it, just as he thought she would. They'd commented and giggled about the movie while eating popcorn in the darkened room, just like a couple of teenagers at the local hometown theatre on a Saturday afternoon.

Sunday, Ben cooked breakfast, letting Janine sleep in a bit. After they ate, she got caught up with administrative work for a few hours, then got into the shower. Once in, she realized that she'd forgotten to grab a towel, and the bottle of conditioner that she'd left on the dresser. She opened the shower door, leaned out, pushed the intercom button, and said, "Ben, darling, I've forgotten my conditioner and a towel. Can you please bring them to me? I'm sorry, but I'm already in, or I'd get them myself." Janine stood there, half leaning in, half leaning out of the shower stall, and getting goosebumps from being cold.

Finally, after what seemed like an eternity Ben answered, "Sure, be right there, babe." Janine happily got back into the warm water and felt the chill leave her body almost instantly.

Ben made it upstairs in nothing flat. He grabbed a nice big towel from the hallway linen closet and went into the bedroom. As he walked towards the bathroom, he saw her laptop sitting over by her pillow, facing him. Her suitcase stood at attention at the foot of the bed, and several pairs of shoes were lined up next to it. He continued towards the bathroom, spotting the conditioner on the dresser. He grabbed it, then entered the bathroom. He hung her towel on the hook next to the shower, and set the conditioner on the floor, just outside the shower door. "There you are Janine. The towel is on the hook, and the conditioner is here on the floor next to your door."

"Oh. Gosh, I didn't hear you come in. Thanks. I'll be out soon."

"No problem. Take your time and enjoy it," he said before exiting back into the bedroom. While there, he decided to get his paperback book out of the nightstand and read for a bit while Janine finished packing. As he got closer to the nightstand, he happened to glance over at Janine's computer screen and noticed the page displayed four columns. It was some kind of elaborate spreadsheet.

Each column had a picture of a person, their name, and a list of their viable organs that they might be able to provide, with a checkbox next to each organ. There was a separate, larger box on top that said, Whole Body next to it, apparently for those who were the healthiest, and had the most body organs and parts to harvest for the open market.

Ben felt waves of realization pass through him, like he was being repeatedly struck by lightning. He backed up fast, as intense fear filled his entire body. So fast, that he fell down, twice, while continually trying to scuttle backwards, as if his life depended on it. His eyes stayed glued to Janine's computer screen the entire time.

Ben tried to recover as fast as possible, but slowing his thoughts down now was taking some serious effort. His heart was racing so fast that he feared he might have a heart attack. He closed his eyes, keenly aware of the sound of the shower still going in the other room.

After a brief moment, he reopened them, and quickly crossed the room to the laptop again. He took his phone out and snapped a picture of her screen, then scrolled it a little. The names seemed to go on forever. Patients who were recently deceased, and others who were still alive. Many of these men, and a couple of the women, were listed as homeless, but included the tent community for the last known or regular spot where the patient can be found. Ben took several more pictures of the list, returned it to its original position, and quickly went downstairs and out to where Andrew would be.

21

THE DEATH PARADE

Ben needed Andrew to be where he'd asked him to be. He felt like he was going to explode. He was full of so much information, and so many things were going on. He needed help figuring out how to deal with these revelations.

Ben looked around not seeing him. Andrew isn't here yet, shit! he thought. Ben checked the time, 1:48 p.m. He should be here any minute. I'll just come back.

Ben decided he would come back out once Janine got back into her final packing. In a couple of hours, Bromley and Decker would be showing up to get her.

Ben still wasn't sure if he should say anything to her at this point. After what he'd just seen on her computer, he knew she was involved in smuggling human transplant organs or even whole bodies. He shuddered realizing that medical science had advanced to the point where virtually any part of the human body could be transplanted into a viable host, creating a multi-billion dollar organ smuggling incentive, making organ harvesting, and delivery, the hot new commodity. Not a lot of drugs and money bags to launder so much anymore. He couldn't discount anything now, including Janine's level of involvement, and her position in the El Rey cartel.

Ben knew their reach went far and wide to many countries around the world. With enough money involved, anything becomes possible, and the cartel leverages that as needed. Janine was likely a soldier for them.

The more things Ben began to realize, the angrier he felt. I cannot accept that Janine would be so deep in with the cartel that she would risk everything for . . . what? Money? Maybe. We just got married and now she has no worries and she knows that. Ben mused a bit more, and felt goosebumps spread from head to toe when he realized that, indeed, she wants it all. Her salary as a specialist at the hospital, great job, great pay and benefits, and an outstanding cover.

A side gig keeping a database on potential organ donors, both willing, and unwilling, dead, and alive, homeless, working class, upper middle class, and wealthy. Listing their viable organs for the cartel to sell on the global black market to the highest bidder. Ben thought, the money from this makes illicit cocaine profits look like child's play. How long would it be before he, too, would meet with an untimely, mysterious death, leaving his entire estate to Janine.

Ben had to work hard to control his temper and not storm right into the house and confront Janine. His insides felt like the outer rings of a tornado swirling around inside him, wanting to rip right through him to get out. His walk back into the house quickly turned into a slow gallop, and then a jog. He was determined to confront her about all of it right now. Not later, now!

He crashed into the kitchen and almost ran her over as he rounded the corner heading towards the stairwell. "Oh, there you are!" he said loudly, his eyes half bulging out of his head staring at her.

"Yes, here I am," she answered matter of factly, meeting his gaze head-on, steady and controlled. She quickly moved past him, and into the kitchen.

"Janine, I have to talk to you right now." Ben shouted.

"Now?" Janine shouted back, "Ben, you know I have to finish getting ready. I don't have time for this."

"Janine, cut the bullshit. I know what's going on, and I know what you're doing. I can't believe all the lies. If you were an actress, you'd have won an Oscar for best actress in a leading role. How dare you marry me!"

"Ben, what the hell are you talking about? What? What do you think I'm bullshitting you about?"

"Oh, for fuck sake, Janine. It's over. I know you're in bed with the El Rey cartel, doing your disgusting little part to make sure the wealthy get the organs they need—on fucking demand! My God, you had me fooled. I really thought you loved me, but now I know this whole thing with you was just to get me to fall for you. It's all been a charade. You saw on my forms that I was a widower, and you knew a lot about me. You targeted me, didn't you? I was just another spoke in your wheel. You used me for my boat, exploiting my past with the cartel, and for my estate."

Janine listened to Ben carefully. Her face flattened even more, and now her gaze grew dark, and calculating. As Ben shouted away, Janine had slowly slid the kitchen island drawer open, the drawer where Ben kept a 9mm pistol in case of an intruder.

Ben kept moving slowly towards Janine, still shouting, angry as hell about her deceiving him and fooling him. It stung, and now he wanted revenge.

"Stop right there, Ben." Janine said, grabbing the gun out of the drawer and pointing it right at him.

"Oh my. Really? What are you going to do with that, shoot me? Come on, Janine. We've been married a whole week, and you're already pulling a gun on me? My gun, I might add."

"Based on what you just said, I know that you likely saw my laptop on the bed upstairs while I was in the shower, and that's why you think I'm still involved. Well, yes, I am, but I do not have a choice. I either cooperate, or I'm dead."

"That's not going to work, Janine. I don't believe you, and, just so you know, there are some people on their way that already know a lot about your potential involvement with the cartel, and other criminal activities."

Janine didn't like hearing that at all. She raised the gun firmly at him now.

Ben pretended to see someone by looking past her with a concerned look on his face. She looked away just long enough for him to duck, and grab a small plate off of the counter. He threw it at her as hard as he could, frisbee style. Right when the plate left his hand, he heard her gun go off.

The bullet zinged past his head, so close to his left ear, that he actually felt the bullet push a little puff of air into his ear canal when it went by. The plate he'd thrown hit Janine hard on her left jaw bone.

Ben saw the impact knock her backwards a few steps, and when she stood up again, the impact point was already three times bigger, and likely broken.

Ben stayed low, and tried to move to the other side of the kitchen by running in a crouched position behind the counter. Suddenly, he heard another gunshot, but didn't feel anything hit him. He heard a heavy thump, and heard Andrew shouting, "Dad! Dad!"

Ben stood up with his hands in the air, and saw Andrew in the doorway holding his Glock. He looked over at Janine lying on the kitchen floor, dead. Her eyes were open, and fixed while staring at something unseen. Her body remained motionless as her blood continued oozing out of her, spreading rapidly across the floor like a knocked over gallon of thick, viscous, blood-red paint. "Thank you, Andrew."

"You're Wel—"

—Ben saw a bullet hit Andrew's right arm just under the shoulder, knocking him backwards. He was lucky, the backward motion caused him to fall behind the corner of the kitchen island, just out of the shooter's line of sight. Without thinking, Ben quickly grabbed Andrew's Glock, and his own 9mm from Janine's hand, fighting the urge to puke from the sight of the massive pool of blood around her head. "Are you okay, Andrew?"

"I'll make it, Dad."

Ben tossed him a kitchen towel. "Tie that around your arm, tightly for now. Where is the shooter?"

"I saw the muzzle flare come through that window," Andrew said pointing to the window next to the dining room table.

"Let's move out of here before we're boxed in. Go out through the garage. I'll go out to the foyer. Look alert," Ben said before sliding Andrew's 9mm back across the floor to him.
Ben barely got out of the kitchen and into the foyer before someone shouted, "FBI! You won't get out alive unless you put your weapons down! I said FBI, put your weapon down. Now! If I see you after this warning, and you are holding what appears to be a gun, or weapon of any kind, I will not hesitate to respond with lethal force."

Hearing this, Ben kept moving on his tip-toes. He went into the coat closet under the stairs leading to the upstairs bedroom. It's an area that people seem to just gaze past, and not really notice. As soon as he backed into the closet, leaving it open a tiny crack, he saw the kitchen door slowly open and watched the hands with the gun emerge, followed by the rest of agent Decker. Agent Bromley followed him as if they were attached. They slowly moved into the foyer, then decided to check out the den.

As soon as Ben saw them go into the den, he came out of the closet, quickly rounded the corner of the banister, and began going upstairs as fast as possible trying to buy some time and make some calls for real help.

Halfway up, Ben heard Bromley say, "You, Ben, hold it!"

Ben turned, and fired several rounds at them causing them to scramble back into the den.

Bromley shouted, "Mr. Scot, you're not getting out of here alive. I hope you realize that."

"We'll see who's left standing in the end, you piece of shit!" Ben hissed back, firing another two shots at them for emphasis.

Ben heard them mumbling to each other for a minute, then it got quiet. Ben moved across the upstairs landing on his belly, peering through the railings at the downstairs foyer, giving him a view of both the den and kitchen doors. The front door was directly underneath him, with a small alcove just inside the door for hanging jackets etc.

The silence was deafening. Ben heard a thump, then Bromley shouted, "Ouch. Fucking statue." He fired two rounds at the statue to punish it for being in the way of his foot, while he walked around in a strange place in the dark.

Ben fired in the same direction to scare Bromley, or better, hit him before he finished crawling to the far left side of the landing for a better view. Suddenly, bullets began ripping through the entire landing, right where Ben had just been laying. It was a fully automatic, military grade rifle, for sure. Every time it fired, it seemed to lay out bullets by the tens in a couple of seconds, destroying everything in its line of fire, almost instantly.

Ben waited and, just as he suspected, Decker came out to check to see if he had eliminated Ben with that last barrage. When Ben saw Decker come out, he was holding the automatic rifle.

Ben shot at him with both guns. Decker immediately fired back in Ben's direction, causing him to retreat on his belly into the nearby bedroom as fast as he could possibly move.

Decker moved into the middle of the foyer for a better angle, one with a direct line of sight to the upstairs bedroom that Ben had just crawled into. He began firing at Ben. The bullets tore the doorjamb to shreds, and knocked huge chunks out of the drywall.
One of the bullets hit the water line feeding the adjacent bathroom, and water started spraying in all directions.

Ben heard more gunfire, but this round sounded different. He slowly and carefully crawled back out towards the door. Someone downstairs shouted, "Drop it! FBI! Drop it!" Then Ben heard three semi-automatic rifles all go off at the same time. He crawled out just enough to see that both Bromley and Decker were now both lying dead on the floor of the main foyer. Two men wearing FBI jackets with bullet proof vests were standing over them, while the other agents were fast fanning out, looking for any further threats. All of them were dressed in black tactical gear, and Ben realized these guys were real FBI agents.

Ben slowly, and carefully stood up with his hands raised. He very carefully walked out, and slowly began descending the stairs.

Someone shouted "Whoa! Got someone. 10 o'clock. Stop right there, Mr."

Ben complied. He stopped, not saying a word. He was so scared that he suddenly began to see his life flash before his eyes. He knew that if he blinked the wrong way, these guys would wallpaper the walls with his body using their bullets. He felt his knees wobbling. "Don't shoot! Please. I'm the owner of this house, Benjamin Scot.

Please. I need to sit down before I pass out. Please let me finish coming down."

"Slowly! Keep your hands up. Move slowly." one of the agents said through gritted teeth.

When Ben finally made it to the bottom, six FBI agents quickly moved in to grab him at the same time, like he was some sort of mob kingpin. They hustled Ben into the kitchen so fast that his feet barely touched the ground. Andrew was already sitting in a chair. Two FBI agents stood over him. They slammed Ben into a chair, and began asking him nearly non-stop questions while he tried to catch his breath. Andrew guided Ben in answering their questions after identifying himself as Ben's son, and attorney. Once he was able to satisfactorily explain himself and prove his identity, they finally backed off, and even apologized to him for scaring the crap out of him.

Ben identified Janine through thick tears, then the agents helped both him and Andrew get into the ambulance waiting to take them to the hospital to be examined. They bandaged Andrew up before leaving, letting him know that he was good to go home if he wanted to, but Andrew decided to go with Ben to the hospital for support.

Despite all of his objections, they held Ben at the hospital overnight for observation. They initially put a mild tranquilizer in his IV drip to keep him calm and relaxed, but when it had worn off completely, Ben, being tired of the program, renewed his objections about being kept there. Unfortunately, no one paid any attention to him at all. He felt invisible, truly invisible for the first time in his life.

He also felt powerless to make his own decisions. His rights were being taken away from him, as if he were some type of criminal who wasn't entitled to the same rights as the rest of society. At a time when virtually everything else had already been taken away from him in a matter of one afternoon, now he had to deal with being a patient. It seems like the lines between being a patient or a prisoner are thin indeed, he thought.

Ben looked around his room. It was virtually identical to the room he had been put in when he had been admitted from his mishap at sea. He flashed back on that day again, meeting Janine for the first time, remembering her sparkling beauty that day. She had seemed extraordinary and magical to him. Then, in a sudden fast forward, his mind flashed to Janine lying on the kitchen floor in a pool of her own blood, lifeless, never to kiss again, never to speak again, never to laugh again.

Ben suddenly felt emotionally overwhelmed, and finally let himself cry. The emotional response triggered his tears. At first, his crying started small, but with so many emotions to process, and with no one else in the room to hear him, he let it all out and cried hard. He let himself rock back and forth from the intense sobbing. His mind played a tragic movie, beginning with Bessie smiling at him, then her dead in her coffin—pale and lifeless, followed by seeing himself diseased and full of toxins from all of his drinking. That imagery morphed into Janine's smiling face and twinkling eyes, then she was screaming from feeling the terror of being lost at sea and surrounded by sharks, followed by the image of her dead body, lying in her own blood. The movie played in Ben's head while he heard Hernandez's voice in the background, mumbling insults at him, and laughing, and taunting him.

Ben's sobbing subsided briefly, until his mind decided to replay the movie again and, this time, included Andrew getting shot in the arm. His baby boy. His smart, squared away, star lawyer, who always made time for him—shot. The imagery made him feel sad and heavy inside, like an anvil had attached itself to his heart.

The next morning Ben texted Celia, and asked if she could please come and get him at the hospital. He said he would be discharged around 10am. after being released by the doctor. He made sure to include that he was only there having routine, age-related tests run, and that there was no need to worry about him at all. She responded almost immediately, and let him know that she could pick him up, no problem. They agreed to meet at the patient pick-up area out in front.

Ben was dreading having to tell her about Janine. He decided to ask her if he could please stay at her place for a day or two to finish recuperating. He texted *Honey, Janine is at a conference out of town right now. Can I stay at your place for a couple of days to finish recuperating?*

Sure, dad, that would be fine. We can swing by and get some stuff for you at the house and then you can come home with me.

Ben hadn't thought about supplies, and he didn't want to go home with Celia. He was sure that there would still be blood and other nasties at his house, and it was still a fresh crime scene. *Honey, if you don't mind, please just come and get me, but come at 9am.*

22

THREE YEARS LATER

Celia and Andrew both took their time walking down the wooden steps leading to the dock where Ben had moored his new lobster boat, *Bessie's My Best Bet*. Ben had bought his new, but used, lobster boat a little over a month ago, when he'd finally realized that his happiness largely depended on him being out on the water, at least a good percentage of the time.

After Janine's death, Ben had received some counseling around his temporary fear of what predatory creature might lie in wait for him just below the surface of the dark, cold water below, and had continued his sobriety by attending Alcoholics Anonymous meetings, and with the help of Cam, his new support sponsor.

Ben spotted Celia carrying a pitcher of fresh made, iced lemonade, and Andrew had baby Benjamin Morse Philips, Celia and Jake's newest addition to the family, in his front mounted chest pack that he really loved to be in. He greeted them, and rushed in to help. "Careful, careful," Ben said, taking a hold of the pitcher. He smiled, watching Andrew close the gap carrying baby Benjamin.

At the bottom of the small hill next to the covered dock, Ben had constructed a large lean-to that covered a series of big saw horses that he'd constructed out of small tree timbers, and were currently being used to support the hull of a canoe Ben was hand crafting.

Celia said, "Wow! It looks great, Dad. This one seems to be coming along very nicely."

Andrew agreed, "I think this one is going to be the best one you've ever made, dad. I hope you're well paid for these."

"Yeah, guess I'm getting the hang of it a little better now. It's still quite a process, but one that I really enjoy. And, yes, they cost an arm and a leg; More than I'd ever pay, but I'm the maker, not the buyer. I simply tell prospective buyers that the price is the price, take it or leave it."

"How have things been overall?" Both Andrew and Celia said, overlapping their questions, surprising them. They all chuckled for a second, then Ben answered,

"Great. I take the new *Bessie* out at least three times a week now, but I don't feel as inclined to as much as I used to. It feels good getting back in the saddle again, though. Seeing Dr. Leonard for the last couple of years has really helped me learn how to better process all the recent experiences and life changes that I've been through, and help teach me how to put things in better perspective, at least enough to get on with my life. Now I'm able to resume doing something that I've always loved to do. I can't believe that I ever considered giving up going out on the water. Funny, Dr. Leonard recently shared with me that he can't believe that I have found enough courage within myself to go out on the water at all. He said he wouldn't blame me one bit if I didn't go out ever again after what I went through. I laughed at him for saying that. I told him he would never say that if he had spent any time at all actually out on the water. I invited him to accompany me on a short run out on *Casco Bay*, but he declined."

Both Andrew and Celia looked pleased. Ben Sr. loved how little Ben seemed so mellow all the time. Ben had started calling him little Buddha, until Celia finally stopped it.

Ben looked at Andrew and said, "Andrew, congratulations on landing that huge contract with the City of Portland to oversee all of their new building contracts."

"Thanks. I thought for a brief time that we were going to end up in second place, but it worked out nicely in the end."

Ben looked at Celia seriously and said, "Celia, I can't thank you and Jake enough for taking that huge, lonely house off my hands, honey. I would've sold it to strangers if you and Jake had decided to not run your own bed and breakfast. I don't know why it took me so long to figure it out. I hated being alone in that huge place. I'm so glad that I was in a position to make it affordable for both of you to own it, and finally get on with making your bed and breakfast dream come true. It was definitely a win-win for both of us. As it turned out, it gave me enough to buy another lobster boat and, with your blessing, I now have a rent free place to stay for the rest of my life. But, by far, the best part is, I get to be a part of this little guy's life everyday," Ben leaned in and gave his grandson a kiss on his cheek. Little Ben giggled, trying to say grandpa, *gandpah, gandpah*, pointing at his grandpa, smiling and gurgling at him.

Celia took a deep breath, letting it out slowly, "Yes, it worked out great for all of us, and we're doing fine, but my gosh, it's a lot harder work than I thought it was going to be. Luckily, we are doing so well that we were able to hire another cleaning person. Finding and keeping, quality help seems to be another big part of it, too. You wouldn't believe some of the deadbeats that come in to apply for work, Dad. You really wouldn't.

"Oh yes I would, honey. Hey, congratulations on having that many paying guests this early on. That's not easy to achieve. Both of you should be proud of making that restaurant/B&B idea work. Bravo, honey. Bravo."

"Thanks, Dad. That really means a lot to me. Without you practically giving the place to us, and then financing us with a zero percent loan on the balance, we would never have been able to make this a reality. The least we could do is be successful.

Hey, it's getting cold, we're going back up. Come up for dinner, okay? It'll be ready in a couple of hours."

"Okay, sweetheart. I'll be up in about an hour. I still have a bit to finish for today."

"Don't forget, Dad, tomorrow is Tuesday," she said looking at little Ben with a big smile on her face, while exaggerating the words and trying to get him laughing. "Grandpa babysitting day." She looked up at Ben, smiling. Andrew stayed silent. He enjoyed watching his father and sister banter.

"Oh, no. I haven't forgotten, not at all. I love my Tuesdays and Thursdays with my little lobsterman," Ben said chuckling. He walked over and gave both of them kisses on their foreheads, patted Andrew on the back and gave his arm a firm squeeze and said, "I'll see you in a little bit, my sweeties."

Ben picked his planer back up and continued reducing the thick plank of wood. Just when he'd become completely focused on the task again, his phone began buzzing. He reluctantly put the plane down and pulled out his phone. It was a voicemail from JSH! Ben tapped to listen to the message:

Señor Scot! It is me, your old pal Hernandez. Que pasa? I know you think I died at sea, but when my helicopter went down, I managed to jump outward enough right before hitting the water to survive. Señors Bromley and Decker picked me up instead of you. Hahahahahaha! Isn't that funny? I think it is. How do you Americans put it? Hilarious? Yeah, I think it's hilarious. Señor, I understood from your former wife that you are known as the Angel of Casco Bay? I did not understand until she shared with me about all the good you have done where you live. I thought, how unlikely, that you would become known as an angel! Nevertheless, Señor, you just lost your wife and I think I will leave you alone now, no? Yeah, that's enough. We're even. My men and some organs, for your wife, and your boat. Yeah, I think we're even. I won't ever bother you again, Señor. You have my word. Besides, I have killed many men, and I could kill many things, but I could never kill an angel. Adiós para siempre! (Goodbye forever!)

THE END